Waking Beauty

Waking Beauty

Dawn K. Lake

Chapter 1

Princess Andromeda was about to get her happy ending, and yet she wasn't happy.

It was the night before her wedding; her husband-to-be had saved her from a terrible fate and it was thus only natural she marry him. Or so everyone said. Tomorrow, they would be wed here in the Summer Palace, and afterwards he would take her away and she would live in his Castle as his Queen.

It had all been decided. She had everything she'd been told she wanted.

Yet something gnawed at Andromeda's heart. There was an emptiness inside her, a restlessness. A sense of something calling to her, wild and dangerous, ever daring her to step beyond the palace walls.

She'd always ignored it before. Her Fairy Godmother had promised Andromeda that what she longed for was simply the Prince who would one day save her from a terrible fate; that once she met him she would feel love in her heart and understand her place in the world forever more.

But things weren't working out like that at all. As one hour after another ticked towards the dawn, Andromeda's dread only grew. Her heart was heavy, not joyful at all, and she couldn't help but feel that tomorrow would mark the end of her life in many ways, not its beginning.

As had begun to increasingly happen of late when her thoughts were disturbed like this, Andromeda's fingers began to worry across her ribs, tracing a long, thin scar hidden beneath her gown.

An assassin had given her that scar two years ago when he tried to kill her. And if Talen hadn't been there, he would have succeeded. Two years. Two years since Andromeda's parents had sent Talen away. Saving Andromeda's life hadn't been good enough for them; not when they'd seen the slash along her ribs and declared her beauty marred forever.

Talen had been Andromeda's bodyguard. She'd come with a previous Prince, the one who broke the sleeping curse, and if Andromeda were to be completely honest with herself, Talen had always fascinated her far more than the Prince ever had.

Talen, with her quick, clever fingers, her lethal skill with knife and bow, her pale skin and fine golden hair, so different to anyone Andromeda had seen before. Like all the people of her kingdom, Andromeda was dark, with springy black curls and brown eyes. She'd asked Talen once where she was from, how many lands she'd crossed before coming to her kingdom, but Talen hadn't answered her. Instead, she'd glanced sidelong at Andromeda and said in a teasing voice, "Isn't that the sort of thing you should ask your Prince?"

But Andromeda had never needed to ask him anything. All he did was talk about himself.

The night the assassin had tried to kill her…Andromeda could still remember the cold fury in Talen's eyes as she slit his throat, sending his blood spraying across the bedsheets. The way her pupils had started pulsing in fear moments later as she took in Andromeda's wound; the sharpness of her voice as she called Andromeda's name and tore up one of her fine silken dresses to stem the bleeding.

Despite her pain, Andromeda had reached up to stroke Talen's cheek, and remembering the softness of the look Talen had given her in return made Andromeda's chest go tight and her blood stir in rebellion as she stood at her casement listening to the enticing whisper of freedom promised by the wind.

There were too few hours left until dawn.

Andromeda's hands balled into fists. "To buggery with this," she muttered, well aware that her parents would have been horrified to hear her utter such a vulgar phrase, and even more horrified if they realised she knew what it meant.

Talen was the one who'd taught her the importance of always having an escape route planned out ahead of time, so Andromeda was not without readiness for fleeing from her destiny.

Underneath the false bottom of the chest at the foot of her bed, she had a labourer's outfit hidden away along with a travel satchel filled with dried fruit and meats and a tidy amount of coin. About a mile away on a humble farm, there was a nondescript horse being cared for which Andromeda had bought several months ago. She'd be discovered almost immediately if she attempted to flee on a horse from the royal stables, and thus she'd secured this horse for... 'Emergencies' as she told herself, though she'd never fully acknowledged just what she might consider an emergency to be.

So Andromeda discarded her Princess finery, dressed herself in the garb of a labourer, shouldered her satchel and climbed down the ancient rose vines as thick as tree trunks that reached from the ground all the way to her bower.

Once outside, it was easy to avoid the guards. Confined so much to her room, Andromeda had had ample time to memorise their movements and to calculate how to slip by. The walls surrounding the palace were tall, but in the Western Wood Andromeda knew of a hollow that went under the wall, concealed by brambles on both sides; probably made by wild pigs.

And it was by this route she made her escape as the moon set, breathing lightly and wriggling silently through the clinging brambles to freedom.

She hurried across the fields in the dead dark to the farm which kept her nondescript horse, and left two gold coins but nothing else when she took the mud-coloured mare and her humble bridle. (Most of the poor could not afford saddles, so Andromeda would have to ride without one too).

During their last meeting, when Talen had come to say goodbye, Andromeda had asked her where she would go. Talen had drawn close to her, so close no one else would hear, and whispered in a voice that made Andromeda shiver, "If you ever want to find me, venture into the wilds. Go into the Endless Forest and leave the path. That will be the beginning."

If Andromeda hadn't still been injured, she might have walked away from everything she knew and followed Talen then and there.

As it was, she was two years late.

There was only a single road that ran through the Endless Forest, and any who strayed from it were said to become lost forever. What would happen to Andromeda if she dared to step off the path? Would Talen be waiting for her? Talen had never said where she was from, but Andromeda knew she'd lived in the Endless Forest for a time before becoming her bodyguard. She used to tell stories about it.

With the pre-dawn mist thinning and the sun threatening to rise, Andromeda mounted her mud-coloured horse in the lane outside the farm and turned her steed's nose resolutely towards the dark bulk of the forest spreading as far as her eyes could see. Before anyone in the Summer Palace was even awake, she had ridden right out of the story that had been prepared for her, and into another entirely of her own making.

⸎

IT WAS NOW five days since Andromeda had stepped off the path. And on each one of those days, she had deliberately wandered deeper and deeper into the trackless wilds of the Endless Forest, intent on becoming lost.

She didn't know whether to be pleased or worried at her resounding success. Even if she wanted to, she doubted she would be able to find her way out of the forest now. Riding Brownie, the mud-coloured mare, Andromeda threaded her way through strange enormous trees, the sound of her horse's hooves muted by bracken and leaf litter. They ate sparingly from Andromeda's supplies and stopped to drink at whispering shining streams before moving on, always on, towards the nebulous hope of discovery.

As the shadows lengthened and the light of the fifth day began to fade, Andromeda found a small clearing and dismounted. She gave Brownie her nosebag and proceeded to set up camp, glad once more of the survival skills Talen had secretly taught her.

Night stole in between the trees, and Andromeda had a growing sense something was different tonight compared to those that had come before. Strange animal cries she'd never heard before sounded in the distance, and the trees seemed to press closer just beyond the fragile edge of her campfire's light. There was a feeling of watchfulness in the air, a sense of tension as if a storm was about to break, but when Andromeda looked up the sky was clear, with a pale crescent moon shimmering like a sliver of silver.

She returned her gaze to the clearing and scanned her surroundings, and that was when she saw it. Something was stirring on the other side of the fire. A figure cloaked in darkness, that wasn't there one moment, and was the next.

Andromeda grabbed her dagger from its sheath at her side. She was next to useless with weapons, for all that Talen had tried to give her some rudimentary training, but she wasn't going to confront a potential threat empty handed. She would meet it with all her pride as a Princess who had thrice faced death and lived.

"Show yourself, whoever you are. I know you're there!"

"Oh hush, child," a voice said, a low, smoky whisper like the hiss of the wind; like the pull of strange magic spoken in an unknown tongue. "You and I both know if I wished to harm you, you'd already be dead."

The shadows fell back on the other side of the fire as the flames danced higher, and Andromeda could see her now. A woman with dusky skin like hers and piercing eyes that shone like a night sky with the glimmer of stars in their depths.

Andromeda's hand shook. She'd never seen this woman, but she knew who she was. She'd heard of her a thousand times before. "You're the Fallen Fairy," she whispered. "You were supposed to be my Fairy Godmother. You were supposed to protect me. But you cursed me when I was born." Her voice began to gain strength as anger outweighed her fear. "You put me to sleep. You put everyone to sleep. I only woke up when the Prince saved me, when he kissed me—"

At that moment, Andromeda had to stop. This was the story. This was her story. At least, that was what everyone said, but it wasn't how Andromeda remembered it. She'd woken to different eyes looking into hers, a different face...Not the Prince's. Not his.

And that Prince hadn't lasted. He was supposed to marry her but after the attempted assassination he'd gotten onto his white horse and ridden away, never to return. Her parents said he must be the wrong Prince, that she deserved a better story...And in time had come the monster, and the rock, and another Prince to save her...

The Fallen Fairy let out what sounded like a sniff of dry amusement. "Cursed you, did I? Are you so sure about that?"

There was something about the way she said those words, something that made Andromeda think she knew what had really happened when Andromeda woke up from the sleeping spell. Keeping her eyes steadily upon Andromeda's the Fairy declared, with perhaps a hint of sadness, "I didn't curse you at all, Andromeda, and I would have remained your Fairy Godmother, in a world with different rules to this."

12

Those words fell like a strange yet hauntingly familiar cadence upon Andromeda's heart. There *was* something familiar here; something she'd once known perhaps but had since forgotten. Or maybe it was an unconscious awareness she'd always carried with her, solidified into cogency by the light of her own fire, taking shape out of the living darkness she could feel all around her.

"But if you didn't curse me, why were you sent away? Why was I given a new Fairy Godmother?"

The woman laughed bitterly. "The new Fairy was just a lackey, doing your parents' bidding. Are you really going to tell me you know so little about how the world works, Princess Andromeda? I would have expected more from you."

Her eyes flashed a dare to Andromeda from across the fire. She didn't speak again, but the air between them was thick with magic. Something was holding the woman back from saying more...not her own desires, but a spell. She couldn't unleash her knowledge, her power, unless Andromeda asked her to. Unless she wished it.

Andromeda already had an inkling of what the Fallen Fairy was going to tell her; not the exact words perhaps, but she'd already worked out that the shape of her longing didn't match the stories her parents were always trying to place her into. There was always that yearning for something else, a yearning that paradoxically used to grow both quieter and sharper in those long ago days when Talen had been at her side.

Meeting the strange Fairy's eyes, Andromeda spoke her wish. "Then tell me," she ordered. "Tell me how the world really works."

With a flash of white teeth, the Fallen Fairy crossed the fire that separated her from Andromeda. It was difficult to tell whether she flew or passed right through it, for the darkness had thickened again as soon as Andromeda spoke. The Fallen Fairy was somewhere behind Andromeda in the shadows now, hidden further by winding tendrils of smoke she'd somehow brought with her from the campfire.

Andromeda turned and turned about, trying to catch sight of the Fairy, but all she'd see was a glint of eyes, or the floating edge of a cloak before the Fairy danced beyond her vision, too quick to follow.

"When a girl makes a wish," whispered the darting, half-unseen Fallen Fairy, "there are some wishes which are permitted, and others which are not. Fairy Godmothers are not supposed to grant a wish to a girl when she wishes for something she is not allowed to wish for. The only wish we are permitted to answer is when a girl makes a wish to be a Princess and marry a Prince. What do you think the effect of that might be?"

The answer was all too obvious, and soured Andromeda's stomach. "If all the other wishes go unanswered, then girls will come to believe they don't have any other destiny besides becoming a Princess and marrying the Prince. They will be pushed into wishing for the only thing they are allowed to wish for, and never think about whether they really want it or not."

"Indeed," said the Fairy. "And those of us who *would* hear the wishes, and grant the wishes...well, we're called devils and cast into the wild. We become Fallen Fairies, and our girls are either never told of us, or they're taught to fear us for our supposed curses. A new Fairy, an obedient Fairy, will be put in our place, and I think you yourself know what that results in, Princess Andromeda.

"After all, what *would* the Princes do if the Princesses stopped wanting them? If the Princesses started making other wishes, and having them answered? The very fabric of our land would be rewoven into something completely different, and thus such fairy tales have been made unthinkable, unwritable, to keep the world weaving in the same old, worn patterns."

Yes—Yes—It made an awful, sickening kind of sense. Andromeda knew the Fallen Fairy wasn't lying; she could feel the truth of her words resonating in the very depths of her heart. This was why Andromeda's destiny, as laid out by her until recent Fairy Godmother, felt not so much like being given a joyous gift as walking into a prison and hearing the door slam shut behind her.

"Why can you appear before me now when you couldn't before?" Andromeda asked the Fallen Fairy. "Is it this place? The Forest?"

There was a faint chortle of laughter. "Very good Andromeda. You're getting sharper. By your own choice, you have entered this Forest and strayed off the path. You have asked to know that which is beyond the bounds of knowable in this world. You've broken the bonds that bound you to the fate the obedient Fairy prepared for you and set me free to help you...if you wish it."

Andromeda was trembling. Talen must know about all of this. The Fallen Fairies, the wishes, the imposition of destiny...why else would she have sent Andromeda into the Forest and told her to step off the path? Was that what the Fallen Fairy was offering? A way to help her find Talen?

That was what Andromeda wanted. She'd stopped denying her longing the night she ran away; even before then she hadn't done a very good job of concealing it. Talen's smile, her courage, her kindness. Andromeda wanted all those things, and still more besides. She used to watch Talen sometimes, trying to be discreet, admiring the strong attractiveness of her form, the way the sunlight glowed in her short golden hair. And as she watched her, Andromeda would think...she would think how nice it would be—

Somehow then, Talen would catch her watching and laugh, and Andromeda would get up and sweep away, feigning offence to cover how flustered she was. She'd never admitted how she felt; nor had Talen for that matter. Not in so many words. Yet it had been there unspoken. Unacknowledged. Something not permitted to take shape in the narrow bounds of Andromeda's previous life.

"Very well then." Andromeda's eyes blazed out in the darkness. "Fallen Fairy Godmother, this is what I wish. Tell me how I can find the one I love. Tell me how I can find Talen, who once lived in this Forest."

At last the Fairy appeared before Andromeda, almost fully visible. The smoke was still at her edges, blurring parts of her into the darkness, but Andromeda could clearly see her face and the hint of pride in her eyes.

She gave Andromeda an approving grin, sharp as the edge of a knife. "Talen has left the Forest and now dwells in a land far beyond your kingdom. If you want to get there, you'll have to follow the Broken Road. It will not be an easy journey."

"What is the Broken Road?" Andromeda demanded of the Fairy.

The Fairy's answer came swift. "It is a Road that will lead you right to the house where Talen resides, if you can follow it far enough. But you have to understand—the Road is broken because generation upon generation, the humans of this world and many others have done all they can to destroy it. As fast as parts of the Road are built, they are torn down, and when they are rebuilt, they are torn down again. This is a Road of rubble, a Road that disappears, a Road you will sometimes despair of ever finding again if you lose the trail. The Road might be nothing more than a signpost hidden in the wilderness or the feeling in your heart. Do you understand what I'm telling you?"

Andromeda's heart was beating hard as the pounding of a wild deer's hooves. She felt like she and the Fairy were conspirators now, in sympathy against the injustices of the world.

"Yes, I understand. Show me the Road."

With a laugh, the Fallen Fairy clasped an arm around Andromeda's shoulders and drew close to her, passing her free hand in front of Andromeda's eyes and whispering, "Open your eyes, Andromeda. The Road is already here."

Andromeda started out of the sleep she hadn't realised she'd fallen into. She sat up, hearing Brownie snorting nearby, and looked everywhere in agitation, but she could find no sign of the Fallen Fairy. The campfire needed stirring back into life, however Andromeda neglected this task and instead thrust a short, stout stick into the embers until its end was ablaze.

With her crude torch she began to search through the thick undergrowth of the forest. Whether it had happened to her in sleeping or waking state, Andromeda didn't doubt that the Fallen Fairy had been here. There was a glimmer in her heart she hadn't been able to feel before, a glimmer that seemed to wax and wane like an inner magical compass as she searched through the forest.

Suddenly she stopped and let out a gasp. It was there, it was really there. Glowing softly, pale as silver moonlight, a Road of broken bricks leading deeper into the darkest part of the forest.

Andromeda broke camp at once and, leading Brownie behind her, set foot upon the Road.

Chapter 2

Following the Broken Road was perilous, as the Fairy had warned, and many were the trials Andromeda braved to follow, and follow, and keep following the Road, beyond the end of her world. More than once she lost the Road and had to search until she found it again. Sometimes bands of enemies barred her way upon the Road and they were tricky indeed to deal with at first, requiring all Andromeda's wits to make up for her lack of physical prowess.

Then there came the day when a strange monster with the face of a man and the heart of a demon chased her on the Road. Andromeda spurred Brownie to go faster and faster as the demon howled behind them, and fear clenched a fist in her stomach as she saw piles of bones and half-rotted bodies scattered alongside the Road. Victims of the demon who would never finish their journeys and follow the Road to its end.

Andromeda saw a wooden hut up ahead, golden light spilling out from its wide open door. A trap? A refuge? Brownie was trembling beneath her; lungs heaving painfully, foam flying from her sides, but Andromeda felt the change that came into her mount as she caught sight of that golden doorway. Her ears pricked, she prepared herself for one final mad dash, and trusting Brownie's instincts Andromeda urged her on, crying to her to go, go, as the demon ran naked on all fours, its speed inhuman, its twisted mouth slack and salivating.

Galloping full-tilt, Brownie barrelled through the blinding golden light of the mysterious doorway, and Andromeda heard what sounded like a door slamming shut behind them. The glow faded; Brownie slowed and came to a trembling stop. Andromeda slid from her back, turning with quick and wary steps in search of danger.

To her surprise, they were in a library, every wall lined with books from floor to ceiling, the space seemingly too large for the small hut Andromeda knew they had entered. On one side of the room was a stout wooden door, now shut. As Andromeda watched, it began to shudder with the force of something pounding into it again and again, and she could hear the demon screaming for the toll he believed he was owed.

Next the walls began to shake, the demon's snarls chillingly close as he sought a way to break into the hut. Dust sprinkled down from the rafters; the floor shook beneath Andromeda's feet, but the library did not buckle against the demon's onslaught. Unmoved it remained, a quiet refuge remote from the demon's howling, incoherent rage.

As the frenzied attack continued, a single book was dislodged from one of the highest shelves and fell at Andromeda's feet, open at its cover page. Brownie snorted and rolled her eye. Andromeda's own heart was thumping unsteadily at the demon's madness, the strangeness of the library, the lung-constricting dread of being trapped with no escape. But she did her best to hide those feelings as she stroked a calming hand over Brownie's sweat-streaked neck, and knelt to pick up the book. Her hands began to tremble as she read its inscription:

This Book sits in the Library of the Shelter that was built to protect those who follow the Road from the demon that rages without. The Books that line the shelves of this hut are Books of Power and it is the spells written within their pages that keep the demon at bay.

The demon cannot be killed, but he can be banished for a time. Go to the door of this hut and with a touch it shall open. When the demon rushes forward, look into his eyes and speak the spell written on the following page of this Book. Do not look away. Do not let your heart fail, or you will be lost.

In the event the bearer of this Book succeeds in banishing the demon, the bearer may take the Book of Magic with her when she leaves to recommence her journey. This Book can only be wielded by one with whom the Book has recognised kinship, and if it is in your hands it has chosen you for the duration of your honourable life. The spells herein are already in your blood and only need instruction in order to be brought forth into the world. When your life of honour is done, the Book will make its way back to this Library and join once more in powering the spell against the demon, until such time as another shall come whom the Book wishes to assist.

May your journey ever be one of courage and honour, Blessed Witch.

"Witch?" Andromeda murmured. "How could I have that kind of power?"

Of their own accord, the pages of the Book turned in a sudden gust of wind. On this new page, beautifully bordered by two fierce-eyed Witches, Andromeda read out loud, "Rejecting an identity imposed by the world leaves room for the self to grow. In cases such as these, the power of magic belonged to the individual always, but she could not see it for the false self to which she was confined, for others' gratification."

Andromeda let out a breath, and felt something stir in her blood. Something powerful as the roar of a newly-wakened titan. Something primal as that which she had felt the first time Talen touched her.

The demon was still hammering at the door.

"No!" Andromeda spoke in a voice of command she had never used before, suddenly silencing the demon's howls. "I will not pay your toll."

Flipping the pages back, Andromeda found the spell that would banish the demon. She marched to the door, her eyes full of the fury of a storm and her hair crackling with lightning. Throwing open the door, she confronted the demon and stared it down. She spoke the spell of banishment and felt a great power coursing through her; the power she never knew she possessed. It was amplified by the power of the generations of Witches who had come before her to safeguard this place and this knowledge, the many Books around the walls glowing and rustling their pages as a great wind stirred and went roaring through the door.

With a howl the demon vanished, and that part of the Road was henceforth safe from his interference for many years.

Andromeda took the Book of Magic with her when she left.

Altogether, Andromeda travelled for six months, through land after land, through world after world. She studied much from the Book of Magic and found it both illuminating and mysterious. Its pages were not constant; as she discovered new worlds so too did she find new parts of the Book. It would describe to her new plants, new myths, new spells associated with whatever world she had entered and thus she began to amass quite the collection of rare and valuable ingredients. After about four months, she noticed that the Book was beginning to increasingly direct her towards healing magic, and that worried her. She could think of only one likely reason, and it was to do with what awaited her at the end of the Road.

The solitude of Andromeda's journey was not always easy to bear; some days she wept at the fear of never seeing Talen again, but she wouldn't allow despair to linger. When she was discouraged, she would force herself to tilt her face up and feel the sun shining down on her, the fresh wind blowing through her hair. She would look towards whatever horizon she could see, and remember that she, who had once spent most of her life staring at castle walls, could now travel as far as her heart could take her. She had won her freedom and she must not squander it; she must have courage and hope to the same degree that any hero possessed.

In this manner, day by day, Andromeda moved forward on the Road and let nothing get in the way of her quest.

Blackheath was to be the land in which Andromeda would finally be reunited with Talen, but she did not know that when she crossed the frozen sea that landed her on Blackheath's shores. At first, she did not even know the name of the land she had entered, for during her first week all she saw was snow and ice. She would have frozen to death had not her Book of Magic taught her how to make her own fire to keep warm.

Gradually, however, the land grew less harsh, and she came to a town called Drakk where the Winter had not yet arrived. Drakk prospered in a golden autumn that seemed almost summery after the cold, and the folk there were friendly enough, though evasive as to the odd behaviour of their country's seasons.

Drakk sat at the foot of what the locals called the Barren Mountains. Andromeda's questions about the mountains were not welcomed, and she was told they were as empty as their name suggested. This she did not think true, for she could see the Road wending its way straight up the steep slope of the nearest mountain, following a rocky, narrow trail. Andromeda could feel in her blood that Talen was near, and ignoring the dire warnings of the townsfolk, she began her ascent of the mountain right away.

The mountain trail proved to be steep, slippery and treacherous. A cold wind chilled Andromeda as she climbed with Brownie in tow, but her sense of Talen's nearness, as well as a growing feeling of uneasiness, kept her climbing at a punishing pace. She allowed herself only a brief stop at midday, looking up at the jagged peak of the mountain all the while and wondering what could have driven Talen up here.

In the late afternoon, as the sun bathed the mountain in a bloody glow, Andromeda heard an ominous roar somewhere above her and doubled her pace despite her growing fatigue. For most of the day, she'd been ascending the mountain's southern face, but soon after she heard the roar the trail curved around to the east. Here she encountered a rotting wooden bridge that spanned a deep ravine and crossed over to the exposed northern slope. Several whispered spells made the bridge strong enough to bear her own and Brownie's weight, but Andromeda wondered how Talen had managed to cross the bridge if she'd come this way.

On the northern face of the mountain, the trail began to climb even more steeply. Andromeda was exhausted by this time; sweating despite the growing chill, her calves and thighs aching, her lungs burning as she gulped in as much air as she could with every breath.

Brownie nudged her from behind, an invitation to ride her the rest of the way, but Andromeda feared for her horse's slim legs and delicate hooves on the treacherous ground.

"It's all right, Brownie," she said, her words breathless. "There's something not far above us. A dwelling of some kind, I think. We'll have to stop there. The light is almost gone."

After another few painful steps, the incline of the path levelled out into a small natural plateau on the shoulder of the mountain. The wind started up again, thin and cold, needling into Andromeda's skin like the rumours of malicious gossip, but she was as oblivious to it as she would have been to the opinions of the court on her absence from her own wedding.

All Andromeda's attention was centred on the figure she could now see lying collapsed beside the rough hut she'd spotted from below; the lean hunter's physique and bright golden hair leaving her in no doubt as to the identity of the person she'd discovered.

"Talen. Talen!" All weariness forgotten, Andromeda dropped Brownie's reigns and rushed to Talen's side, but Talen didn't respond to Andromeda's calls. She didn't even stir as Andromeda approached.

Andromeda tried to prepare herself for the possibilities—injury, illness, some kind of spell—and still her face crumpled in horror as she reached Talen's side and took in her condition. Talen was burned, horribly burned; her flesh red and charred and blistered all over her body. Each harsh, painful breath she drew seemed to require so much effort Andromeda feared any one of them might be her last.

"Talen." Talen's left shoulder seemed to be the only part of her still uninjured, and it was the only place Andromeda dared to touch her as she whispered her name. "Talen, what happened?"

There was a strange red mark on the unburned shoulder. Not a tattoo. Not a scar. Not something that had been there when Talen left. Though she'd never encountered anything like it before, Andromeda somehow knew what that mark meant as soon as her fingers brushed over it. A curse. The curse of fire.

Her brows drew together in worry, but she quickly tried to wipe the expression away as Talen groaned and opened her eyes, large beautiful eyes blue as the cornflowers she sometimes used to bring Andromeda from the fields beyond the palace. Talen's eyes widened in surprise when she saw Andromeda hovering over her, and, though the motion was obviously a painful one, she smiled, the incredulous smile of a dreamer who sees her desires made flesh before her yet knows that what she sees cannot be.

"Your highness," she managed, her voice ravaged and broken. "How..."

A weight of dread lifted from Andromeda's heart to see Talen conscious, no matter how weak she may be. Returning Talen's smile with one of her own, she said, "I am not a Princess in this land, Talen. Call me by my name."

Talen reached out to her, yearning in her eyes as she touched blistered fingertips to Andromeda's cheek. "Andromeda," she husked. "How can you possibly be here?"

Andromeda knew her gaze was filled with equal longing as she leaned into Talen's touch. "I did not wish to be a prisoner of destiny, so I left. I went into the Endless Forest, and found the path that would lead me to you."

As a spasm passed through her body, Talen closed her eyes with a groan. "I'm glad," she whispered, when she could meet Andromeda's eyes again. "I've missed you..."

Beneath Talen's words, her touch, there were shades of goodbye. She knew how far gone she was; she knew she couldn't reasonably expect to live for much longer. But Andromeda hadn't come all this way to only have a few moments with Talen before losing her to death. Determination shored her up against the overwhelming wreckage of Talen's body, for her Book of Magic had been preparing her for this.

With shaking hands Andromeda searched through her pack until she found an elixir she'd brewed a world or two ago, a recipe her Book had been most insistent upon her making. Crafted from ground giants' bones and unicorn hair amongst other ingredients, the potion was guaranteed to give strength to the sufferer of any wound or sickness no matter how grievous, as long as she still drew breath.

"Here." Cradling Talen's head, Andromeda held the unstoppered bottle to Talen's lips. "Drink this. It will help."

Talen barely had enough awareness left to understand what was happening, but she instinctively swallowed as Andromeda carefully trickled the liquid into her mouth bit by bit. Once the bottle was empty, Andromeda gently laid Talen back on the ground and watched her anxiously.

Nothing much seemed to change, except that perhaps Talen's breathing grew a little easier. Andromeda had hoped for more improvement, but maybe Talen had been so close to death that merely keeping her alive had taken the elixir's full power.

Well, in that case Andromeda was just going to have to move quickly to try what else she could while there was still time.

She got to her feet and checked the interior of the hut to see it was safe. In the dying light, she picked out a few rough pieces of furniture set around a single empty room. Good enough. Giving Brownie a command to wait, Andromeda wrapped Talen in a blanket and helped her stagger into the hut.

She laid her down on the narrow bed by the large open fireplace and ignited the black, powdery rocks in the hearth with a simple spell. Andromeda didn't know what the rocks were exactly, but she'd seen similar substances used as fuel in other worlds where wood was scarce.

Talen's injuries looked even worse with the benefit of greater light, but Andromeda made sure no hint of that showed in her voice as she reassuringly brushed Talen's uninjured shoulder once more. "Talen, I have to step outside to bring the rest of my supplies in, but I won't be long, I promise. Just hang on until I get back. Can you do that?"

She wasn't sure Talen would respond, and was heartened when she stirred and opened her eyes. "Andromeda," she said, her voice terribly weak, "what can you do? Nothing can heal these injuries."

"I can heal them," Andromeda insisted. "I've been learning magic, Talen. I promise I can help you, if you'll stay with me." She bowed her head and leaned close to Talen, smelling seared flesh and blood. "Please," she whispered. "I've just found you. I don't want to lose you so soon."

When she drew back to meet Talen's eyes, Andromeda could see she still had her doubts. The fear of never being whole again, even if Andromeda succeeded in keeping her alive. The prospect of a future in which pain and infirmity may come to be her only steadfast companions. But Andromeda could also tell that her entreaty had awakened Talen's desire to fight. She could see the spark of determination brightening her gaze, she could see the trust Talen was willing to place in her.

"All right," said Talen hoarsely. "Go get your supplies. I...won't go anywhere."

Andromeda nodded and let out a fervent expression of thanks. With a last reassurance she would soon return, she hurried to the door of the hut and went out into the early evening. Brownie, still standing fully laden next to the Road, gave her a worried look and whickered.

"Brownie, oh Brownie. I've found her. I've finally found her." Burying her face in Brownie's flank, Andromeda allowed herself the luxury of a few overwrought tears. She knew she could not allow herself to be like this for long, not with the monumental task of healing Talen still before her, but it was such a relief to allow her tangled and conflicted emotions an outlet, however brief.

Brownie turned her head and nibbled comfortingly on Andromeda's curls, making her laugh tearfully.

"Right," she said. "Let's get you unloaded."

There was a small pasture next to the hut, ringed by dry stone walls with a wooden gate that was somehow still in good repair. After unloading Brownie, Andromeda turned her out in the pasture with an apology she didn't have time to do more. She could see the outline of a small stone building in the pasture, hopefully a shelter of some kind Brownie could use if she needed it.

From what Andromeda had seen so far, the Barren Mountains were very much like their name. Stony and inhospitable, with sparse animal and plant life. But someone, some time, had placed a spell on this pasture to cultivate soil and the growth of rich, green grass. It must have been a long time ago, for the spell's power was fading, but there was still enough grass that Brownie would be able to eat.

There was water too, from a trickling brook that ran through the pasture. Andromeda collected some in a bucket and carried it back to the front door of the hut, her heart beating anxiously the whole time at what felt like too long away from Talen's side, too long a delay in starting the treatment she desperately needed.

It was a tense moment for Andromeda when she re-entered the hut. She held her breath, fearing she'd be met by the silence of death, despite Talen's promise. She listened to the crackling fire, her cheeks reddening in the sudden warmth of the room, straining to hear the sound she longed for.

Talen's breathing. Talen was still breathing. She even reacted as Andromeda approached, jerking out of an unconscious haze to regard Andromeda with a befuddled expression. "You came back?" she asked, the wistful longing in her voice threading its way straight into Andromeda's heart.

"Of course I did," Andromeda replied, placing the bucket of water down by the fireplace. "I'm nearly ready, Talen. There's just a few more things I need."

Talen closed her eyes, her face drawn with pain. "Don't be much longer."

Andromeda paused to brush Talen's shoulder comfortingly before hurrying back to the door to get the supplies she'd unloaded from Brownie. After dumping everything near the fire, she likewise dragged over one of the hut's rickety chairs, placing it between Talen's bedside and the hearth.

Next she found the numbing potion she'd brewed several nights ago. That had been another occasion when the Book of Magic had fixedly kept returning to the page detailing the recipe until she made it.

"It should stop the pain," she said as she helped Talen drink.

"How...did you learn magic?" Talen asked fuzzily as Andromeda settled back in her chair, intent on the next task.

"I found a spell book that taught me, after I ran away from the palace. But you, Talen. How did you end up like this?"

Talen's gaze settled on the fire, looking as if it reminded her of far more terrifying flames. "Dragon," was all she said in a strained, quiet voice.

Andromeda paused in alarm. "A Dragon? There's a Dragon nearby?"

Talen swallowed and nodded.

"Are we safe here?"

"I don't know. I don't even know...how I managed to survive."

"Don't dwell on it," Andromeda said quickly, realising that adding to Talen's burdens was the last thing she should be doing right now. "I'll take care of everything."

With a slow exhale, Talen closed her eyes. "I can't feel the pain anymore," she murmured, and Andromeda fervently hoped that was because of the numbing potion, and not because Talen was dying. "That's something, at least."

She didn't speak again, and nor did she stir. Andromeda swore, biting back tears, knowing death was already here lingering in the dark shadows of the hut, ready to claim Talen's life should she make even one small mistake.

Moondust was the only hope she was clinging to, a fine silver dust said to be capable of healing any wound or sickness. Andromeda had learned of it by chance in a small, stormy world she'd passed through during her search, and with the Book already prompting her towards healing magic she knew she couldn't leave until she'd attempted to find it. Most in that world had told her Moondust didn't exist, but she'd persisted and sought out the long-lost mermaids who were said to be the only ones capable of guiding humans to where the Moondust could be found.

Eventually, when learning of Andromeda's plight, one of the mermaids had agreed to take her to the single outcropping of rocks surrounded by turbulent seas on which the Moondust grew. As Andromeda discovered, the substance was actually a kind of lichen, which only glowed in the moonlight when the mermaids sang and was otherwise invisible and unusable. Buffeted by the wind and soaked by the sea-spray, Andromeda had spent all night scrambling over the sharp, slippery rocks harvesting the Moondust.

Opening the pouch in which the Moondust was stored, Andromeda let the sparkling silver dust fall through her fingers, muttering a brief plea to the Fallen Fairy to lend her good fortune. She didn't even know if the Fairy could hear her so many worlds away from her home, but at least it made her feel less alone.

Talen remained frighteningly still as Andromeda mixed the Moondust into a salve made with oil and crushed herbs. Even when Andromeda began to tentatively apply the salve to Talen's blistered skin, hesitating and gritting her teeth for fear of the pain she might cause, Talen did not react. Her breaths were becoming so faint Andromeda could barely detect them.

All the magic she had was Moondust and hope, and so all Andromeda could do was continue grimly on, tearing away the singed rags of Talen's clothes to reveal still more burns, slathering and lathering until finally the Moondust began to solidify into a soft, flexible coat like a second skin, completely sealing the burns and leaving Talen a shimmering silver creature.

It was then that Talen gave a sigh and briefly opened her eyes once more, looking in befuddlement at the shimmering hand she raised before her.

"What—?" she said weakly.

"It's called Moondust," Andromeda said, her voice steady and quiet. "It will help your body heal."

Lowering her hand, Talen nodded, though Andromeda wasn't sure how much she had really understood. "Thank you, Andromeda. For coming to find me." The words were barely audible over the low crackle of the fire. "I always hoped I'd see you again."

With a smile more trembly than she meant it to be, Andromeda caressed Talen's sparkling Moondust-coated cheek. "These last two years, I spent a lot of time thinking about you, wishing I could see you too." She paused. "I'm sorry I didn't come sooner. I should have."

Talen's eyes were already drifting closed again, but this time Andromeda wasn't so afraid they would never reopen. "You should have come sooner," Talen agreed. "But since you just saved my life, I'll think about forgiving you."

Despite the circumstances, Andromeda let out a low laugh, surprising herself. She was about to respond, but saw that Talen had already lapsed back into a sleep-like state. So instead, she caressed Talen's cheek once more, and said, "There's one more thing I need to do, to give this the best chance of working. I hope you can lend me your trust, Talen, for a little longer."

Andromeda wasn't sure if Talen heard her.

The coating of Moondust needed to remain undisturbed for seven days. The Book of Magic claimed the best way to achieve that was to place the patient into an enchanted sleep. Having been in an enchanted sleep herself before, Andromeda felt ambivalent at best about placing someone else in that state, especially without Talen knowing.

But, remembering the trust in Talen's gaze, Andromeda had to believe she would understand. And she had to have faith that she herself would do this right, and be able to bring Talen out of the enchantment when the time came.

She had already memorised the spell from the Book; all she need do was put her palm to Talen's forehead and speak it.

Her hand shook as she placed it against the dazzling sheen of Talen's skin, but her voice did not. Andromeda spelled the enchantment in a voice of power, the voice of a Witch, feeling the magic flowing through her, responding to her; melding with the enchantment of the Moondust and sending Talen into a healing sleep that would be her best chance of survival.

At the end of it, Andromeda was trembling with exhaustion, but still she did not allow herself to rest. She picked up the Book of Magic and began to read again, looking for guidance on what she needed to do to get Talen through the week safely. For now, Andromeda had saved Talen's life, but there was still a long way to go before her task here was done and the woman she cared for was whole again.

Chapter 3

For three days and three nights, Andromeda did not sleep as she sat by Talen's bedside. She renewed the coating of Moondust whenever she saw its radiance fading, and passed many hours running her hands over Talen's damaged skin whispering magic under her breath.

The incantation Andromeda spoke had, for want of a better word, appeared in the Book that first night she spent by Talen's side. As she leafed through the Book, the spell had been there, a few pages after the entries on Moondust, even though Andromeda was sure it hadn't been there before.

The Book of Magic described the incantation as a supportive spell which would help to amplify the Moondust's healing powers. The stronger the bond between healer and patient, the more powerful the effects of the spell would be. And so as Andromeda healed, she imbued her feelings and her memories into her touch; thinking back to her days as a sequestered Princess, to the way that meeting Talen had expanded the possibilities of her world.

Talen had been so many things: a hunter, a tracker, a warrior, someone who faced the wilds without fear. Someone who could make Andromeda laugh, whose very presence brought a light into her heart. Talen had shown Andromeda there were other ways to live besides what she'd been taught; that the unknown was full of possibility and joy as well as danger.

Because of Talen, Andromeda had been able to transform from the inhibited creature she had been into a woman who revelled in her own new-found strength and abilities, who could now hope for a future of growth side by side with the one she loved.

It was undeniably difficult work. Andromeda didn't understand the means by which the spell worked, but sometimes she almost felt as though it was her own strength she was pouring into Talen's wounded body, giving her what she needed to heal. Often she was left weary, but she continued on for she could feel that beneath the membrane of Moondust Talen's skin was mending.

The way that Talen sometimes stirred or smiled in her sleep in response to Andromeda's touch was a further indication of hope— Andromeda took it to mean that Talen could feel the connection between them too, and welcomed what Andromeda gave her.

Thankfully, there was little Andromeda needed to do besides concentrate on healing. She kept the hut clean with a few basic spells she'd learned soon after finding the Book of Magic. She left for only a small amount of time each day, in order to fetch water and groom Brownie, using the opportunity to work the kinks out of her spine and sharpen her senses in the cold mountain air. The stone structure Andromeda had noticed in the pasture when she first arrived was indeed a rough barn, and with a few spells she was able to reattach its door and refresh the mouldering pile of straw in one corner so Brownie had a comfortable bed.

On a rare exploration when she felt safe enough to venture further, Andromeda followed the brook in Brownie's pasture upstream and found a small waterfall tumbling down the side of the mountain with a deep pool at its base carved out by the water. It would have been perfect for swimming if the weather had been warmer. As it was, Andromeda only dipped her fingers in and shivered.

Despite keeping a watchful eye out, she found no clues as to who had constructed the hut or why.

About mid-morning on the fourth day, Andromeda was surprised to hear footsteps outside the hut. The people of Drakk had insisted the mountain was impassable and that no one lived up here (neglecting to mention the Dragon), so Andromeda couldn't imagine why anyone would go to the trouble of climbing the treacherous path up the mountain, unless they too were curious about Talen's fate or were foolhardy enough to want to face the Dragon themselves.

As a precaution, Andromeda had already woven some basic defensive spells of protection around the hut—thinking of the Dragon more than human assailants—so she was not unduly alarmed when a knock sounded at the door. While she wasn't entirely certain the spell she'd cast would be able to withstand a prolonged assault from an angry Dragon, a single human shouldn't be a problem if they proved to have ill intent.

An elderly woman with tanned skin and keen brown eyes was standing on the threshold of the hut when Andromeda opened the door.

"Excuse me for the disturbance," the woman said, "I realise this must seem strange. But...I just had to see for myself whether you found the Hero. Whether she still lives."

Andromeda frowned. "The Hero? Do you mean Talen?"

The woman nodded, her gaze looking past Andromeda towards where Talen was laid out on the bed, all a-shimmer. Her eyes widened slightly, but she did not otherwise react.

"Talen is still alive, but she's badly injured. I'm caring for her, as you can see." There was a pause, in which Andromeda tried to decide whether she should invite the woman inside, and the woman waited to see what Andromeda would do, studying her intently with an astute gaze.

While the woman's appearance on the mountain was undeniably odd, Andromeda couldn't sense any malice or deceit from her. Besides, if she knew Talen, she might be able to tell Andromeda what had sent her up the mountain to fight a Dragon in the first place.

"Come in and rest," Andromeda said, deciding to trust her instincts. "The path up this mountain is not an easy one."

"Thank you," the woman said, following Andromeda into the hut and taking the second chair Andromeda placed by the fire. She gladly accepted the mug of hot tea Andromeda poured out, and sipped it appreciatively with a sigh.

"Been a long time since I climbed the mountain," the woman admitted ruefully. "Not since I was a young woman." With self-depreciating humour, she added, "I did not perhaps fully account for that when I decided upon this course of action. I couldn't even make it up here all in one day; I set out yesterday and had to spend last night in the open on the mountainside."

"Why would you take a risk like that?" Andromeda asked. "Do you know Talen? Are you a friend of hers?"

"No, I don't know her, but I know of her. Everyone does in this land." Giving Andromeda a direct look with her intelligent eyes, the woman said, "Forgive me, I should properly introduce myself. My name is Lezith. I live in Drakk, the town at the base of the Barren Mountains. I saw you when you passed through, asking if anyone lived up here. I watched you set off. When you didn't return, I got curious. I thought perhaps you'd found her. The person you were obviously looking for. And that she hadn't died, like all the others."

"Why did the people of Drakk not tell me the truth? They must have known Talen had come up here to fight the Dragon."

"Ah, so you know about the Dragon now."

"Talen was able to tell me before I put her into this slumber to help her heal."

"She faced the Dragon then?"

"Yes. But it happened before I got here. She was badly burned."

Lezith grimaced. "Now those injuries are not easily healed. You must be a great Sorceress to have saved her life. And that sparkling stuff on her skin—I've never seen anything like it." She looked with interest at Talen's shimmering form over the rim of her mug, making no effort to hide her scrutiny.

"I'm not a great anything," said Andromeda, cautious of giving too much away. "But I do have some herblore. The substance you can see is a kind of lichen with healing properties, just a very rare variety."

"So rare it did not come from this world," Lezith guessed astutely.

She held up a worn hand as Andromeda began to protest. "All right, I'll not push the matter. It's of no account to me anyway. You asked why the people of Drakk didn't divulge what they knew. I'm not proud to say it, but it's because of fear. They fear the Dragon. They fear its wrath. They think that if the Dragon should spy any townspeople helping the Dragon Slayers, it might destroy us. They all pass through our town before they ascend. Great lords and warriors and heroes. We do not speak to any of them, nor offer them succour. Each one comes to this house and readies themselves for battle in whatever manner they deem fit. And then each one climbs alone to the peak of the mountain where the Dragon dwells, and until your Talen, they have all died alone in the Dragon's flames. The pact is between the Hero and the Empress; to slay the Dragon for reward and renown. We just have the misfortune to be caught up in it."

"And why does this Empress want the Dragon slain?"

"It's not what you think," said Lezith, hearing the note of disapproval in Andromeda's voice. "It's not for sport, it's not so some vain fool can have a trophy made of a Dragon's head. The Dragon used to be the protector of these lands, but it has all gone wrong. No one knows why."

Andromeda poured them both fresh mugs of tea. Lezith was indeed proving herself to be a knowledgeable conversationalist, and Andromeda was eager to do what she could to keep her talking. "What do you mean it has all gone wrong?"

After thanking Andromeda for the tea, Lezith explained, "The Empress's clan have been our rulers ever since this land came to be.

They are said to share the Dragon's blood. The Dragon guards this mountain. It has always guarded the mountain. But now, it lets nothing through. We cannot cross the mountain, and what we need cannot cross over to us."

"And what is that? What will the Dragon not let through?"

A wistful look came into Lezith's eyes. "Spring," she said softly, her gaze wandering over to the open door and the chill day beyond.

"Spring?"

Glancing back to Andromeda, Lezith nodded. "Since the founding of our land, it was the tradition for the reigning Emperor or Empress to call the Dragon at the end of Winter, and the Dragon would always answer that call. It would leave this mountain and fly across the land, and in its wake Spring would bloom. The warm, fragrant air would come through the portal that lies at the peak of this mountain, and the Dragon's wings would create a mighty wind that carried the Spring throughout the land. After bringing rebirth, the Dragon would return to the mountain, and remain there as Spring turned to Summer, Summer to Autumn, Autumn to Winter. The Dragon would sleep through the Winter, and awaken again in the Spring to answer the Imperial Family's call..."

With a sigh, she lapsed into silence, as if she didn't have the heart to continue.

"How long has it been since Spring came to this land?"

"Ten years. For ten years the snows of Winter have been deepening without respite. Much of Blackheath has become uninhabitable. The further one goes from the Dragon's Mountain, the worse it gets."

"The Dragon's presence still creates enough warmth to keep nearby towns like Drakk liveable?" This explained those peculiarities of weather that had puzzled Andromeda when she first encountered them.

"Yes, but even we are locked in Autumn. Soon enough, the Winter will probably claim us too."

"How much longer do you think the people of Blackheath can go on like this?"

Pain glittered in Lezith's eyes. "Not for long. The land can't sustain us like this. I doubt I will get to see another Spring before I die."

Moved by Lezith's sorrow, Andromeda couldn't help but grasp her hand in sympathy for a moment. "I can't imagine what your people have been through, trying to survive like that. It sounds as if the Empress is acting out of desperation. You said before the people of Drakk don't like to get involved with the Heroes, for fear of angering the Dragon. That's understandable, given the circumstances. So I wonder again—why did you decide to climb the mountain? Why tell me all this?"

Her manner lightening, Lezith chuckled. "I suppose you could say I was curious. I'm old, and there is nothing a Dragon can take from me that death is not already coming to collect. I wanted to see for myself what had become of you. There was a look in your eyes when you passed through the town; like you could see marvellous visions that were closed to the rest of us. It's foolish, but a part of me wondered whether you would climb this mountain and find the Spring that has been hiding from us, all these years."

Andromeda gave Lezith a smile tinged with sadness. "I wish I could, but I think I probably used up all my luck just finding Talen still alive."

"Perhaps. It's a curious thing, your coming here. All the others before Talen, they came up this mountain alone, and they died alone. So Talen would have died, yet she lives because you came after her. It marks a change in the pattern. I don't pretend to know what it means but...I would be very surprised if we have reached the end of this story already."

"Will Talen have to fight the Dragon again? She bears a curse mark on her shoulder that I much mislike." Andromeda looked at Talen's sleeping form, frowning without realising it as worries for the future crowded into her mind. "She is very dear to me. I don't know if I could bear to lose her. I was searching for her for such a long time."

Lezith rose and patted Andromeda on the shoulder, an understanding look in her eyes. "I've told you as much as I can. I don't know what pact Talen made with the Empress, or why. You will have to wait to hear the rest from her when she awakens. And now I really must be starting back. It's a long way down, and if I'm gone for too long everyone will start to worry."

"You want to leave already?" said Andromeda. "You must be exhausted after two days climbing. Why don't you stay the night?"

"It's all right," Lezith insisted. "Even if I have to sleep outdoors again, I'd rather get as far down the mountain as I can."

Andromeda shook her head in disbelief as Lezith rose and made for the door. "Can I at least ask how you managed to cross the wooden bridge over the gorge? I barely made it."

"Oh, the bridge," said Lezith dismissively. "That's just a test. After a while, you remember which parts of it will bear weight and which won't."

"But I used magic to help me cross. If the bridge is meant to be a test, why didn't I get punished for cheating?"

Lezith paused at the door. "Who said there was only one way of passing the test? Now, do I have to see myself out or can I expect a proper farewell?"

Giving Talen a caress and a whispered promise she'd be back soon, Andromeda joined Lezith outside the hut. The cold mountain wind whistling down from the peak sent her black curls flying, while Lezith clutched her tattered cloak tighter around her shoulders.

"I wish you a safe journey home," said Andromeda, adding a touch of the solemnity she had often imbued into the blessings she used to bestow as a Princess.

"Thank you," said Lezith warmly. "I'm glad to have met you, Andromeda. There is not much of novelty left in the world when one has lived as long as I. One day, I hope I will have the chance to hear more of your story, for I can sense it is an interesting one. But for now, I leave you with a parting message. The Empress will know of what has happened here soon enough. She will be coming. I would tell your Talen that, when she wakes up. She will need to prepare herself."

"Very well. I'll be sure to tell her." Andromeda wanted to ask Lezith what she meant, for there was a clear warning in her voice, but Lezith's expression did not invite further questions.

Looking towards the peak of the mountain, Lezith added, "The death of the Dragon, for the life of the land. It's not how it's supposed to be. As the Dragon awakens, so should the land awaken too. What will happen when the Dragon dies? Even if Spring returns, it will not be the same Spring. Only the Dragon can bring that. What stories will we tell ourselves, when the Dragon is gone from the world? Will we forget who we once were, and what the Dragon meant to us?" She shook her head. "It's a bad business, and I'm afraid I've often wished I'd already been safely in my grave before these strange days afflicted us."

"Has no one tried to solve the mystery? There must be a reason for the change in the Dragon."

"Many have tried, including the Empress herself. No solution was found. Not even a clue. And now it's too late for all that. Your Talen has sworn to kill the Dragon, and that oath must be fulfilled. Death is the only option left and we must all bear the consequences, whatever they may be."

She looked back to Andromeda. "I'm sorry, I've disturbed you with my ramblings. Just you concentrate on getting Talen well. The rest doesn't matter for now."

Andromeda nodded and smiled, though Lezith's words had left her uneasy. "Thank you for coming all this way to see me. I hope the rest of the townspeople are not too angry with you."

As she set foot on the mountain path, Lezith made a dismissive noise. "They know haranguing me will only make me more stubborn. I've always been the sort to take my own counsel. Good luck, my dear, and blessings to both you and Talen. Come and see me in Drakk if the two of you get the chance."

"We will," Andromeda promised as she waved goodbye. She watched until she was satisfied that Lezith was safely managing the steep descent, and then went back inside, closing the door behind her.

As Andromeda watched over Talen throughout the afternoon and into the night, she ruminated on everything Lezith had told her. Why would the Dragon behave in such a strange manner? Why hadn't the Empress been able to communicate with it, when her family had always had such close ties to it before? And why had Talen agreed to fight the Dragon? She'd never been the sort to care for glory.

Andromeda sighed and stroked Talen's face as she slept. "What have you gotten yourself into?" she whispered.

And then she rubbed her eyes to chase away her growing tiredness and resumed chanting healing incantations under her breath while the Moondust coating Talen's skin shimmered and sparkled in the firelight.

Chapter 4

On the morning of the seventh day, Talen awakened. Andromeda had been watching her anxiously since dawn, waiting for any sign of consciousness. The Book of Magic had claimed Talen would awaken on her own without assistance, but only if there had been no missteps in the weeklong healing.

The waking was a gradual process, and not a gentle one. First Talen thrashed and groaned in her sleep, her fists clenching and her teeth grinding. Then her breathing grew laboured as if she could not draw enough air into her lungs, and finally she began to mumble incoherently in what might have been gibberish or merely some language Andromeda didn't understand.

Finally, in response to Andromeda's voice, she sat bolt upright and opened her eyes, looking about in panic and confusion that gradually eased as she began to realise where she was.

"Andromeda," Talen's voice was rough from days of disuse, and there was still fading panic in her eyes as her gaze settled on Andromeda. "You're really here. I thought I'd dreamed the whole thing...I was sure I must still be dying..."

Andromeda soothed her with a touch. "You're not dying. I put you to sleep for a week to help your body recover. That time has just passed. You should—" Despite trying to appear calm, Andromeda couldn't stop her voice from faltering.

"I should be healed?" Talen hadn't missed the uncertainty in Andromeda's manner.

"I hope so. How do you feel?"

Talen gave a hollow laugh. "Like I've been to the Underworld and back again." She rubbed at her shimmering skin. "This stuff is itchy. Is it supposed to be like that?"

"I don't know. My Magic Book didn't say anything about the Moondust itching. But now that you're awake, the coating does need to be washed off. I have fresh water here—"

"No." Dumbfounding Andromeda, Talen threw back the bedcovers and stumbled to her feet. Her breathing was elevated, but otherwise she appeared steady enough. With a stubborn set to her jaw, she said, "I want to have a proper bath. There's a pool at the base of the waterfall. I'll go there."

"Talen, the water will be freezing."

The writings in the Book of Magic had been vague in the extreme about what would happen after Talen's awakening. Andromeda had no idea if her seeming strength and energy were typical; if it would be safe to let Talen out of the hut so soon.

"I don't care if the water's cold. I'm not going to be able to get this stuff off without immersion. There was a satchel I left here in the hut. Spare clothes and such. Have you come across it?"

Andromeda stood, still struggling to figure out what she should do. Seeing her doubt, Talen walked back to her, and, after hesitating, reached out to tangle her fingers with Andromeda's own. "I'll be all right, Andromeda," she said, looking into Andromeda's eyes reassuringly. "I just...need to do this alone." Beneath the Moondust, Andromeda saw Talen's expression tighten. "I have to know what I've got to work with. How bad it is."

"If I've done everything right, you should be as you were before," Andromeda said, though it was still without confidence.

Talen nodded. "Right. But this is your first time doing something like this, isn't it?" Her tone was surprisingly gentle. "It might not have gone perfectly."

Letting out a breath, Andromeda nervously readjusted her grip on Talen's fingers. The fact that Talen was the one comforting her right now was upsetting enough to almost make her cry. "All right. If you're really determined, I'll wait for you. Your satchel is in the corner over there, with the other bags."

Talen gave Andromeda a smile that did not entirely disguise her dis-ease. "Thank you. I won't be long."

Andromeda paced up and down restlessly by the fire after Talen left, but she soon felt too confined indoors. She went out into the morning sun and looked over the bleak mountain range, wondering where the Dragon had gone. Unusually, there was little wind this morning, and Andromeda could hear the gushing of the waterfall even though she couldn't see it from here.

Eventually she sat down on the rough stone bench that had been placed outside the hut at some point—probably many years ago from its worn and lichened state—and found herself shaking—from relief, from tension, from the sheer exultation of knowing Talen was going to live.

Her breath caught as she heard Talen approaching. It was odd, how easily she recognised her footsteps after two years. She looked up and started to her feet. Talen was pale, even paler than Andromeda remembered, her eyes and cheeks were underscored by hollows, she was thin and wasted—but her skin was whole. No burns. No scars. No suggestion she was still in pain.

"It worked?" Andromeda asked, reaching out her hand to stroke Talen's cheek.

With a nod, Talen leaned into the touch. "Thank you," she whispered. She closed her own fingers over Andromeda's hand, her lips parting as her breath sped. She seemed as taken with the wonder of being here with Andromeda, able to see her, to touch her, as she was at her recovery from the Dragon's attack. "I don't know how you managed it, but I don't have a single mark. Not one scar."

Andromeda raised her free hand to touch Talen's shoulder, able to feel the curse mark beneath the fabric of the shirt she was wearing. "You do still have one mark," she pointed out.

She saw Talen's eyes widen slightly. "You know what that is?"

"Not entirely. But I know it's a curse of some kind. I can feel that much. I'm a Witch now, remember?"

Talen gave a bark of laughter. "You think I'm likely to forget, when it was your magic that saved my life? But...how did you become a Witch? Why would a Princess want that?"

"I couldn't stay a Princess. Not if I wanted to find you. So I changed into something else. That's the short version, anyway."

"I don't want the short version," Talen said.

With a smile, Andromeda drew even closer to Talen. She'd spent so many hours watching over her, agonising every time she had to touch her damaged skin, fearing what pain she might be causing. It felt like a glorious indulgence to simply be able to reach out now, to embrace her, to feel the warmth of her body.

"I'll tell you," Andromeda promised. "But first...I have to do something I've dreamed about doing ever since I first got to know you."

She looked into Talen's eyes and saw the same rising desire she felt in her own chest. She felt Talen's arms encircling her, felt the steady beating of her heart.

"Andromeda." Talen said her name in a low, trembling voice, husky with want. "I realise events have rather gotten away from us here, but are you sure you know what you're doing? Have you really thought—"

Their lips almost brushing together, Andromeda replied, "You ask me that after I crossed so many worlds to find you? After I healed you when you were dying? Of course I know what I'm doing." Closing the last gap between them, Andromeda kissed Talen. Not for long, and not for as long as she wanted to; a kiss of happiness and yearning with an untamed edge that promised future passion.

She laughed when she drew back and saw the disbelief lingering in the depths of Talen's eyes, beneath the bright shine of bliss.

"Why the shock, Talen?" she teased. "These feelings have always been between us."

"I know," said Talen, a slight stammer in her voice. "It's just...the last time I saw you, you were a long way from even acknowledging to yourself what you felt, let alone anyone else." Her eyes wandered to the bench where Andromeda had been sitting before. "Come," she said, taking Andromeda's hand and pulling her towards the bench. "Sit with me and tell me what's been happening to you since we parted. I'm not eager to stay on this mountain longer than we have to, but I doubt I'd make it far if we left today. Have you been disturbed at all during the time you've been here?"

Andromeda gladly sat down next to Talen, close enough that their bodies touched, her hand still twined with Talen's. "I've seen and heard nothing the whole week. Are you sure the Dragon is still here?"

"Oh, it's up there all right," Talen said, looking towards the peak of the mountain with a dark expression. "But if it hasn't bothered to come down and kill me so far, I guess I'm safe until I face it again."

"So you are going to fight it again?"

Talen switched her gaze back to Andromeda, regret darkening her eyes. "I took an oath, Andromeda. I don't have a choice."

"Why Talen? Why did you do it?"

Running a hand through her hair, Talen again looked away. "For a stupid reason. I'll tell you about it, but you promised to tell me your story first. I know—I can sort of remember—feeling you in my mind while I was asleep, talking to me, but it's all slipping away like a dream. I just have these blurred impressions."

"All right, I'll tell my side first," Andromeda agreed. "Before I do, though, I'm going to bring out some food for both of us. You've gone a week with only magic to sustain you, and I haven't eaten since before dawn."

Talen agreed she was starting to get hungry, which Andromeda took as a good sign. She brought out bowls of stew and the last of her dried fruit supplies, and later they sipped sweet tea as Andromeda told Talen what had befallen her in the two and a half years since they'd parted. She told it out of order, starting with her adventures on the Road, her encounter with the demon, the finding of the Book, and finally her journey through Blackheath and up the mountain to this very hut.

"And so that tells me how you learned to wield magic," said Talen, tucking away one of Andromeda's curls, "but it doesn't tell me why you decided to leave. What made you come after me."

Andromeda smiled. "I stopped being able to pretend I wasn't in love with you. That's all."

Talen's hand stilled for a moment, then trembled. "Yes, but what was the trigger? That's what I'm trying to ask."

Diverting the question, Andromeda started on a different track. "You know, I've always wondered how you came to be travelling with that Prince. The one—"

"I know which one," said Talen, unhappiness edging into her voice as she recalled. "There was no particular reason for it. We met by chance and he asked me to travel with him. I had nothing better to do, so I went. The castle where you were put to sleep...the wilderness had grown up and hidden it so well he didn't even realise anything was there. He would have ridden right past it. I was the one who hacked a path through the thorns and found the castle door. Everyone was asleep inside; the guards, the servants, the entire court. And you, lying on your bed beneath a bower of roses. I didn't even realise the Prince had followed me until he barged in and kissed you."

A look of anguish crossed Talen's face. "I didn't want to leave you after that, even though I knew I was getting myself into a world of pain. So I became your bodyguard, and watched him woo you." She sighed and shook herself. "What happened with him in the end? Did you marry him?"

"No!" Andromeda was shocked to realise Talen even thought it a possibility. "I mean...as I was back then, I suppose I would have, if he'd stayed. Not because I had feelings for him; I honestly found him rather dull. It's just that in those days I thought I had no choice but to let other people write my story for me."

"What made him leave?" Talen asked the question too calmly, as if she was trying to hide the emotional impact it was having on her to rehash this particular chapter of the past.

"He didn't give a reason, but I think it was probably the scar. From the assassin's attack. My parents didn't let him see it, but they did have the court physician describe it in detail, mapping out on my body where it was and what it looked like, while I was standing there fully clothed."

This revelation completely shattered Talen's attempted composure, and she gave Andromeda a horrified look. "That's utterly barbaric. I truly wish you hadn't gotten hurt, that I'd done my job better, but to humiliate you like that, for something that wasn't even your fault—"

Andromeda leaned into Talen's shoulder, taking her hand as she did so. "If you hadn't been there, I would have been killed. I don't care about the scar. It's not painful or debilitating. But you're right; the way my family behaved was abominable. As I stood there, I kept thinking about how you'd been after the attack; the fear in your eyes when you saw the blood. That wasn't because you were worried about my beauty being damaged. You were afraid of losing me. You showed me more tenderness than the Prince who'd given me a thousand gifts and countless declarations of love."

She felt Talen exhale. "I'm sorry, Andromeda. I should have told you I loved you before I left. I should have given you the option to come with me, even if I thought there was no chance you'd take me up on it."

Andromeda turned her face to Talen's collarbone, a ridiculous smile on her lips as she heard Talen say that she loved her. Even if she'd already known it, the spoken affirmation was a powerful thing, a confirmation of the reality Andromeda most definitely wanted.

It was the very opposite of how she'd felt two and a half years ago, standing with flaming cheeks while others judged the value of her body, the Prince's dispassionate eyes looking her up and down like a chipped jewel no longer worth the asking price.

"I honestly don't know what I would have done if you'd asked me to leave with you," she admitted, straightening up to meet Talen's eyes. "But even if I'd said no, I would have regretted it. I regretted it anyway, even though you never asked me."

With an understanding smile, Talen kissed her. "Leaving behind everything you know isn't a small thing. It takes a lot of courage."

Smiling back, Andromeda wondered if Talen too had once had to make a choice like that. She still didn't know much about her past. There were a lot of questions she intended to ask, but in all fairness, Andromeda had agreed to tell her story first, and she might as well finish it since she was already drawing close to the end.

"Well, to continue on. After the Prince left, my parents said he must have not been my true love after all, and consulted my Fairy Godmother. She advised them to put me in peril, and wait and see who rescued me. She said that was how my true love would be revealed."

Talen groaned. "And they went ahead and did that, I'm guessing?"

"More or less. There was a monster, and another Prince came along to rescue me. So everyone decided he was the one I was supposed to marry. But by that point, I was sick of everything. I hated my life, and I hated what I knew it would be if I married him. The night before my wedding, I ran away and made for the Endless Forest. You'd told me before you left I should go there if I ever wanted to find you."

Lightly scolding, Andromeda paused to add, "Which, incidentally, was very misleading advice. Since I knew you'd lived in the Forest before, I thought you meant I'd find you in the Forest, or you'd find me. But you were already several worlds away. Why did you tell me to go there? How did you know I'd figure out a way to follow your trail?"

"Funny thing, you know," Talen said, half-amused and half-serious. "I've travelled through many different worlds, and all of them have their own version of the Endless Forest. It's not always called that, it's not even necessarily always a forest. It could be a desert or an ocean or any number of things, but what all the places have in common is that they are borderlands where the imposed rules of the world fall away. The place where those go who have been deemed not to have a place in the world. I had a feeling you would find someone to guide you, if you could make it there."

"You did turn out to be right," Andromeda confessed, though not without some grumbling at the accuracy of Talen's prediction. "I met my Fairy Godmother in the Forest. My real one. My parents had always told me she was evil, because of the sleeping curse. But I realised everything about that was the opposite of what it seemed. She told me to follow the Broken Road, and that's how I was able to find you."

"I always thought Fairy Godmothers a very odd quirk of your world, but I am grateful to her if she helped you. I have no knowledge of this Broken Road, however. I have not been following any particular path these last two years."

Andromeda had to laugh at that, and tangled a hand into Talen's hair, combing her fingers through fine, silky locks. "You've been following the Road your whole life. You're so far along it you're probably treading the unbroken ground that hasn't even been paved yet, let alone destroyed."

Talen raised a confused eyebrow. "Andromeda, I don't know what you're talking about."

"I'll explain it to you sometime. But now I want to hear your story. How did you get caught up with the Empress of this land? Why did you agree to fight the Dragon?"

Shaking her head, Talen gave Andromeda a tired smile. "I know I said I'd tell you, and I will, but...later? When I have the rest of my head together."

Despite the many questions she had, Andromeda nodded. "All right. I don't want to push you. Shall we go in? As nice as it is out here..." Andromeda scanned the sky, thinking of the Dragon.

"Yeah, we can go in," Talen agreed. "But don't worry about the Dragon. It's not coming for us yet."

"What do you mean?"

After getting to her feet, Talen paused, looking confused. "I...don't know. It just came to me."

"Does that mean the Dragon will come for us later?"

Talen met Andromeda's worried gaze. "I don't know. I certainly hope not."

Despite the sunshine, they both shivered.

❦

THE UNUSUAL WARMTH of the day started to dissipate as the afternoon shadows lengthened. Andromeda stirred herself to complete the chores that had to be done before nightfall: building up the fire, fetching more water, preparing an evening meal. Talen had been asleep off and on throughout the afternoon but woke up as Andromeda was cooking, her stomach growling loud enough for Andromeda to hear.

They talked over supper, mostly confining themselves to the past, for they both knew that the shadow of the Dragon hung over the future and Talen was still reluctant to tell how she had come to make her pact with the Empress.

Andromeda found her asleep once more when she came back from putting Brownie away for the night, and left her be with a smile and a caress. She settled in her chair by the fireside with the Book of

Magic open on her lap, still not quite willing to give up her vigil, and continued to watch over Talen's bedside as she had done on so many nights before.

Chapter 5

Sometime during the still darkness of that night, Andromeda was awoken by the slide of sheets shifting on Talen's bed. She jolted out of her uncomfortable rest with a fast beating heart, imagining the burns returning, spreading across Talen's skin in a spectacular failure of magic.

But she opened her eyes to see Talen blinking at her sleepily, her hair rumpled, her skin touched by nothing worse than the glow of firelight.

"Why are you sleeping like that?" Talen asked, her voice low, barely rising above the crackling fire.

"I have to watch over you. I've barely dared to sleep at all since I found you."

"You had to watch over me," Talen corrected. She propped herself up on one elbow, and held out a hand.

Andromeda looked at Talen's outstretched hand, then up to her eyes, earnestly sincere and bright in the dimness of the room. When she'd kissed Talen earlier today, Andromeda's stomach had tingled with excitement and warmth had bloomed between her thighs. She knew she wanted Talen, yet right now, she was also stiff and weary, more grimy than clean, and thinking she would much prefer a roomier bed.

A half-smile curved Talen's lips. "I still feel like I've just been dragged out of the Underworld. I'm not exactly thinking—" She broke off for a moment. "Of anything besides wanting you to lay down with me." With a mischievous gleam in her eyes, she added, "Unless you think it improper for a former Princess to share the bed of her former bodyguard?"

"If I thought that, would I really have come all this way?" Though Andromeda had meant to match Talen's teasing tone, her reply had a sober note.

Her own expression growing serious, Talen shook her head. "No. And you've already told me you've thought this through. So..." She waggled her hand. "Hurry up. My hand is getting cold."

Rolling her eyes and letting out a laugh, Andromeda took Talen's hand and allowed herself to be pulled down into the narrow bed. Talen shifted to make room for her, but it was still a tight squeeze with the two of them. They could hardly help being pressed against each other, and that was a sensation to Andromeda both unfamiliar and very welcome. Beneath the blankets already warmed by Talen's body, Andromeda allowed her fingers to wander with light touches, retracing the paths she'd followed so many nights when Talen's skin was withered and burned.

"You really don't have any scars, do you," she said, hearing the wonderment in her own voice.

"Not from the burns," Talen agreed. "But in the interests of full disclosure, I do have a few old ones from past adventures."

Talen's breathing had sped a little, and she soon moved an exploratory hand lightly over Andromeda in return, starting at her hip and working upwards until she was tracing the sweep of Andromeda's cheekbone, her chin, her lips.

Seeing the look in her eyes, Andromeda leaned in and kissed Talen, holding her, revelling in the warmth of her; knowing this was all a near miracle given the state she'd found Talen in a week ago.

After they parted, they lay curled into each other's arms, not speaking, listening to the rhythm of each other's breaths, each other's hearts. It was a moment of much needed peace for both of them; the end of Andromeda's long journey upon the Road, the end of Talen's tortured wonderings about what had happened to the Princess she left behind.

The uncertain, chaotic future would sweep this night away all too soon, but for now it was enough to be here together, stubbornly celebrating life in this ramshackle cottage perched on the mountain of a dying world.

Heavy-eyed, Talen kissed Andromeda's shoulder, then sighed and shifted back enough to look at her. "I think I'm ready to tell you now. How it is that I came to take up the task of slaying the Dragon. This land has been locked in Winter for ten years—"

"I know," said Andromeda. "I already know the story of the Dragon. A woman from Drakk named Lezith came to visit a few days ago, and she told me what she could." She brushed her hand over Talen's left shoulder. "This mark came from the Empress, didn't it? Binding you to your fate of taking the Dragon's life. But why Talen? You were never like that; boasting of slaying beasts and monsters. You always said you preferred a forest over any castle. So what did the Empress tempt you with?"

Andromeda hadn't known she was jealous until she heard it in her own voice, bitter and hurt. Talen obviously hadn't expected it either, though it paradoxically seemed to lessen the tension Andromeda could feel in her body.

"I already told you it was a stupid reason," Talen said softly. "I still prefer forests over castles, I still prefer the solitude of the wilderness to a city full of people. But I couldn't stop thinking about you. For two years I racked my brains about how we could be together, and it always came back to the same thing. You were a Princess, and as far as your parents were concerned, I was a nobody. I knew you were supposed to marry that Prince, but I also knew you didn't love him. Despite wanting to please your parents, I had my doubts about whether you'd be able to bring yourself to do it. So I kept thinking that if I could return as a somebody, I might have a chance with you. I could be your suitor if I had the power of a Prince. And that's what the Empress was offering. An estate, a title, and a tidy sum of gold."

It was evident from the rueful tone of Talen's voice that she already knew her strategy had been flawed. Nevertheless, Andromeda smoothed a hand down her chest and whispered, "It's because you weren't a Prince that I fell in love with you. I never would have spurned you because you couldn't give me riches and a title."

"I know. But I wasn't thinking of you. I was thinking of your parents. I thought if I could prove myself to them, using the standards they adhered to, they might be willing to consider me."

"Talen, no matter what you did, it never would have been enough to satisfy my parents. Not if you had ten castles gilded in gold. Not even if you found out you were the long lost royal heir of some great empire. It would not have been acceptable to them for me to form a union with a woman instead of a man. You'd have been thrown out of the court if you dared to suggest something so outrageous, and if I'd suggested it, I probably would have been married off to the nearest Prince before the day was out." She stroked an apologetic hand through Talen's hair. "It's not fair things are like that in my world, and I know now it isn't the same everywhere. It means a lot that you were willing to go that far for me, but it wouldn't have worked."

There was a frustrated look in Talen's eyes. "And part of me deep down already knew all that. That's why I'm so angry at myself. I should have trusted you. I should have waited instead of trading away my future."

Cold dread trickled into the pit of Andromeda's stomach, and her mouth was suddenly dry. "What do you mean by that?"

With tears glinting in her eyes, Talen said, "In a year's time, either the Dragon will be dead, or I will be. That's what the curse mark is; it binds me to those terms. There's no escape, no running away. I'm not free anymore."

"Oh Talen." Andromeda leaned her forehead against Talen's, breathing in her scent and listening to the sharp mountain wind moaning outside. Her blood soared to be here with Talen as she'd longed for, and it hurt in a way she didn't have words for to know this curse could take Talen from her arms. "I wish I'd come sooner. This never would have happened if we'd been together. I never wanted to live my life within the constraints my parents laid out for me. That's why I left. I wanted—"

"You wanted freedom. I know. I could see the hunger for it in your eyes. That was why you used to watch me." Talen gave her a flirtatious smile. "Why it started, anyway. Because you knew I was free, and it fascinated you." Sadness creeping into her eyes, she added quietly, "but I've lost that now."

"No. There has to be a way to break the curse. I was under a sleeping curse once, and I woke up from that. I'm a Witch now. I can perform spells, enchantments. There might be something in my Book—"

Her words died at the incredulous and disapproving look Talen gave her. "I took the mark freely, Andromeda, of my own will. Any spell you might cast to try and undo that would explode back on both of us.

"I have no aptitude with magic, but I know yours must be extraordinary to have gained the abilities you possess in just a few months. But if you think you can meddle with a curse like the one I bear, you don't understand magic as well as you think you do. It works on a primal level. Try to betray it, and it will betray you right back. There is no way to weasel out of what I have done, and nor would I try. I have to deal with the consequences of my decision."

Andromeda remembered the hollow expression that had been on Talen's face earlier that day as she looked towards the mountain peak, saying she would face the Dragon again. She thought of how she had found her, burned and dying, and how that nightmare could soon play out again. Andromeda didn't want this. She didn't want Talen to be right.

A dark, cold hatred bloomed in her heart for this Empress who had ensnared Talen with her curse. Even if she had no hidden motives and was only trying to save her people, Andromeda was not prepared to forgive her.

But she didn't say any of this aloud, only found Talen's hand and held it. "I understand. But I won't let you face this alone. Whatever happens."

Talen nodded, and put her free arm around Andromeda. "I know." After a pause, she added, "We should head down the mountain tomorrow."

"Are you sure you'll be strong enough?"

"To walk? Probably not. But I'll be able to ride Brownie if you have no objection to that. The sooner we put some distance between us and the Dragon the better."

"All right. Lezith mentioned something else as well. She said the Empress would already know what had happened up here, and that she'd be coming. She said you'd want to prepare. She obviously meant something by it, but I don't know what."

Talen grimaced. "The Empress is very keen on recruiting new Heroes. After ten years of failure, that isn't going well. If the Empress knows you came up here to help me, she'll probably try to convince you to become another Hero if I fail. Or she might try to claim you're already entangled. But she can't do anything unless you agree. It's very important that you don't."

"She only gives the mark to one Hero at a time?"

"So it's always been in the past. There have been cases when she's convinced a second Hero to try and take vengeance on the Dragon after they had a friend or lover fall. All that has resulted in is more death."

Andromeda touched Talen soothingly. "Don't worry, I won't let the Empress manipulate me into anything. I think I have a far better chance of helping you if I steer clear of whatever machinations she has going on."

She felt Talen relax. "Thank you. I feel a lot better hearing you say that."

It wasn't long after this that Talen fell asleep, burrowing into Andromeda with a murmured goodnight and a noise in her throat like a contented sigh. Andromeda stroked Talen's hair, her mind busy with what she could do to try and free Talen from the curse, but soon enough she slept too; a former Princess in the bed of her former bodyguard with no regrets.

⸎

As DISCUSSED, Andromeda and Talen made their descent the next day. Brownie seemed rather proud to have the honour of bearing Talen, and enthusiastically chewed on Andromeda's hair several times as if to highlight the importance of her contribution. She was becoming very self-important for a horse that had only ever known life as a peasant's beast before meeting Andromeda. But imagining the drudgery of her previous existence, and the loyalty she'd shown her on the Road they'd travelled together, Andromeda could not bring herself to scold the formerly-humble mare very hard.

When they came to the Bridge, Andromeda asked Talen how she'd gotten across last time. She said she'd sought out an ancient text which described how to safely navigate the bridge, but was more than happy to let Andromeda use her magic this time.

After they'd crossed it, Andromeda offered Talen her dagger. "I know you're far from peak condition, Talen, but if we run into any difficulties, I think this will be of more use to you than me. I kept practicing after you left, but I never improved very much, I'm afraid."

Talen didn't hesitate long before taking it, and once armed she looked more at ease. "I'll give it back after I get a new one," she promised.

Andromeda nodded. She did want the dagger back, but mostly because Talen had originally given it to her as a gift. One kept secret from the King and Queen, who most definitely would not have approved of their daughter wielding a weapon.

It took Talen and Andromeda the full day to get down the mountain, and dusk was already falling as they emerged near Drakk. Talen wasn't keen on visiting the town, despite Lezith's invitation. Too many people, too many questions, too much trouble if anyone objected. Instead she suggested they travel a bit further and camp by the road. The Empress lived to the East, in the Imperial City. She didn't like to come too close to the Dragon's Mountain, but she'd been known to set up court as little as a few miles away when she needed to.

Since Talen thought it likely the Empress was already travelling towards them, they decided to keep going East until they ran into her. Talen told Andromeda that the Imperial City was about two weeks' ride away, so they should still have a fair bit of time before their paths crossed.

"I'll tell you more about her in the coming days," Talen said, "but in brief, what I would say is to be careful of the Empress. She has a way of sniffing out your weaknesses."

They travelled perhaps another mile in the coming dark, passing through lands frozen and bare, watched by the occasional wary-eyed family in whose fields struggled sickly winter crops.

Andromeda was just about to suggest they stop for the night when both she and Talen heard pounding hooves on the road ahead, drawing closer. Talen pulled Brownie to a halt, and extended her arm to Andromeda, who'd been walking alongside on foot.

"Get up behind me," Talen said, her voice apprehensive. "I cannot imagine the Empress's emissaries have reached us so soon."

But that was exactly who the riders proved to be. After Andromeda had scrambled up onto Brownie's back, a troop of six armoured guards took shape out of the oncoming darkness, bearing burning torches and a banner with a Dragon. Their leader, a woman, reigned up her horse beside Talen and handed her a scroll.

Without preamble, she said, "Her Imperial Majesty requires your presence, and the presence of your companion, in keeping with the agreement of the sacred pact you made when you took Her Imperial Majesty's mark, and became her servant."

Talen frowned and snatched the scroll. "I am not the Empress's servant." She unrolled the scroll and read it before rolling it back up and stuffing it into her belt. After casting a quick glance over her shoulder towards Andromeda, she said to the woman, "How far away is the Empress? My companion and I have already travelled a full day, and I cannot make a tired horse fresh again."

The Captain signalled to two of her guards, who immediately dismounted. "Our horses are fresh," she said. "The Empress is only two miles ahead." She nodded to the two dismounted guards. "My guards will follow with your beast and possessions. Come. We must make haste."

This was surprising news, considering that Talen had said the Empress was likely two weeks away. Andromeda could tell Talen was taken aback as well, and her reluctance wasn't lost on the Captain, whose hand moved to hover over her sword.

Talen noticed the gesture and said dryly, "My companion and I were already on our way to the Empress. Bringing us in by force will not be necessary. I am just...perplexed to learn the Empress is so close. I expected her to be at the Imperial Palace."

"The Empress anticipated the need of her presence, and made the appropriate preparations to be here," the Captain said. Her hand did not move away from her sword.

It was an explanation that seemed to make more sense to Talen than it did to Andromeda. Breaking eye contact with the Captain, Talen nodded to Andromeda that it was okay to dismount. Despite the unpleasantness of an armed escort, resistance under the circumstances would have served no purpose. But Andromeda did wonder if the Captain realised Talen could have thrown her dagger and buried it in the Captain's throat before she would have been able to draw her sword.

After Talen had dismounted, Andromeda whispered a few words of instruction to Brownie and then mounted one of the riderless horses while Talen mounted the other. Since Andromeda was already carrying her Magic Book and most of her magical supplies, even if the guards decided to be less than honest with their possessions they wouldn't lose much.

The Captain told the two guards with Brownie to follow on foot and then gave the order to move out, spurring her horse into a swift canter. Not surprisingly, Andromeda and Talen had been wrangled into the middle of the column, with the Captain and another guard ahead and two behind.

It felt odd to be riding with a saddle again after having gone so long without one. Andromeda briefly had time to realise how much she now preferred the feeling of connection she got with her mount from riding bareback before Talen spoke to her quietly.

"The Empress respects strength. She also respects intelligence. Don't make yourself smaller than you are in front of her; it won't be to your advantage."

Andromeda nodded. Interesting that the Empress liked strength in others. That suggested she wasn't a tyrant, whatever else she might be. Tyrants typically saw the strength of others as a threat, not a virtue.

"There's one more thing you should know," Talen added. "The Empress lost her family to the Dragon. She'll try to use it. Remember what we discussed, and be careful."

"I will," said Andromeda, meeting Talen's eyes reassuringly. She had no intention of being recruited into killing the Dragon, especially when she didn't know why it was apparently intent on destroying the world it had always previously protected.

Chapter 6

The Captain kept the horses going at a fast pace that made the two miles pass quickly. She drew the party up before a Manor House that looked as if it had been abandoned some time ago, and after dismounting banged her fist on the front door.

A richly dressed and rather fussy looking man opened the door, commenting in an affected drawl, "Your summons is as delicate as ever, I see, my dear Valouria."

Valouria rolled her eyes at him, though not in a way that suggested she was really annoyed.

"Guests to see the Empress," she said, gesturing towards Talen and Andromeda who'd also dismounted along with the rest of the guards. "Talen you've already met before, and this is Andromeda, Talen's companion. Please do your best to make them presentable."

"Of course." The man bowed. "And since Valouria has neglected, as usual, to finish the introductions, my name is Jasper. I am so fortunate as to serve as retainer to Her Imperial Majesty. Please do come in." He ushered Talen, Andromeda and Valouria into the Manor's hall. Valouria paused to give instructions to the remaining three guards, telling them to see to the horses and then return to their normal duties. She also said she wanted to be informed as soon as the two guards with Brownie arrived, and that if they were late getting back she was to be informed of that too. Andromeda had travelled through lands with roads more dangerous than those Blackheath offered, despite its problems, and she doubted anyone would be foolish enough to tangle with the Empress's guards, but she still liked to see the care Valouria had for those she commanded.

Once Jasper had closed the door, Valouria excused herself, saying she would inform the Empress of Talen and Andromeda's arrival. Having gotten them this far, it seemed she didn't think it necessary to keep them under armed supervision until they were actually in the Empress's presence. Or perhaps her trust in Jasper was such that she knew he would ensure they kept their appointment.

"Well." Jasper looked Talen and Andromeda over with a sigh. "These primitive conditions are far from ideal, but please follow me. I have baths prepared and a selection of fresh clothes waiting. It is the absolute minimum I insist upon before allowing guests to appear before Her Imperial Majesty. Come, this way."

The halls of the Manor were ablaze with many tallow candles that only served to highlight the building's disrepair. Dust and leaf litter covered the floor and parts of the plastered ceiling hung loose, exposing wooden rafters and roosting wild birds who chattered uneasily at the disturbance passing by beneath them.

Andromeda wondered what had happened to the people who used to live here. Dead? Gone in search of somewhere warmer? And why had the Empress decided to receive them here? Simply for convenience? Judging by how Talen was covertly checking their surroundings, Andromeda guessed she hadn't been here before either.

Jasper stopped outside a door where a female servant waited. "The bathing room," he said, cracking open the door with another bow. "Malina here will see to any needs you might have, though as I recall, Talen has always been a most self-sufficient guest." This last comment was made in a slightly disapproving tone.

"Yeah, I learned how to wash my own back when I was five," said Talen bluntly. "I don't need someone to do it for me. Andromeda and I will be fine on our own. No disrespect to Malina, of course."

The female servant—Malina—nodded. "I understand. But please do not hesitate to call upon me if you should need anything. It is an honour to serve the Great Hero and her companion."

Talen nodded, looking uncomfortable at the title which seemingly went with being the Empress's Dragon Slayer.

"Come on," she said to Andromeda, grabbing her hand and pulling her through the door Jasper was holding open. It closed softly behind them, and Talen let out a sigh. "Thank goodness. You have no idea how much I had to fight Jasper on the bathing attendant thing last time."

Andromeda laughed. She could well imagine Jasper's horror at being presented with a charge who preferred independence to pampering. "Well, since thanks to your prior efforts we have our privacy, shall we enjoy these baths?"

Talen smiled back at her, though there was something wistful in her eyes as she reached out to caress Andromeda's cheek. "It could probably be more enjoyable, under other circumstances."

Desire fluttered in Andromeda's belly, and she too wished there was more in the way of time and less in the way of servants and Empresses awaiting their presence. She took Talen's hand in her own and kissed it.

"You have no idea how much—how many times I've thought about—being with you. I wish—"

"I know," said Talen in a low husk, responding to the searing edge of want she could hear in Andromeda's voice. "But...another time. In better circumstances. For now..." Talen sighed and dropped her hand. "I suppose we'd better hurry up."

The baths were on the far side of the room, hidden behind decorated partitions. Approaching them, Andromeda and Talen found the two leftmost tubs had been filled. Here, not without some regret, they parted ways, Andromeda taking the bath on the far left while Talen entered the next stall.

No speech passed between them for the next few minutes. Andromeda couldn't say in which direction Talen's thoughts tended, but she knew what was occupying her own mind, and those thoughts were not the kind that would have made for easy verbal intercourse.

"How's the water?" She was relieved when Talen's voice floated over from the other side of the partition, asking a bland question which broke the awkward silence.

Over her many months of journeying, Andromeda's opportunities to enjoy hot baths had been few and far between, and despite the less than ideal circumstances she was blissfully thankful to be able to immerse herself in the steaming water. There was thus only one answer to Talen's question, which Andromeda gave with indolence dripping from every syllable: "Wonderful."

She heard Talen chuckle. "Try not to get too comfortable. Since we're here now, I want to get this meeting over with as quickly as possible."

Making a noise of reluctant agreement, Andromeda got to work making good use of the abundant fragrant soaps and oils with which the bath was equipped, thoroughly scrubbing herself clean and softening some of the roughness from her hands that hadn't been there before she started this journey.

All too soon she heard the water in the next stall sloshing as, presumably, Talen exited her bath. Closing her eyes, Andromeda allowed herself a few more moments of luxuriating in the glorious hot water before following Talen's example, her skin getting goosebumps from the sudden cold shock of the air. She dried herself off with the nearby towel that had obviously been supplied for that purpose and slipped into the plain white robe that was likewise waiting.

Talen hadn't bothered with a robe. She was standing naked by the bench near the door, rubbing a similar towel through her short blonde locks and investigating the variety of outfits laid out on the bench.

Despite the earlier flare of feeling between them, Andromeda knew Talen's current decision to forego clothing was unlikely to be connected. Talen had never been self-conscious about her body; she'd always had a sense of ease and ownership over herself that Andromeda had found both fascinating and alien when she'd first met her.

It had taken a while before Andromeda understood Talen's confidence. Talen used her body. She trusted it. She knew what it could do. Whether it was riding a horse or shooting an arrow or tracking a deer through the woods, Talen never doubted the ability of her body to respond to her needs.

It wasn't until then that Andromeda began to realise she'd never been taught to think of her own body as belonging to her. She'd been raised to believe her body was supposed to be for someone else—the Prince who would one day marry her. His was the approval that had to be gained, and that meant any activity which might damage her body in his eyes could not be pursued.

Not until her escape from the palace the night before her wedding had Andromeda fully learned to live in her own body. Living on the road, she'd had no time to worry about what others might want, only what tasks she needed her body to do to help her survive.

Tasks that had roughened her hands, as Talen's were roughened and calloused from years of archery and carpentry and knife work.

Perhaps Andromeda shouldn't have worried so much after all about trying to soften her hands with oil.

Having finished with her hair, Talen was starting to dress, choosing an outfit much like that which she normally wore. Andromeda could only assume that Jasper had included the garments knowing Talen's preferences: black hose, a long, cream hooded tunic and an archer's leather vest.

With the full expanse of Talen's naked skin before her, Andromeda could see that it was true the burns were completely gone from Talen's flesh. It still staggered her that with her own power she had done this, wresting Talen back from the brink of death and thus re-writing all the possibilities that were to come in the future.

However, the ordeal had taken a toll on Talen's body. She was thinner than Andromeda remembered, her muscles wasted more than they should have been after a week of bed-rest. The Book had warned Andromeda things like this could happen—while the magic had done the bulk of the work in healing Talen, it had still required her to use a lot of her body's own reserves as well.

Hopefully the Empress wasn't going to immediately demand Talen go back up the mountain to face the Dragon again.

Turning her attention to her own clothing needs, Andromeda began to look through the different garments, hesitating over a maroon robe with green trim. It was plainer than most of the other clothes on offer, but would be far more practical for travel if the Empress was going to be generous enough to let them keep whatever clothes they chose.

"Those colours would suit you," Talen commented, noticing Andromeda's interest.

"I was mostly thinking it would be practical," Andromeda admitted, though she added with a smile, "but of course if I look well that is no bad thing either."

She dropped her robe and began to dress, noting Talen's eyes flick briefly to the scar along her ribs.

"Did your parents ever discover who the assassin was?" Talen asked, as she re-fitted her leather bracers over her arms.

"Not exactly," said Andromeda, "but they found out who sent him. It was one of my uncles, hoping to secure his own son's claim to the throne."

"Was there any punishment?"

Andromeda gave Talen a bitter smile. "Once I married, I would have lost control of the kingdom anyway. The Prince you remember; the Prince of the sleeping curse—he had no kingdom of his own. He wanted to marry me to gain a kingdom, but…that didn't work out, as you know. The next one, who rescued me from the monster, he was different. He already had a kingdom. I was supposed to go away and live with him. My parents were going to pay him off so he wouldn't expect to get a cut of our kingdom as well.

"They were planning to give the crown to my cousin, the one whose father had sent the assassin after me when I was engaged to the Prince of the sleeping curse. They thought it more important to carry on the line than to punish my uncle for trying to kill me."

She felt Talen's hand on her shoulder. "If it means anything," Talen said, her large eyes full of sympathetic outrage, "I think you did well to leave, under those circumstances. You would have gained nothing from your marriage, and lost a great deal."

"More than I ever would have been able to recover," said Andromeda, grasping the hand on her shoulder and looking into Talen's eyes.

She felt Talen's fingers interlacing with her own. "Do you have… any regrets?"

"No." Andromeda shook her head emphatically. "No Talen. I'm glad I chose as I did."

Talen smiled, colour tinging her cheeks, and bent to lace up her boots while Andromeda finished dressing.

"Before we go," said Talen, once they were both more or less presentable, "I've been considering how the Empress might have known to come here. As I said before, it's a two week journey from the Imperial City, and you found me outside the hut on the mountain a week ago. So the only way the Empress could have made it here is if she set out *before* you ever started up the mountain to find me. Is there any way she could have known of your movements, your intentions? Did you tell anyone you were following me who might have relayed that to the Empress?"

71

Frowning in thought, Andromeda replied, "I think I have only been in this world about a month. The first three weeks, I was mostly on the Road, following your trail. I did come across a few travellers, but I didn't tell any of them what I was doing. Even in Drakk I didn't ask about you specifically, just whether anyone lived in the mountains. Though some of them seem to have guessed I was looking for you anyway. Could the Empress have learned of what was happening then? What about when the Dragon attacked you? Would the Empress have felt that?"

"I think so. The mark I bear does connect me to the Empress."

"How deep is the connection?"

Hearing the odd tone in Andromeda's voice, Talen said reassuringly, "She has a general sense of where I am. She knows whether I am staying faithful to the oath I took. But my thoughts and feelings are entirely my own. As long as I am working towards slaying the Dragon, I don't think she cares what I do." After a pause, she continued, "There are magical objects that can communicate over great distance in this world. Such objects are rare, but I would not be surprised if the Empress had an agent in Drakk who was in possession of one. It would make sense to have someone who could keep her informed of anything to do with the Dragon. If that's the case, the Empress could have learned about you quite quickly. But that was still only a week ago. Not enough time for the Empress to have gotten here."

Andromeda sat down on the bench. "Any ideas then?"

Talen nodded, seeming oddly disturbed. "I suppose the stars must have told her."

"The stars?"

"It's what the people of this land believe. Maybe it's true. They think everyone's fate is written in the stars. All they have to do is decode it." Glancing at Andromeda, Talen added, "I've never been much of a believer in fate. I like the thought of having free will better."

"I like it better too," Andromeda said with a smile. "I never wanted my destiny. But if the stars in this world foretell everyone's fates, has the Empress told you what yours is meant to be?"

"No. But her strongest Sage apparently saw that the stars would favour me in a fight with the Dragon. Perhaps a faulty reading given how things went."

Andromeda caressed Talen's arm in sympathy. "How did you meet the Empress?"

With a wry shrug, Talen said, "When I first came to this land, I heard the Empress was looking for Heroes; that there was great wealth promised to any who could slay a dangerous Dragon. So I went and offered my services. You already know why. But the Empress wouldn't accept me right away. She had a lot of questions, a lot of tests. And she said she had to ask the Sages, though I never saw any of them while I was at the palace. Even after I took her mark, the Empress still spent a few weeks parading me around before finally letting me go to the Dragon's Mountain."

"If the Empress had paraded you around a bit longer, I might have caught up with you on the way up the mountain," Andromeda speculated. "I remember hearing a roar as I was climbing; that must have been when you were fighting the Dragon. I found you outside the hut not long afterwards when your injuries were still fresh. You said then you didn't know how you survived. I didn't want to push you at the time, for obvious reasons, but...what did you mean by that? How did you get away?"

Talen sighed and shook her head. "I wish I knew. I remember climbing to the peak of the mountain and facing the Dragon. I remember the flames. I don't remember anything after that until you found me. The hut isn't far below the peak, but there's no way I climbed down by myself, given the state I was in."

"You would have died if I hadn't found you when I did. There's no way you still would have been alive if I'd had to climb to the top of the mountain to find you."

"I know," said Talen. "The same thought has crossed my mind more than once. I'd really like to know who in the world I need to thank for getting me down that mountain so you could find me."

Could it have been the Fallen Fairy? No; Andromeda didn't think her powers worked like that. The Fairy could influence events and situations but ultimately action had to be taken by the humans involved. It must have been some other force that had taken Talen to the hut.

"Anyway." From the reluctant, drawn out way Talen said the word, Andromeda knew what was coming next. "We really should get this meeting over with. Are you ready?"

Andromeda nodded and got to her feet. She noticed that Talen's fingers had strayed to her left shoulder, worrying at the curse mark hidden by the fabric of her shirt. Covering Talen's hand with her own, she smiled reassuringly. "Don't worry. I was once a Princess. I know how to handle court politics and tricky royals. The Empress isn't going to fool me into anything."

Talen's fingers twined with her own, and she nodded.

Taking a breath, she went over to the door and pulled it open.

Jasper was waiting on the other side, looking more patient than Andromeda would have expected. His expression grew somewhat less congenial, however, as he examined both of them with a critical eye.

"I was hopeful your extended absence indicated a desire to properly prepare for the honour of being in the presence of Her Imperial Majesty, but I can see I was mistaken. Still, there is no time to do more. The Empress was quite clear I was to bring you as soon as possible." He turned sharply on his heel. "Please follow me."

Talen looked at Andromeda and held out her hand. The gesture she used was deliberate and specific; that which was used only between betrothed couples at court in Andromeda's homeland. It caught Andromeda off-guard, and gave her a rather surreal moment. During her days acting as Andromeda's bodyguard, Talen had seen the Prince perform this gesture many times, watching while Andromeda took his hand, watching as they went ahead, waiting and walking behind them.

Not until she saw Talen perform that gesture now, not until she saw the intensity of emotion in her eyes, did Andromeda realise how deep the cost of that silence had really been for Talen.

Still feeling rather dreamlike, Andromeda responded by taking Talen's hand, making a declaration unintelligible to their current company and yet full of significance.

"When all this is over," said Andromeda, a tremour breaking through her voice for a moment, "would you consider paying a visit to the Endless Forest with me? I think my Fairy Godmother would be glad to see us together. We could ask her to bless our union. I don't have anyone else left...who could do that."

"I lost my family while I was still a child," Talen said softly. It wasn't something she'd ever mentioned before. "And you might not have made it here without your Fairy Godmother. I too would be glad of her blessings, if she is willing. Once all this is over, we'll return to the Endless Forest and find her."

They both knew that if things went ill, this might be a promise Talen couldn't keep, but at least Andromeda knew that in making it, Talen was giving her a tacit pledge she would fight for their future together as hard as she could.

Breaking eye contact, Talen looked away to where Jasper was waiting for them a little way ahead, his impassive expression doing an impressive job of hiding his impatience.

Then she looked back to Andromeda, and asked a question that was about more than their immediate situation, her gaze falling momentarily on their still entwined hands. "Shall we?" she said.

Andromeda smiled, her heart speeding in the way that she'd always been promised it would when she met the person she was meant to be with. "Yes." She didn't add anything else. She didn't need to. The light in Talen's eyes told her that her answer was enough.

They walked up the hall towards Jasper hand in hand, and proceeded towards their meeting with the Empress.

Chapter 7

J asper led Andromeda and Talen through another maze of candle-lit halls until they came to a pair of elaborately carved double wooden doors. The doors were closed, with one guard standing watch on either side.

"The Hero and her companion, here to see Her Imperial Majesty at Her Majesty's request," Jasper drawled.

The guards nodded and opened the doors; their party was clearly expected.

In Andromeda's experience, even when royalty travelled, they rarely did so lightly. They liked to take all the trappings of authority with them wherever they went, and thus she was surprised by the simplicity of the audience chamber on the other side of the doors.

There was a raised platform at one end of the room with a carved wooden chair upon which sat the Empress herself, but the chair was very far from being a throne. The similarity of its colour and style to the chamber doors suggested it belonged to the Manor House.

A few standards had been placed around the room, and there were silks hanging upon the walls that probably covered those belonging to the Manor's original occupants. Valouria stood to attention behind the Empress's chair; an interesting choice of positioning clearly meant to show the trust the Empress had in her Captain.

Several more guards were stationed around the room, and there were two servants standing to one side below the dais. By the standards of Andromeda's kingdom, this was travelling very lightly indeed.

They had not been disarmed upon entry, which may have indicated either that the Empress wished to demonstrate her gracious trust, or that she trusted those around her enough to repel any attempted attack.

Bowing deeply before the Empress, Jasper announced their presence:

"Your honoured guests, Your Majesty. Talen the Hero, returned unharmed from the Dragon's Mountain, and her companion Princess Andromeda."

Andromeda hadn't told Jasper anything about herself, and was taken aback to hear him announce her title. How had he known she was a Princess? A lucky guess?

The Empress did not speak, but she did incline her head slightly towards Talen and Andromeda. From the surprise that leapt briefly into Jasper's eyes before he schooled his expression blank, Andromeda guessed that was a most unusual mark of respect.

Talen was still holding Andromeda's hand, as if about to present her; a detail which was not lost on the Empress.

"Your Imperial Majesty," Talen began. "Allow me—"

"I see you still have not learned to bow properly, Talen," the Empress interrupted her, disapproval evident in her voice. She spoke in a tone that was deeper than that of most women; a trait she had likely been trained to master.

What the Empress said was true. Talen's bow had been a stiff incline from her waist barely discernible. She'd been the same during her time as Andromeda's bodyguard, much to the displeasure of the King and Queen. Andromeda had asked her about it back then, and with immovable calmness Talen had told her that her people had stopped bowing to royalty a long time ago and that she wasn't about to break the tradition.

"Talen comes from a people who are ruled by no one," Andromeda said, releasing Talen's hand and bowing herself, but only as much as she would to another royal in her own land. "I have never yet seen her bow to anyone simply for their station."

"Princess Andromeda," the Empress said, speaking Andromeda's name in an oddly hushed way while staring at her intently.

The Empress was about forty, with pale skin, black hair and the darkest eyes Andromeda had ever seen. In contrast to her plain surroundings, she was richly dressed in silks of red and gold glinting with jewels that looked similar to the rubies and emeralds valuable in Andromeda's kingdom. Upon her head she wore a golden tiara with five sharp points. Set into the tip of each point were small shimmering objects which at the time Andromeda assumed to be more precious stones, though she was to learn later they were actually Dragon scales.

She made a striking figure, this Empress, and a rather terrible one too for there was grief etched deeply into her face that gave her a gaunt and tormented look. The sole survivor of the Dragon's massacre, who had watched her kingdom crumble for ten years. While not discounting Talen's warnings, upon this meeting Andromeda couldn't help but acknowledge that the Empress must lead a difficult and lonely life.

Flicking her eyes from Andromeda to Talen, the Empress commented, now suddenly casual, "So you have won the love of your Princess after all, Talen, and without the need of riches. How is it this came about? I am most curious to hear."

What sympathy Andromeda had for the Empress quickly began to evaporate. It discomforted her to her very bones to think of Talen sharing her innermost fears and desires with the Empress, speaking of her feelings to her long before she had ever voiced her feelings to Andromeda herself.

She also quickly realised that the Empress had caught her discomfort; that she had perhaps spoken in the first place to see what impact her words might have. This was all part of some obscure test then. Maybe to see if she could rattle them. To test their trust in one another. But to what end?

Talen had begun to answer, but Andromeda placed a hand on her arm. Stopping, Talen indicated with a nod that she understood, and waited while Andromeda addressed the Empress instead.

With no apology in her tone, she said, "You are mistaken, Imperial Majesty, in thinking Talen was ever required to win my approval by great feats of conquest. I gave my love to her freely, because of who I already knew she was. The only obstacle was the custom in my kingdom which dictated that a Princess could only marry a Prince. That is why I am no longer a Princess. I left that life behind me many months ago."

Andromeda wanted to see how the Empress would react to being contradicted, and she had to admit she handled it well.

Though her smile was cold, she graciously inclined her head in acknowledgement of Andromeda's statement. "Of course. I did not mean to misrepresent the nature of your feelings...Andromeda." There was a slight hesitation before the Empress said Andromeda's name, as if she could only just restrain herself from using Andromeda's title despite Andromeda's disavowal of her royal status. "But the fact remains that when Talen offered herself as Hero, her stated motivation should she succeed was to use the reward to become your suitor."

"Why did any of that come up at all?" Andromeda directed the question to Talen more than the Empress, but it was the Empress who answered.

"You think I send simply anyone to slay the Dragon? Selfish fortune hunters full of vanity and petty greed? No, I must find out what is in the heart of every prospective Hero who would take up arms against the Dragon. I must always hear their story. Talen was reluctant to speak at first, but once she did, the strength of her heart—the strength of her feelings for you, Andromeda—was quite evident. And I deemed that love would give Talen the courage to face the horrors that awaited her. In that, I was not mistaken. She is the first Hero to return alive from the Dragon's Mountain."

"Well, I'm not sure it counts, since the Dragon is still alive too," Talen commented dryly.

The Empress bored into Talen with her dark, intense eyes. "But you will face the Dragon again," she said. "You must."

Talen looked back without blinking. "I know. I understand the terms of the pact I made. I will slay the Dragon."

Relaxing slightly, the Empress continued, "Now, I must hear what happened on the mountain. For though you survived, your fight with the Dragon did not go well, Talen. This much I already know. That mark you bear connects you to me, and I felt it when the Dragon struck you down. The life was fast draining out of you, and I feared you would fall like every Hero before you. But then—something changed. Something stopped death in its tracks."

The Empress's gaze switched to Andromeda. "Your magic," she said, a tremour breaking through her voice. "It was your magic that saved her."

How did the Empress know about that? Had she been able to feel Andromeda using her abilities? Well, if she already knew there was no point lying about it. A shallow attempt at deceit would only earn the Empress's contempt.

"Yes," said Andromeda simply. "I was able to heal Talen with my magic. I had been searching for her for many months, and finally found her moments after her fight with the Dragon. She was badly burned. It took all my skill to save her."

Something akin to desperate hunger kindled in the Empress's eyes. "There are many wielders of magic in my land, Andromeda, and not one of their spells has ever been effective against the Dragon. Yet you come to us from across the frozen sea and reverse the ravages of the Dragon's flames as if they are nothing."

Beside her, Andromeda heard Talen draw in a sharp, quiet breath. Talen had warned her already that the Empress would try to recruit her into her web of Heroes, but Andromeda could only assume from

Talen's reaction that she hadn't realised the Empress would have a special interest in Andromeda's magic.

Talen still kept her silence, however, despite her dis-ease. It was probably the best move. Had she tried to speak on Andromeda's behalf, it would have only given the Empress the impression that Andromeda was too weak to speak for herself.

Examining Andromeda closely, the Empress said, "Talen never told me of your magical abilities, Andromeda. I find this a most curious omission."

"I only learned I had those powers once I left my kingdom," Andromeda replied. She did not go into the story of how she found the Magic Book and banished the demon with the face of a man.

The Empress made a noncommittal noise. "I must admit, I do not fully understand your willingness to abandon your kingdom so easily. Talen told me you were the only child of the King and Queen, the sole heir to the throne. What will become of your people, now that you have run away to your lover's arms? Whatever your feelings for Talen, was it not a selfish act to abandon your responsibilities?"

Earlier, the Empress had mentioned she liked to hear people's stories. Was that part of why she was asking? Covertly probing to see whether Andromeda might be another candidate for the Hero's role? Wondering what the Empress would make of her answer, Andromeda told her the truth.

"I would have stayed," she said. "If my parents had allowed me to keep Talen by my side, and given me the freedom to become the Queen and rule my own kingdom."

"You speak nonsense, surely," the Empress said with a frown. "You were the sole heir. Who else would rule your kingdom?"

"As I explained, Imperial Majesty, my parents required me to take a husband. The Prince I nearly married already had a kingdom of his own, and my parents did not wish our kingdom to lose its independence. So they offered him gold in return for agreeing to give up his claim on the kingdom. My cousin was to become King instead, and I was to be sent away to live in the Prince's kingdom as his bride. No matter what, they were never going to let me rule. At least this way, I have kept my freedom."

The Empress looked as if she couldn't quite believe what she was hearing. "Your own parents denied your birthright, and denied your kingdom their Queen?"

"In all truth," said Andromeda unhappily, "the people of my kingdom will be glad for my cousin to become the heir. He is already married, and has a son. Even if I'd married a Prince with no kingdom of his own, he would have been given mine. He would have ruled instead of me. Then my people would have been ruled by a stranger. This is the better outcome for them." Andromeda couldn't stop her voice from wavering, nor the pinprick of tears in her eyes. It was painful to drag all of this up; to go over the injustice of her kingdom being stolen from her no matter which path she took.

For a moment, the Empress was silent, giving Andromeda a compassionate look that acknowledged the impossibility of the choices she'd faced. She understood Andromeda's pain as only another ruler could, and while it didn't make Andromeda like the Empress any better, she couldn't deny that this exchange had created a certain shared sympathy between them.

"It is a pity your parents were fools," the Empress said, in what probably passed for a gentle voice. "You would have made a formidable Queen." She paused, then continued, "In the realm of Blackheath, the heir to the throne is always the oldest child born to the reigning Emperor or Empress, no matter whether male or female. It has been thus since the founding of our kingdom three thousand years ago. More informally, however, it is a well observed phenomenon that the Dragon is happiest when an Empress reigns, or when a female heir waits to take the throne. For many years, the Imperial Family and the Dragon shared in the sacred duty of safeguarding the land. A partnership that could only continue as long as the royal line endured, for the Dragon will only answer to those in whose veins flows Imperial blood.

"Thus it has always been that those who carry royal blood are encouraged to be plentiful in the number of children we have, to ensure the line never dies out. But not every ruler desires to wed, and long ago my ancestors recognised the injustice of forcing that state upon an unwilling participant. Instead, it was decided that any children begotten by those of royal blood would be acknowledged, regardless of the wedded or unwedded state of their parents. We became free to choose our own partners, and from the court of the Imperial Palace that new tradition spread. Today, all my subjects are likewise empowered to choose the relationships they wish without censure or coercion, thanks to the work of my forebears.

"However, in such a system, there are bound to be instances in which the identity of a child's father is in doubt, though never its mother. It has thankfully not occurred in recent memory, but there are several documented historical instances in which an Emperor or another male of the royal line presented a child to the Dragon which he assumed to be his, only to find out it was not so.

"Naturally, such questions do not arise when an Empress rules. She births her children from her own body, and it matters not whether the father is known. That is why it used to please the Dragon to be presented with a female heir, but we would never become so barbaric as to disinherit anyone for an accident of sex."

"I would hope that one day, my kingdom might come to hold similar views," Andromeda said, since the Empress was expectantly awaiting her response. In other circumstances, it might have been an interesting discussion, but as it was Andromeda just wanted to bring this audience to an end as quickly as possible. She was tired, after a week of little sleep and a long day of travel, and she knew that Talen must be feeling the same.

"Perhaps you can re-take your kingdom one day," the Empress said, meaning to be kind. "In the meantime, however, there is the matter of the pact your lover has made with me. Has Talen informed you of its terms?"

"Yes, I've told Andromeda everything," Talen said, breaking her silence. "She knows I will die in a year's time if I do not slay the Dragon. She knows that every Hero before me has fallen. But I do not intend to leave her alone and grieving. As I swore to you, I will slay the Dragon. I need new weapons, a night or two of rest; that is all. You chose me to be your Hero, Imperial Majesty, so I beg of you, allow me to fulfil my oath."

What she was really asking was for the Empress not to involve Andromeda, her tone carrying the sort of servility she had always refused to display in the past. It was against everything Talen believed to behave like this, and Andromeda hated that she was doing it.

"Of course you shall have ample opportunity to fulfil your oath, Talen," the Empress said, but her gaze on Andromeda was as intense and hungry as ever. She rose from her chair, and descended the dais with smooth grace. Indicating Andromeda and Talen should follow, she led them to a table laid out with fruit, cheese and wine.

Dismissing the forthcoming servants, the Empress herself offered food and drink to her guests. As she poured out three glasses of the deep red wine, she said, "Now that you have been so kind as to tell me your story, Andromeda, please allow me to tell you mine." She placed the wine carafe gently back on the table, not spilling a drop.

"The Dragon has brought a curse upon this land. Ten years ago, it went mad. Instead of bringing the Spring to us as it always had before, it made its pilgrimage to the Imperial City and there it slaughtered all those who carried Imperial blood. I lost my entire family that day. The late Emperor who was my older brother, his children, my own three children, too many uncles and aunts and grandparents and cousins and lesser relations to count. All wiped out in the Dragon's flame.

"No doubt I would have perished too, had I been there. It was customary for the Imperial Family to gather and pay respects to the Dragon every year, and absences from that duty were not encouraged. But that year, I was ill with a difficult pregnancy and staying in seclusion far from the demands of court.

"You can imagine my reaction when I heard what the Dragon had done." The desolation in the Empress's voice, the darkness in her eyes, spoke more clearly than words could of her pain. "In an instant, everything I knew, everyone I loved, was ripped away. But I could not crumble under the immense weight of pain in my heart, for my people needed me during the chaos that followed.

"Ever since that day, my land has been dying, Andromeda. The Dragon who once protected us now hides on its mountain and watches as Blackheath freezes into a wasteland of snow and ice. It has ignored every offering I have made, every attempt at reconciliation. If Blackheath is to survive, the Dragon must be slain."

"That is a terrible story, Imperial Highness," Andromeda allowed. "I am sorry your land has fallen under this shadow, and you have my deepest sympathies for the loss of your family. But you already have a Hero in Talen, who has vowed to free your kingdom of this curse. What assistance could I be?"

"Your magic—" the Empress paused. "Its like has not been seen in this kingdom before. I have told you already that no spell, no enchantment, has ever been effective against the Dragon or its flames until now. You could be a great help to Talen in achieving her task. However, only those who bear my mark can reach the peak of the mountain where the Dragon dwells. As the situation stands now, Talen will face her fate alone."

Slowly, the Empress took a long sip of wine. "Alas, I have never been able to bestow my mark upon more than a single Hero at any one time. But I have spoken to my Sages, and they tell me that if two hearts were aligned closely enough, it may be possible for two Heroes to share a single mark. Doing so would not be without consequence, for the length of the pact would be shortened to six months, and both would live or die together at the end of it. Still...most worthy Heroes try their might against the Dragon long before the year is done anyway. What do you think of that, Andromeda?"

So, this was the Empress's overture. Even if she had not asked directly, she was testing to see whether Andromeda would be open to becoming another Hero, just as Talen had warned.

Andromeda glanced at Talen, seeing the warning in her eyes. Looking back to the Empress, she answered in the same indirect way in which the Empress had asked her question. "The dedication you show towards freeing your kingdom does you great credit as a ruler, Imperial Majesty. However, you cursed the one I love, so that she too was nearly taken by the Dragon. For that, I will not forgive you. Nor would my magic allow me to enter into any bargain to slay a living being without knowing why that being acted as it did. That is the condition upon which I wield this power; that I must act honourably at all times. Should I lose my honour, my magic will go with it. Talen has all my trust in this matter. She should have yours too. You are the one who chose her." Andromeda couldn't keep the bitterness out of her voice as she said this last.

Her tone was not lost upon the Empress. Nor did she seem surprised by Andromeda's answer. "I could show you an entire library in the Imperial Palace filled with tomes and scrolls written by hundreds of learned individuals who attempted to divine the source of the Dragon's behaviour. Nothing worked to appease it. Believe me, I did not take the decision lightly to kill what was once the guardian of this land. Having said that, your faith in your lover does you credit, Andromeda. I hope it serves you well."

Abruptly, she looked away and summoned Jasper to her side. "Have our guests accommodated for the night. Tomorrow, Valouria and her guards will escort Talen and Andromeda to Drakk."

"To Drakk?" said Talen. "That town will have nothing to do with the Heroes."

"I have given a proclamation to Valouria which will change that situation. There is a talented Blacksmith in Drakk who can forge new weapons for you, Talen. You would have to travel all the way to the Imperial City to find a smith who could match Ferris's skills, and I am sure you are as reluctant as I at the prospect of such a delay. We are coming now to the end of our long struggle with the Dragon; I can feel it. May whatever power still watches over this forsaken world have mercy upon us all."

She motioned towards Jasper again, but with a quiet cough, Valouria stepped forward from where she had remained beside the Empress's chair. "Please, Your Imperial Majesty, allow Jasper to stay here and tend you. He will be most anxious to see to your needs. I can take our guests to their chamber; I know where they have been placed."

The Empress nodded. "Very well, I have no objection if our guests do not."

Once she had Talen and Andromeda's assurances, the Empress kissed the palm of her own hand then placed it upon Talen's forehead. "Go with my blessings, Hero. May fortune smile upon you."

And to Andromeda, she gave a slight bow, saying, "I maintain it a great pity you gave up your birthright, Princess. Perhaps one day you will find that keeping Talen and your kingdom both is not as impossible as you deemed. Goodnight."

With that, she indicated Valouria should lead them out of the chamber. Andromeda's last glimpse of the Empress was of her sitting back down in her chair while Jasper topped up her wine glass. She saw her look up at him with a soft expression Andromeda would not have thought the Empress capable of, and from the returning look Jasper gave her, Valouria had evidently not been wrong in her assertion of where Jasper's priorities would be.

Chapter 8

Valouria escorted Andromeda and Talen through another set of crumbling halls until they came to a door located in the part of the Manor that had probably once been the private chambers of the family who lived here.

She showed them into the room which had been cleverly decorated to hide the worst of the decay and indicated a table in the corner laden with an assortment of food and drink more substantial than that which they had been offered at the Empress's table.

"Thank Jasper for that," she said. "He organised it all."

"Thank him for us if we don't see him tomorrow," said Talen. "If the plan is acceptable to you, I'd like to set out early for Drakk tomorrow."

"I have no objections," Valouria said. "Your horse and possessions arrived safely. I had my guards place your packs at the foot of the bed."

Talen nodded her thanks, and Valouria turned to go. She paused at the door, however, seeming to hesitate before saying, "I owe you for today, Talen. I know you didn't want to come. It still would have been my duty to make you, had you not agreed, and I know the ensuing conflict would have cost lives."

It was clear she meant potentially her own life and those of her guards.

Talen gave her an unhappy look. "It's not your fault I'm in this mess, Valouria. I wouldn't want you to pay for it. I bound myself to the Empress, and thus I must answer when she calls, whether I want to or not."

Valouria nodded, and spoke again, including Andromeda in her response this time. "Blackheath has become a harsh kingdom, but it wasn't always thus. I wish both of you could have come to know us before the calamity that befell us. You would understand why we fight so hard to regain the peace and prosperity we once knew." After even more hesitation she continued, "I was there, the day the Dragon killed the Imperial Family. I was only a raw recruit at the time, and nearly all the guards I knew perished as well, trying to stop the Dragon. It was... more gruesome than any battle I have ever seen. Everything we knew about our world was shattered in the moment of the Dragon's attack, and I don't think the darkness of that day has ever really left any of us.

"The Empress knows there is little time left to save Blackheath from becoming a wasteland. That is why she is willing to resort to the methods she does. If we should meet again after tomorrow, I would beg both of you to remember that. I expect no mercy for myself, but those I command...some of them are not much different from the young recruit I myself once was."

"Yes, I noticed the Empress let us off too easy," Talen said bluntly. "She must have some other scheme in mind. Do you know what it is?"

"I know nothing more than what I have said," Valouria insisted. "The Empress does not lie; I will take you to Drakk tomorrow and from there you will be free to do as you wish, within the confines of what the mark allows. I am simply...aware of the precarious circumstances."

From their familiarity, Andromeda guessed Talen and Valouria had gotten to know each other during Talen's days at the Imperial Palace, and developed a sense of mutual respect. It couldn't be pleasant for either of them to find themselves in possible conflict over their relative positions.

"I'm sorry Valouria," Talen said. "I can't make you any promises without knowing what the Empress might do."

Valouria's expression stiffened, but she nodded in understanding. "Very well. I can't say your answer is a surprise, though I wish it were otherwise. Goodnight." She bowed to both of them. "I will see you tomorrow."

Taking her leave, she closed the door. Once they were alone, Talen went and sat down on the edge of the large double bed. She took her boots off with a sigh and sat slouched over with a hand tangled into her hair. "I've made such a mess of things. I should have guessed the Empress would be interested in your magic. She *did* let us off too easily. She barely tried to persuade you at all. I cannot believe she is simply letting us go on our way with no further interference. She must have some alternative plan in mind."

Andromeda approached Talen and placed a soothing hand on her shoulder, making her look up. "If she does, we'll figure it out and deal with it together. Who do you think told her that I healed you? Would her Sages have known? I hate to think it was Lezith."

"It could have been Lezith," Talen said. "But I think the Sages more likely. It's also possible she knew because of the mark itself. That would make sense."

"If the Empress can sense things like that; whether you're hurt, where you are, does that mean...Can you ever sense anything from the Empress?"

Talen shook her head, drawing Andromeda down beside her. "No, not at all. I assure you of that." She stroked Andromeda's cheek, an apology in her eyes. "I know you don't like that I've bound myself to the Empress. I know I've hurt you by it, though I never meant to. I'm sorry. I wish I could take it back, but I can't."

Somewhat embarrassed by her jealousy flaring up again, but grateful for Talen's understanding, Andromeda said, "This isn't your fault, Talen. I know my feelings are irrational, I just...hate the thought of you making such a desperate bargain. Things never should have come to that."

Talen drew her fingers down Andromeda's spine, making her shiver, and said in a low voice, "I've pledged myself to you and no other."

"I know, Talen." Andromeda kissed her before answering, "As I have to you."

"We'll get through this, Andromeda. We'll be fine."

Andromeda suspected Talen's seeming confidence was more bravado than conviction, but she was glad of the reassurance either way.

"Do you know what happened to the child the Empress was carrying ten years ago? Did the pregnancy fail?"

"So everyone says," Talen replied with a shrug. "Besides, if the Dragon shares a bond with those of the Imperial bloodline, then it would surely know if the Empress had an heir. It would take action, the way it did with the others. The fact that it hasn't probably means the child is already dead."

"But why was the Empress spared in the first place if the Dragon's intention was to purge the Imperial bloodline? Nothing about this makes sense, Talen."

"I know it doesn't," said Talen. With a half-weary glance, she added, "But I'm not sure if I have the energy for further speculation tonight. All I want to do is eat something and fall into bed."

"Right, of course," said Andromeda, squeezing Talen's knee in apology as she realised she'd been ignoring her growing tiredness.

Andromeda took off her boots, and watched as they tumbled to the floor to lie with Talen's. Back when she was still trapped in her old life, if she'd dared herself to imagine what she truly wanted it would have been something like this. Living an independent life with Talen, in a space that belonged just to them. Being surrounded by others who easily accepted what they meant to each other and who didn't care that they shared a bed at night.

If not for the Dragon, she and Talen could have already been planning out their life together, seeking the blessings of the Fallen Fairy, physically consummating their bond. And Talen's past—Andromeda still didn't know much about it, and wished she did. She would have to ask her sometime, but not tonight.

Getting up, Andromeda held her hand out to Talen. "Come on. Let's try Jasper's food. We'll worry about everything tomorrow."

Talen nodded and took Andromeda's hand. "Thanks," she said, and let Andromeda pull her to her feet.

They made short work of the food, and then fell into bed. Talen was asleep almost instantaneously. Despite the many questions circling in her mind Andromeda soon followed, with her last sleepy thought being that they'd get the opportunity to visit Lezith after all.

TALEN WAS UNEASY and restless the next morning, but Valouria arrived early as she had promised and they set out with two of her guards towards Drakk while the sun was still rising. The Empress did not see them off. Andromeda rode Brownie, who seemed very happy to see her again, while Talen borrowed a horse from the guards.

There was little talk on the road. The air had the bite of Winter, and frost glittered on the abandoned fields. Andromeda wondered how much of the kingdom was still habitable. Drakk seemed to be doing better than most other parts of Blackheath that she'd seen, but if it was one of the last refuges from the cold she would have expected refugees to be flocking there. Was there somewhere else where people were gathering? Or were they simply dead?

It did not take long to reach Drakk. There were few people awake to observe their party riding boldly into town, but Lezith was one of those who saw them. She was sitting in the town's central square, around which most of the shops and traders were located. Her hands were busy with some kind of needlework, and she did not appear at all surprised by the sudden influx of visitors.

"Lezith," Valouria greeted her, without dismounting. "Why am I not surprised to find you waiting for us?"

Lezith folded her work in her lap, and glanced at Andromeda with a mischievous, conspiratorial look before replying to Valouria. "I had an inkling something might happen this morning, so I decided to rouse my old bones early."

"Humph. Well, I must ask you to rouse them again. I have a proclamation from the Empress to read to the town. This is Talen, the Hero, and Andromeda—"

Getting to her feet, Lezith waved her hand. "Yes, yes. I've already met Andromeda and Talen."

Valouria frowned. "You mean you saw them when they passed through the town?"

The twinkle showed in Lezith's eye again. "No. I climbed the mountain a few days after Andromeda did. I wanted to find out what was happening. We had a nice chat. In fact, I invited both her and Talen to be my guests." She inclined her head to Andromeda. "An offer which still stands, of course."

"I should have expected something like this," said Valouria, her voice long-suffering. Andromeda was curious about the relationship between the two; they clearly knew each other and seemed friendly. Yet Valouria was also obviously vexed by aspects of Lezith's behaviour, a fact of which Lezith was not unaware and rather seemed to tease her with.

Lezith had taken up the rope hanging from the clapper of the large bell set in the town square. "You should be grateful," she said, in the moment before she started to ring the bell. "Since I'm here, all of you get to stay atop your fancy horses."

She was right of course. It wasn't an accident that Valouria and her guards hadn't dismounted. It was the same when the criers travelled in

Andromeda's kingdom. Stay mounted. Stay visible. Make the people look up as they heard the King's proclamations.

The bell pealed out, and faster than Andromeda would have expected an assortment of worried-looking townspeople began to emerge, casting wary glances towards the sky as if, perhaps, they expected to see the Dragon circling.

"Fear not," said Valouria, speaking in a clear, ringing voice Andromeda could imagine carrying on the battlefield, "there is no calamity afoot. I have come with a proclamation from the Empress. She bids me tell you that the time for fearing the Dragon's wrath has passed. We stand now on the brink of victory, for Talen the Hero has returned from the Dragon's Mountain."

With a sweeping hand, she gestured to Talen. Talen fiddled with her reins and looked like she wished she was elsewhere.

"Is the Dragon dead then?" someone called from amongst the gathering crowd.

"Not yet. Talen struck the Dragon such a mighty blow that her sword shattered and she had to retreat. She is in need of new weapons, and they must be forged before the Dragon has time to recover. That is why the Empress bid me bring her to Drakk and tell all of you to give Talen and her companion Andromeda every manner of assistance possible."

While the response to this news was lukewarm at best, the townspeople did not look as wrathful as Andromeda had feared they might. Their reaction seemed mostly stoic, taking the Empress's orders as they would the inevitable judgements of the Dragon which came down from the mountain.

"Where is Ferris, the Weaponsmith?" Valouria asked. "The Empress has most particularly requested that she forge the new blades Talen requires."

"Ferris is not here," Lezith responded laconically.

Valouria gave Lezith a hard look. "Then perhaps someone should rouse her, if the bell did not. I see the smithy right over there."

"I will talk to her later," Lezith countered. "If the bell did not summon her, then she is not within its range. She spends much of her time wandering beyond the town."

Valouria looked as if she wanted to question Lezith further, but she was distracted by a nervous looking man pushing his way through the crowd. He was half-bald, and in his haste had pulled on odd-coloured stockings and buttoned up his fine jacket crookedly.

"You do us great honour to bring us tidings from the Empress, oh noble Captain!" he said enthusiastically, bowing deeply. "We are of course Her Imperial Majesty's humble servants. However, I must say these plans seem very radical. What if the Dragon should attack us in retaliation? Are we to have guards to defend us?"

"Most of my guards are busy evacuating the ever-increasing number of people who are losing their homes to the Winter," Valouria said, looking down her nose at the man with distaste. "In the ten years since it went mad, the Dragon has never attacked this town. We shall just have to hope your luck holds, and if it does attack, well, I think the Empress's chosen Hero stands the best chance of protecting you all. Unless you are telling me you have no faith in the Empress or her champion."

The man went pale. "N-no, of course not. But surely we deserve a little extra support—"

"I have no time for this," said Valouria impatiently. She thrust a scroll into the man's hand. "I give you the Empress's official written decree. Disobey and I shall return to take you away and throw you in the Imperial dungeon. The future of all Blackheath is at stake here, and I have better things to do than listen to your whining." She looked away from the man and focused on Lezith. "Make sure Ferris understands she is to forge new weapons for Talen. Strong enough to slay a Dragon."

"I will," said Lezith. She approached Valouria and handed something up to her. The needlework she'd been working on before. "A handkerchief I just finished embroidering. Would you be so good as to take it to Sorrel for me? And this letter for her as well. Few folk are abroad in these times, and I fear I'd wait long before I got another chance to send them."

Valouria's response was quite different to that which she'd given to the hastily dressed nervous man. "Of course. I'll be glad to take these. If you or any of the other townspeople have letters or small gifts, give them to my guards. We are soon bound to return to the Imperial City, and I promise I'll do everything I can to make sure all messages and keepsakes reach their destinations."

This caused a flurry of activity, during which Talen and Andromeda were able to dismount mostly unnoticed. Lezith approached them with a smile. "I am glad to see you again, Andromeda. And you, Talen. We have not officially met, but I saw you when you were, er, sleeping." She chose the word carefully, so as not to convey the truth of the situation to any who might happen to be listening. "Shall we slip away while everyone is occupied? I'm sure you've both had enough of being gawked at for one morning."

After exchanging an enquiring glance with Talen, who indicated she didn't object, Andromeda said, "If you are truly happy to provide lodgings to Talen and I, we would be grateful to accept."

"Of course," said Lezith. "I am too old to make offers out of politeness to people I don't like. Sorrel, my granddaughter, serves the Empress in the Imperial City. My daughter...passed away a few years ago, so Sorrel is the only family I have left. With her so far away, it can get rather lonely around the house. Some good company will be welcome."

While Lezith spoke, she had been leading Andromeda and Talen away from the bustling activity of the town square, to a quiet cottage tucked away on a tree-lined lane. She waved away Andromeda's stumbled condolences for her daughter's death, quickly switching the subject to more prosaic matters.

"There is a field and stables behind the cottage that will do for your horse. I'll show you, and then we can go in."

It didn't take long to unburden Brownie of her supplies and set her loose. She appeared quite happy with her new accommodations, sniffing at the grass before lowering her head and starting to munch with focused intent.

"Well, that's her taken care of," said Lezith. "Come now, this way."

She took them through the back door of the cottage, into a kitchen with a large stone hearth hung with highly polished brass pots and pans. "I'll light a fire soon," she promised. The room was rather chilly. "It's just…We have to be careful with coal these days. The miners can't dig it up fast enough, with all the need there is."

"Coal?" asked Andromeda.

"The black rocks that burn," Talen clarified. "It gets dug up from underground. Since most of the trees aren't flourishing there is little wood."

"Indeed," Lezith agreed. "I hope you'll enjoy staying here," she continued conversationally. "No doubt my cottage is not as grand as whatever accommodations the Empress offered, but it's the home where I've been happy."

She halted outside a door and opened it, showing them into the neat bedroom within. "This is Sorrel's room, but since she is unlikely to be spared from her duties anytime soon, I'm sure she wouldn't object to your using it."

"It's lovely, thank you," said Andromeda.

"What does your granddaughter do for the Empress?" Talen asked. Andromeda could tell she was, if not suspicious, then at least cautious of Lezith. Which was reasonable enough. While Andromeda's own instincts said they could trust Lezith, intellectually she understood that they knew little about her.

"Sorrel reads the stars," Lezith replied. "In Blackheath, the stars tell our future, but being able to decipher what they mean is a rare gift. The Empress employs several such Sages who guide her."

Talen's eyes widened slightly. "Your granddaughter is one of the Empress's Sages?"

"Yes," said Lezith. "Though I don't imagine you got the chance to meet her, or any of the others. The Empress keeps the Sages secluded these days. It's a pity. I remember when the Sages had pride of place in the Emperor's court."

"You told Andromeda that the Empress would be coming when you went to see her on the mountain. Did you know that because you can read the stars too?"

Lezith shook her head. "My powers are nothing like Sorrel's. I merely...sensed it was going to happen. But I will tell you this: if Andromeda's presence was enough that I could feel something had shifted, then the Empress or one of her Sages most definitely felt it too. That is what would have caused her to ride out, perhaps even before Andromeda reached Drakk."

"Talen tells me that the distance to the Imperial City is such that in order for the Empress to meet us when and where she did, she would have had to set out about a week before I even arrived in Drakk," Andromeda said.

"Yes, that sounds about right," Lezith agreed. She let out a sudden laugh. "Poor Jerrard."

At Andromeda and Talen's confused looks, she explained, "Jerrard is the man who was complaining in the square. He acts as the Empress's eyes and ears and thinks the rest of us don't know, reporting to her via a communication stone that allows people to converse over great distances. He would have been bursting with importance when he told the Empress that Andromeda had come seeking Talen, and very disappointed to realise she already knew."

"Indeed, poor Jerrard," echoed Talen, her lips quirking. "Do you know how long the Empress and her retinue have been waiting at that Manor?"

"Some of her representatives came to Drakk a few days ago, buying supplies. That is probably when they arrived. Rumour was the Hero would be descending from the mountain victorious any day and that the Empress was preparing a victory feast."

Talen's voice was dry. "Not exactly what happened."

"No, but you're the first Hero to come back alive, Talen. Folk will not ignore the significance of that. Nor the part Andromeda played in your recovery. The Empress especially will be seeking guidance on what it all means."

Andromeda considered telling Lezith that the Empress had already asked her to become another Hero, but decided against it, at least for now. She could pick her brains about it another time. "What about this morning?" she asked instead. "Were you waiting for us because you sensed we were coming?"

"The earth told me a party of riders approached," Lezith answered. "It is a more immediate and humble kind of instinct, compared to reading the stars. I knew of no one else it could be besides more emissaries from the Empress, and I had a hunch you and Talen might be among them. Now." Lezith went to the door. "I'll leave the two of you to get settled. Come out and have some tea when you're ready." She nodded and closed the door, and Andromeda and Talen once more found themselves alone together in strange accommodations, far from knowing when that might change.

Chapter 9

Upon their venturing out a short time later, Lezith provided Talen and Andromeda not only with tea, but freshly scrambled eggs, bread and vegetables as well. She waved away Andromeda's promises to recompense her, saying that her garden and flock were still thriving well enough to feed half the people of Drakk if need be.

Talen was anxious to meet with Ferris as soon as possible, but Lezith said she'd spoken the truth. Ferris wasn't currently in town and they would have to simply wait until she returned.

"Perhaps you'll take my meddling amiss," she continued, "but I think it would be better for both of you to take some time for yourselves today. You've been reunited so recently, and you've barely had a moment's peace. That seems no way for a young couple to be. Lay your cares aside for a little while. There's an abandoned garden at the end of this lane where nobody goes. You will be quite safe from interruption there."

"Where nobody goes except lovers, I suppose you mean," Talen commented, not seeming sold on the idea.

"No, not even lovers go to the garden."

"Why not?"

"Superstition," said Lezith. "You'll understand when you see it. But I assure you it's perfectly safe."

Andromeda looked at Talen and gave a light shrug. "It can't hurt to go and take a look." Her casualness was only feigned; in truth she dearly wanted some time alone with Talen, and was grateful to Lezith for suggesting it. But since Talen appeared to have some reluctance about the idea, she didn't want to push too hard.

Shrugging back, Talen replied, "If Ferris isn't here, then I guess we might as well do something while we wait for her." Addressing Lezith, she added, "When do you think Ferris will return?"

"Well, let us hope for tomorrow, but I can give no guarantees," Lezith said.

Talen held her gaze for a moment, seeming to assess the veracity of her words, before refocusing on Andromeda. "Shall we go then, to see this garden?"

Andromeda answered with a nod, and mouthed a silent thank you to Lezith when she exited the cottage behind Talen.

Outside, a chill autumn morning greeted them, the clouds shot through with hints of golden sunshine. Andromeda would have welcomed the crispness of the day had she not known that this was a land locked on a course towards endless Winter, with death creeping ever closer.

It wasn't difficult to find the garden, and as Lezith had said, once they saw the sign announcing the garden's name, they understood why no one came here anymore.

They had come to The Garden of the Dragon, nestled right at the foot of the Barren Mountains where the Dragon dwelled.

The garden's large iron gates stood perpetually open, choked with weeds, inviting entry into what must have once been a place of worship and celebration. Talen loosened her dagger in its sheath as she and Andromeda paused at the gates, "Just in case", as she said in answer to Andromeda's questioning look.

"I don't think anything will attack us here," Andromeda commented. "This place feels sad and abandoned."

Indeed, they experienced no challenge as they passed through the rusty gates and the crumbling stone walls to follow what remained of one of the garden's main thoroughfares. The path was bordered by many flowerbeds which had long since stopped growing anything but some kind of tangled spiky bushes, and most of the trees Andromeda could see looked dead.

As they went deeper into the garden, Talen got out her knife and began scraping bark off of tree branches, intently examining the results. Andromeda could tell she was easier here amongst the trees, the tense lines of her body relaxing, her expression becoming less drawn.

"What are you doing?" Andromeda asked her, resulting in Talen giving her a sheepish smile.

"Sorry. I was checking the trees to see if any of them have wood suitable for a new bow. My last one burned up on the mountain. But there's nothing I can use here. Most of these trees are on the verge of dying." She rested her hand against the rough trunk of one of the trees, as if consoling it, her eyes sad. "This garden is only a shadow of what it once was. I wish I could have seen it before. Look how tall some of these trees are. They must have been magnificent in their prime."

"Perhaps some of them will manage to survive if the land recovers soon."

Talen looked up towards the peak of the Dragon's Mountain, easily visible from the garden and probably designed to be so. "Perhaps," she echoed doubtfully.

They continued to wander deeper into the garden, straying off the main path and following winding tunnels with no particular purpose in mind. At one point, they came across a shattered glasshouse covered in, of all things, tiny climbing roses that filled the air with a scent that took Andromeda back to her sleeping princess days.

"How strange," said Talen in wonder, fondling one of the small, velvet flowers. "I've never seen roses grow in any land but yours." She picked one of the deep red blooms and tucked it behind Andromeda's ear. "The colour suits you," she said with a smile.

"Talen," said Andromeda, unable to contain the question any longer, "why didn't you want to come here? Did you not want us to do...whatever it is we're doing right now?"

Seeming surprised, Talen answered, "It's not that I didn't want to spend time with you, Andromeda. Of course I want to do that. I just didn't want to do it in the way I thought Lezith was suggesting. Remember the Maze in the grounds of your palace? And the Lemon Grove? They were always filled with young couples. Anywhere like that is the last place I'd want to go to be with someone."

"Then...where would you go? If you could take me somewhere right now, where would it be?"

Brushing a caressing hand down Andromeda's arm, Talen said, with barely any hesitation, "Into the wilds of a forest somewhere, as far as I could get from Dragons and civilisation. But I'm more curious to know where you would take me, now that you've seen something of the many worlds out there."

Drawing closer, Andromeda thought for a moment then said, "Perhaps to the ocean of the world where I found the Moondust. Empty beaches stretch all along the coast as far as the eye can see, and the storms, when they come, would be wild enough even for you."

Her voice trembled as she felt Talen's hand circling her waist, saw the intent look in her eyes and the flush of colour on her cheeks. They kissed, not gently, but with a sharpness and hunger brought on by the decay surrounding them, by a need to declare to themselves and each other that they were indeed alive.

Andromeda couldn't seem to get enough of Talen into her arms, couldn't hold her close enough, couldn't get enough of the warmth she offered against the chill.

She began to drag her fingers up Talen's thigh, slow enough that Talen could stop her if she wanted to, but Talen simply moaned into her mouth and shifted even closer.

As they continued to kiss, Andromeda slid her hand higher, until Talen gasped and pressed into her touch, her back arching, her fist twisted into the fabric of Andromeda's shirt.

Glass crunched beneath their boots, an unwelcome reminder that, unlike in the Maze or the Lemon Grove of Andromeda's former home, no lush grass was inviting them to further take their ease.

They parted breathing unsteadily, examining each other's faces for hints to the answer of the question they were both considering.

"Not in sight of the mountain," Andromeda said instinctively, barely wanting to part long enough from Talen to get the words out. "You nearly died up there. I don't want to see it. I don't want to think about it, if we're—"

"Everywhere in this garden is in sight of the mountain," Talen pointed out. Her voice was rough in a way Andromeda had never heard before, raw with arousal and desire.

"I know, I know." Andromeda closed her eyes and held herself still, forcing her roaring blood to quiet a bit. It wasn't easy, with Talen so close, her obvious willingness making Andromeda's own cravings flare even more.

But Andromeda hadn't come here for this. Or maybe she had. Maybe part of her had. Not all of her, though. Questions were still crowding into her mind, all the things she'd never been able to ask Talen before, and some part of her stubbornly insisted this was important; that everything had to be done in the proper way.

She opened her eyes again, and smiled at Talen, half apologetic. "Let's find somewhere to sit down for now. It's been over two years since we last met and we've barely gotten to talk. I feel like...there are still so many things I need to ask you."

Talen gave a soft sigh, but she nodded in understanding and said, "I can see a bench over there. Would that suit?"

"It looks fine," Andromeda agreed, reluctantly untangling herself from Talen's arms.

There were several fruit trees overhanging the bench Talen had selected, but like all else in the garden they were struggling, with only a few withered red berries clinging to their branches.

The two of them sat, and Talen looked up towards the Dragon's peak, her expression betraying an almost comical annoyance at its inconvenient presence, combined with an underlying worry as, Andromeda guessed, she thought of what might be waiting in the future.

With a touch, Andromeda drew her attention back. "Try not to think about it for now, Talen. There will be plenty of time to worry about the Dragon later, once your full strength has returned."

Talen's manner did not grow any easier. "It's not just the Dragon I'm thinking about, Andromeda. It's the Empress. I can't fathom what she's planning, but I know she must have something in mind. I'm worried she'll be back to claim you."

"Then let her come. I'm not afraid of her."

"I know you're not, but—" Seeing Andromeda's expression, Talen broke off. "Never mind, you're right of course. We should enjoy the rest of this peace, while we have it. I get the feeling it will be gone soon enough." Talen's eyes were as sombre as her words, but they softened as she stroked Andromeda's cheek and said, "The Empress was right about one thing. You would have made an excellent Queen. I'm sorry it's a chance you'll never have. And—I know you said you had things you want to ask me too—but was it really your uncle who was behind the assassination? Why didn't your father ever punish him?"

"I'm fairly sure my father did punish my uncle," Andromeda replied. "Just not publicly. And since there were no further attempts made on my life, I'm guessing my father found a way to dissuade him from trying the same thing again. But no one ever told me any of this officially, of course. I put all of it together myself. As to being Queen..." Andromeda paused to gather her thoughts. "I would like it if I could one day get the chance to change things in my kingdom for the better.

And I know I told the Empress I would have stayed if I could be with you, but in reality, that would have brought its own challenges. Even if the situation had been much different, if there had been no objection to our being together, can you truthfully tell me, Talen, that you would have wanted to become royalty, ruling over others and living in idleness and luxury? You said your people stopped answering to kings a long time ago."

Andromeda held Talen's gaze as she asked the question, and Talen didn't attempt to look away as she answered. "I can't lie. As much as I wanted to be with you, I never wanted what you represented to all those Princes. I didn't care about any of that. I even used to tell myself that falling for you was a bad idea, because you were part of the same system my people turned away from. Which didn't work, of course," she added with a wry smile. "I suppose, when I found myself dreaming in unguarded moments back then, what I thought of was running away and taking you with me. Building a cottage deep in the forest, living off what the land offered, letting the seasons roll by peacefully. But I didn't think any of it was really going to happen."

Linking her arm through Talen's and laying her head on Talen's shoulder, Andromeda said, "In the stories of my land, Witches are nearly always found living in forests. I think I could be very happy, living that kind of life with you. Brewing spells and potions from ingredients I'd gathered in the woods."

Talen gave an odd hollow laugh that made Andromeda sit up worriedly and ask, "What is it?"

"Nothing. Just—There was also a Witch who lived in the forest where I grew up. A decidedly less nice Witch than you." After a beat, Talen said astutely, "That's what you want to ask me about, isn't it? Where I grew up, what my history is. You used to ask me about it all the time at the palace, and I never really answered, did I?"

"I understand why. I never offered you anything, and the situation was painful enough for you as it was. Giving even more of yourself to me when I gave nothing back..."

"I knew that you wanted to, Andromeda," Talen said reassuringly. "I just also knew that you couldn't, because of circumstances that were unlikely to change, however much I might wish them to."

"But they have changed now, those circumstances."

"Beyond anything I could have imagined," agreed Talen, giving Andromeda a smile. She drew Andromeda back to her, until Andromeda was once more resting against her shoulder. "So I don't mind telling you now, but it's not a short story. Will that be all right with you?"

Andromeda settled her arms around Talen's waist. "Of course," she said softly.

She felt Talen's lungs expand, and then Talen began to speak, her gaze angling upward with a kind of inevitable trajectory towards the looming mountains. "I grew up in the forest of a world many worlds away from this one. My father was a woodcutter, and my mother kept the house and cared for us. I was the oldest of three; I had a younger brother and sister, neither of whom showed as much aptitude for forest lore as I did. My father taught me how to track and hunt, how to use a bow, how to defend myself against the wolves and bears. I learned the names of all the plants and creatures of the forest, and how to coppice so our woodcutting did not destroy the trees.

"A handful of other families lived in the forest too. We were a tiny community with no money but it didn't matter since the forest could supply us with everything we needed. It was a good life. Or it would have been, if not for the Witch."

"The Witch who was not a good Witch," put in Andromeda.

She felt Talen nod. "I know there are many different kinds of magic throughout the realms, and I've met many who use it for good, but this Witch...was a creature of the dark. Only children could see

108

her, and it was children she was most powerful against. She would make them lose their way in the forest and stray into her territory, and there she would kill them and devour their flesh.

"Even though the adults couldn't see her, it didn't take them long to realise there was an evil presence stealing their children away, and they tried to expel her. But it didn't work. The Witch couldn't harm adults directly; she wasn't as powerful against them, but she could make the forest hurt them. Crazed packs of wild beasts began to attack the village, falling trees caused maiming and death, the food my people gathered began to wither away in their hands.

"In desperation, those who survived came to an agreement of sorts with the Witch. They would give her a certain number of children each year, and she would spare the rest and let the community live in peace. That had already been going on for several generations before I was born."

Andromeda reflexively tightened her grip on Talen's waist. Her stomach soured as if she'd eaten too many unripe apples, imagining the horror that must have haunted every day of Talen's childhood. "That's...ghastly," she said, though she wished there were a stronger word to express her feelings.

Talen took her eyes from the mountain and gave Andromeda an unreadable look. "It is," she agreed. "But you have to understand my forebears had fled to that forest to escape a war-mongering king who was drafting all their children into his army. He took their crops to feed the troops, took their animals to carry supplies, took anything valuable they had to fund his campaigns. There were already dark rumours surrounding the forest; it was why no one lived there. However, the king's subjects were mired in such misery already that they thought it better to take the risk than stay where they were.

"And things were good at first. My forebears lived free and proud and swore they would never bow to any king again. Then came the Witch, and they had to struggle to protect their children all over again.

They tried, but because the adults couldn't see her, they couldn't fight her. They couldn't kill her. None of the children succeeded either, despite some of them already being veterans of the king's wars.

"Then, there was a child who fell ill. He wasn't going to survive. My forebears knew if they left the forest and went back, the king would put all of them to death for defying him. So what were they to do? Giving up a dying child so the rest might have the chance at a better life seemed like the lesser of two evils to them, and I can't be easy my people did that, but I do understand they didn't want to die.

"That was how the pact with the Witch came to be made. They would give her the weak and sick children whose chances of survival were slim, and the Witch was happy with that. She didn't ask for the strongest child, or the most beautiful. She feasted on the dying while the living flourished."

The sour feeling in Andromeda's stomach was growing stronger.

"The system wasn't perfect, of course. The poorly were always sent first, but we were a hardy people. There were not always sick children when the Witch wanted to eat. In the times those situations arose...I don't pretend to know what process the adults used among themselves to work out whose children should be fed to the Witch. My mother was soon to have another child at that time; I've often wondered if that was something to do with it. If my parents sent me as a prime sacrifice meant to deter anyone from asking for the baby. If I'm being charitable, I imagine they selected me because they knew I was stronger than my younger siblings, and would have the best chance of surviving against the Witch, even though no one had ever managed to kill her."

Despite having guessed what was coming since the moment Talen started this story, Andromeda still let out a shuddery breath of horror. Before she could say anything, however, Talen was already continuing:

"My father and I often worked in the forest together. I didn't know anything was different when we set off that morning. My mother's farewell was just the same. My father did not act strained or uneasy in any way. They were good actors, I'll give them that."

Talen's tone was as bitter as the peel of the bright yellow lemons that grew throughout Andromeda's kingdom.

"The forest was beautiful that day. I can still remember it. A bright spring morning when the sun finally had warmth again after the long winter we'd endured. There were carpets of wildflowers covered in dew and glittering like fallen stars, birds singing their joy on every tree branch. Lizards venturing out to test the warmth of rocks, and an undergrowth alive with the rustling of creatures newly woken from hibernation.

"We spent the morning coppicing, and at midday, my father suggested we break our fast, as was our normal routine. We ate pies and sandwiches and drank a special cordial my father said my mother had made for us as a treat. That was the last time I saw him. Soon after drinking the cordial, I went to sleep. And when I awoke, I was in the Witch's domain. I wasn't naïve enough not to understand what that meant. I knew I'd been selected as a sacrifice, and that no one was coming to save me."

"Your father drugged you with the cordial?" Andromeda angled her head up so she could see Talen's expression, sympathetically running a hand through her fine golden hair.

Talen nodded, her jaw tight. "It must have been the cordial. The food was all wrapped up together; I think it would have been too risky to put anything in there. I thought he was drinking the cordial too, but I wasn't really paying attention. Why would I? I had no reason to distrust him." Her fingers drummed an uneasy tattoo at her side. "I was twelve years old then—older than sacrifices usually were. The Witch wouldn't take children after their thirteenth birthday, and so the closer that milestone was, the less likely we were to be sent. It made my predicament all the more painful to me at the time."

111

"I'm sorry you went through that," Andromeda said softly. "It would be a terrifying experience for anyone, let alone a child."

Her voice darkening, Talen said, "Oh, I haven't even gotten to the worst part yet. The domain of the Witch herself. On the very edge of the territory we'd carved out for ourselves was the dark part of the forest where the Witch lived; a maze-like place full of traps and spells. No one who went in there came out again. The children given to the Witch were left unconscious on the border of her territory, and under cover of darkness she would come and drag them away.

"When I awoke, I wasn't shackled or imprisoned; I was free to run as much as I wanted, but I couldn't escape. I think the Witch enjoyed the sport of hunting us down. There were so many bones scattered throughout that forest, and I knew they were all the children who'd died before me. Some of them she'd built up into grotesque monuments surrounded by offerings of hair and teeth and blood. I'd never known terror such as that which I felt in those hours, desperately fighting against my fate."

All these years later, the memory of that fear still strained and quieted Talen's voice.

"What happened?"

Talen glanced at Andromeda, a grim smile flickering across her features. "I decided I couldn't let the terror control me, if I wanted to live. I picked up a rusty sword that must have belonged to one of the soldier children sent in long ago, and I killed the Witch before she could kill me. After centuries, I set my people free of her curse. But I couldn't go home. Not after what my parents had done. I couldn't forgive them. So I wandered deeper into the Witch's wood and eventually I went so far I stumbled upon the Endless Forest that joined my world to the next. I crossed over into that new world and didn't look back. After that, I developed a talent for finding those borderlands where one world bleeds into the next, and soon that became my life. Travelling an endless stream of worlds and never regretting what I left behind."

Shifting back so she could stroke Andromeda's cheek, Talen finished softly, "Until I met you."

"Because you fell in love with me?"

"Not just that. I could see how much you wanted freedom. I could never forget that yearning in your eyes. It never felt right that I walked away and left you to a fate I knew you didn't want. I—know what it is to be trapped in a horrible situation all too well. I went through that in the Witch's forest."

"And hence your pact with the Empress."

"Exactly," said Talen, nodding ruefully.

"It's probably for the best," Andromeda said, letting out a sigh, "that I had to find a way to save myself. I wouldn't have learned to believe in myself in the same way if I hadn't." She looked into Talen's eyes, remembering the awful sight of her lying crumpled and burned outside the mountain hut. "Besides, if I'd kept waiting, I never would have seen you again."

"I really thought I was hallucinating when I saw you appear. It seemed so impossible." Talen smiled. "But I'm glad you came to find me. I've missed being with you."

"I've missed you too," Andromeda replied, smiling back. "Every day after you left, I was so lonely." Her expression grew serious, and she touched Talen's knee. "Talen, I know there's nothing I can say or do to make it better, but I'm sorry you had to endure that as a child. And...I'm glad you told me. I know it can't have been easy to speak of such painful memories."

"It's fine, Andromeda. I've made my peace with what happened. As much as I can, anyway." Talen clasped Andromeda's hand for a moment, then rose to her feet. "I think I'm just about done with this place. Ready to head back?"

Andromeda hesitated. There were still other matters she wanted to discuss, but looking at Talen, she thought it was probably best they took a respite for now. Whatever Talen said, retelling that story from her childhood had taken a toll on her.

"All right," she said, following Talen's lead. "I'm starting to get hungry anyway."

A short time later, Andromeda and Talen passed back through the broken gates and left the Garden of the Dragon to its dying dreams. They turned away from the towering Barren Mountains and the uncertain fate that awaited them amongst the lonely peaks, and held hands as they walked to Lezith's cottage through drifting golden leaves.

Chapter 10

L ater, after midday, Andromeda used Lezith's kitchen hearth to brew a restorative potion for Talen, the recipe for which she'd discovered in her Book of Magic. Talen was certainly doing better, even just two days on from her awakening, but they didn't know how much time they had until Talen's next encounter with the Dragon, and she would need to be at full strength if she was to have any chance of surviving it.

The potion made Talen sleepy, and while she dozed on a sofa in the parlour, Andromeda sat at a small table nearby pouring over the Magic Book, looking for anything that might give her further insight into the situation between the Dragon and the Imperial Family.

She'd been planning to ask Lezith about anything else she might know, however inconsequential, but before she could a note arrived, carried by a young girl who gawked curiously at Andromeda and Talen. After reading the note's contents, Lezith frowned, and then gave Andromeda an apologetic look.

"I'm afraid I will have to step out for a bit. There is a situation requiring my attention that won't wait. Forgive me, I'll only be gone an hour or two."

"Of course," said Andromeda. "I hope nothing is amiss."

"In this kingdom, a great many things are amiss. But with any luck making headway on this specific situation may help with others."

With that cryptic comment, Lezith departed.

Andromeda's Magic Book remained stubbornly opaque. There were many pages relating to Blackheath; its plants, its culture, its practices, places of note. Only a single line was written about the Dragon:

> *The Dragon once brought Spring every year to the kingdom of Blackheath, but now she stays on her mountain and does not descend.*

Which did at least tell Andromeda one thing she didn't know before—that the Dragon was female. But it didn't give her any clues as to why the Dragon's behaviour had changed so drastically.

Talen woke up from her nap after about an hour, by which time Lezith still hadn't returned. Giving up temporarily on the Book, Andromeda went to sit with Talen on the sofa, saying, "Talen, there's something I've been thinking about in relation to the portal on top of the Dragon's Mountain."

"Mm? What's that?"

"Well, it's not the only point of connection to another land, is it? I didn't enter Blackheath via the Dragon's Mountain; I crossed a frozen sea of ice. It was to the West of here. That is why I haven't seen the Eastern part of the kingdom, where the Imperial City is."

"Yes, I entered Blackheath the same way."

"I know you have spent many more years travelling between worlds than I have, but in no case did I encounter a phenomenon where the weather or events of one world could impact what happened in the next. It's almost like the 'Endless Forests' as you call them act as buffer zones, that allow the transition from one world to another. Somewhere within that buffer is the border between the different worlds."

"It's not something I've encountered either," Talen said. "But the borders that separate the worlds cannot be completely impenetrable, otherwise you and Brownie and I never would have been able to leave our original lands in the first place. Perhaps the border between

Blackheath and the neighbouring world beyond the portal is just thinner than most."

"Do you think the world on the other side of the portal is also suffering? Perhaps they've been trapped in summer for ten years."

"It's possible, but I don't think the Dragon is about to let anyone through to see. And there are no stories of anyone ever crossing the Dragon's Mountain to go to another world. You'd think if it was known there was a portal on the mountain, someone would have gotten curious back in the days when the Dragon took its annual flight."

"Her flight," Andromeda said.

"I'm sorry?"

"I've been looking through my Book to try and find something useful. The pages don't always stay the same; they change. It has not yielded much that can help us, but in the only brief mention of the Dragon, the Book stated she was female."

For a moment, Talen got a strange look on her face, as if some memory was trying to push itself into her mind.

"What is it?" Andromeda asked.

"I don't know," said Talen. "Just...When you mentioned the Dragon being female, it stirred something in my mind. But I can't grab hold of it; the more I try, the further it retreats."

Andromeda made a show of tidying her curls, examining Talen out of the corner of her eye as she did so. She didn't seem strained as she had been in the garden, and not knowing what the coming days held, Andromeda decided to raise what she hadn't been able to before. She started circling indirectly, beginning with,

"There's something else about the Book too. I haven't had the chance to tell you this, but when I was looking for you, the Book began to progressively give me more and more information about healing plants and spells. Almost like...it knew you might be in danger."

"More predetermined fate?" Talen asked, not sounding particularly thrilled.

"Well...I don't know if I would go quite so far. I was already following the Road to find you. It is not impossible that the magic of the Book could have sensed you far ahead of us, about to embark upon the perilous course of dragon slaying. Knowing I loved you, it could have decided to take measures to prepare me for what might eventuate from that. But that is not the same as a fated outcome. I could have ignored the warnings in the Book. I could have been insufficiently skilled to save you. You could have died before I reached you. We were lucky."

Talen nodded, but it was a tentative gesture, as if she didn't understand what Andromeda was getting at.

"In my old kingdom, girls could only aspire to being a Princess who married a Prince. That's what our Fairy Godmothers were meant to ensure. They weren't meant to answer any other wishes we had. The Fallen Fairy told me that when I met her in the Endless Forest.

"On the mountain, do you remember when I said that everything about the Fallen Fairy putting me to sleep wasn't what it seemed? I know now she did that not to curse me, but so I could be awakened. So I would realise who had the power to do that."

Talen gave her an uncertain look. Her eyes were shadowed with the remembrance of old conflict and heartache; feelings rekindled from her days as Andromeda's bodyguard. Feelings she'd never let Andromeda see back then.

"Go on."

Andromeda touched Talen gently, regretting more than ever the pain she must have caused her in the past. She didn't like bringing back those unpleasant memories, but nor did Andromeda want to let this go unresolved. No matter how strong their emotions for each other, this relationship was still very new, and the more that remained buried, the more potential pitfalls could undermine their future.

"The story goes that the Prince kissed me and broke the spell, but I know that isn't what happened. It was you." Andromeda had to stop to steady her voice, her clasp on Talen tightening. "All you did was take my hand, and your touch was enough to wake me. I remember opening my eyes and seeing you looking down at me. I remember the warmth of your fingers stirring my blood back into life. But the Prince didn't even notice. He shoved you out of the way and he kissed me, while you had to stand there and watch. And you watched silently for months after that, as he was hailed as my rescuer, my soulmate, my betrothed, when it should have been you. You were the one who should have been at my side, not him."

Talen drew in a breath, her face crumpled with emotion, the lines of her body collapsing into a satiated peace that replaced a torment she'd been carrying for far too long. She looked away from Andromeda for a moment, passing a hand over her eyes and wiping away the wetness that began to stain her cheeks.

"I always wondered if you knew what really happened to break the curse," she said quietly. "But you know—I've told you—that I don't believe in destiny. I think it is too often used as a way to justify the established order of things." Cold fire kindled in her eyes as she looked back to Andromeda. "The king who used to oppress my people told them many times it was their destiny to be his servants, but they didn't listen to him and I'm glad of that. Whatever the shortcomings of our forest community, I'm glad I didn't grow up a slave who was sent off to war before I'd even started to bleed."

Talen's expression lost its harsh edge as she continued to examine Andromeda's face, and she gave a smile as she reached out to touch her, caressing her in a way that sent heat skittering through Andromeda's stomach.

"I can't deny that the day I met you, something had been calling to me, long before I reached the castle where you slept. And when you woke up and looked into my eyes, I felt like...I wanted to know you.

You have no idea, how many times I wanted to tell you that I was the one who woke you; how much I wished I could be at your side instead of the Prince. But if you didn't remember what had happened, how could I prove it? I didn't want to be like him, saying you owed me for waking you up. Getting you to be with me out of obligation was the last damn thing I wanted."

Frowning, Talen continued, "I don't know what spell the Fallen Fairy used to draw me to you—if we do see her, I'd be curious to ask her about it—but whatever she did; that's not what made me fall in love with you. I know that. Were you worried I would think otherwise?"

Andromeda shook her head. "If you had those kinds of doubts, you wouldn't be with me like this. I just wanted to tell you that I know what happened back then, and I wish I'd spoken sooner. I didn't because it was hard for me to accept at first. I couldn't understand it. All my life, I'd only ever been given one story, and what I experienced with you didn't match that, at all. I knew what had happened. I knew what my heart felt. But...everything in my life told me it couldn't be. I didn't know what to do with any of it, so I stayed silent."

And because of her silence, Talen now bore a mark that bound her to another when Andromeda wanted Talen bound only to her. Every time Andromeda touched Talen she could feel the curse mark on her skin, drawing her towards death. Because Andromeda had waited too long to act, she was now competing for Talen's life with an implacable foe. An immortal Dragon who had already nearly killed her once.

She tangled a hand in Talen's hair and kissed her, tasting the salt of tears and the lingering floral sweetness of the restorative potion. "It's a mistake I won't make again."

"I know," said Talen, her lips still brushing against Andromeda's. "And I'm glad you remember. I'm glad you told me."

Her eyes grew troubled, and she drew back. "On the subject of the Dragon, I know there must be more to the situation than the Empress says. I didn't want to acknowledge it before because she promised me something I thought I needed to be with you. But I'm not sure we can change things now. The Empress is in a state of dangerous desperation. I bear a curse that won't let me turn aside from what I've committed to do. I think a solution without bloodshed is probably no longer possible."

"We do have my Book of Magic now, Talen," Andromeda reminded her. "That may yet help us."

It was clear Talen was doubtful. "We cannot rely only on that, though. I want to meet with Ferris and have her forge weapons for me. Slaying the Dragon is still the fastest way out of this situation."

"You would do that, even when you know you're being used?"

"The Dragon is killing this land, and everyone in it. That much is true at least."

There was a certain stubbornness in Talen's reply, and perhaps a vain hope that by wiping out the Dragon she could wipe out the foolish choices she'd made. Andromeda didn't think it was going to be that simple.

"And if I should find another way out of this?"

"Then I'll take it, Andromeda. In a heartbeat."

Recognising this was a fair compromise in the circumstances, Andromeda nodded and tucked herself close to Talen on the sofa. "All right. I'll work on it," she said softly.

Talen wrapped an arm around her, and they stayed like that, not speaking much, until Lezith came home.

UPON RETURNING, Lezith explained that she'd had a hunch about where Ferris might be, and had sent the girl they'd seen before with a message requesting her help. Initially, Ferris had refused, prompting Lezith to go and see her personally. Ferris didn't give a flying fig about the Empress's orders, and had not been easy to persuade. Lezith did not reveal her arguments or methods, but she said she'd managed to gain Ferris's agreement to at least meet with Talen and Andromeda the next day.

Talen expressed her gratitude, though not without a raised eyebrow or two. Andromeda guessed it was because Lezith hadn't given them any indication that morning that she might know where Ferris was. Andromeda hoped the reason why was because Lezith had realised Talen's hours would only have been spent fretting impatiently if she'd known there was a chance Ferris could be contacted.

Lezith was talkative that evening, reminiscing about her younger days when she would see the Dragon take flight every year, heading East into the rising sun, and feel the warm winds of Spring come sweeping down from its mighty wings.

Andromeda asked her if she could remember anything that might have happened to make the Dragon change its behaviour so drastically, but Lezith only shrugged. Every great mind in Blackheath had been grappling with that riddle for the last ten years, and none had solved it. Which was exactly what the Empress had said as well.

"I'm not all that interested in what great minds think," said Andromeda. "What do you think, Lezith? You have lived your whole life beneath the Dragon's Mountain. That must bring its own insights."

After a pause, during which Lezith seemed to be debating whether to tell them something, she said, "My daughter once told me the Dragon was sad. This was a long time ago, when she was still a child. She said she was playing in the mountains—not on the Dragon's Mountain itself, but nearby at least. There used to be a swimming hole much loved by the children in the summer months, and that was where she had gone, though it was cold that day so no one else was there. She said the Dragon descended out of the sky and told her it was sad. She asked it why, and it said because it should have had a friend but it had none. My daughter told the Dragon she would gladly be its friend, but it said she wasn't what it needed. And then it flew away, back to its mountain. I remember my daughter was quite indignant when she told me about the Dragon rejecting her friendship."

A smile curled Lezith's lips at the memory.

"My daughter wasn't given to making up stories, but I never quite knew what to make of her meeting with the Dragon. The Dragon cannot talk, for one thing. And aside from its yearly flights around the kingdom to deliver the Spring, it rarely strayed from its mountain."

"If that really happened, what do you think the Dragon meant about being lonely and not having a friend?"

"I don't know," said Lezith, shrugging helplessly. "There are no other Dragons in this land. There never have been." After a further, more stilted pause, she went on, "I buried my daughter six years ago, when a sickness brought on by the never-ending cold swept through the kingdom and took far too many. She was delirious towards the end, but for some reason, she talked about that meeting with the Dragon. I think it must have really happened, and I've often wondered what it meant."

Andromeda clasped Lezith's hand in sympathy. "I'm sorry you lost your daughter that way. But thank you for telling me. I know so little that any bit of knowledge is valuable, and what you have told me is more than I have learned from the Empress or my own Book of Magic."

"It was hard, losing her," Lezith agreed, pain welling up from the depths of her eyes before she made an effort to recover herself. "But I still have my granddaughter. There are folks in this kingdom who have lost everyone they ever loved. Ferris, the Blacksmith, she—" Lezith checked herself, before saying carefully, "She is one of those who has lost a great deal."

Despite questioning, Lezith would not be drawn further on what she meant, only saying that Andromeda and Talen would understand tomorrow when they met her. As the chill of the night deepened, Lezith went to light some precious coal reserves in the bedrooms, leaving the kitchen fire to gradually die out.

The three of them waited while the fire flickered lower, the dark encroaching on their circle of chairs, telling stories in murmured voices that spanned a multitude of realms. Lezith pretended not to notice the looks Andromeda and Talen were casting towards one another, but when the time came to retire, she gave them something.

A single white flower on a long thin stem, its five pointed petals shimmering with a glow like starlight. "The Lovers' Star," Lezith said. "This flower was common here once, but can rarely be found now. It's an old tradition to gift these to young lovers, in the hopes of bringing them good fortune. The petals were often scattered over the bedlinen of newlyweds."

She gave a mischievous smile. "Not that I was ever one for bossing others around, of course. The flower is yours, to do with as you will."

Andromeda could feel the flush on her cheeks as she thanked Lezith. Talen thanked her too, in a way that was peculiarly formal, her words not flowing naturally.

Lezith smiled again, fondly this time, and said, "There's no need to thank me. I would say this is a well earned respite for both of you, and I'm glad to do what I can to make this time what it should be, even if only a little bit. Now." She got to her feet. "My old bones are creaking, and I really must take myself off to bed. Sleep well. I hope you find the accommodations comfortable."

Her gaze lingered on the flower in Andromeda's hand before she left.

Chapter 11

As few as they were, the petals of the Lovers' Star released a sweet heady perfume as Andromeda crushed and scattered them over the turned down bed in the chamber she and Talen were sharing.

Talen had been the one who turned down the covers, moving afterwards to stand before Andromeda, reaching out a single finger to stroke the luminescent petals. "You want to, don't you?" she said, referring both to the scattering of petals and something else.

"Yes." Andromeda had nodded, looking into Talen's eyes, her voice husky with desire.

She'd plucked and scattered the petals as Talen watched, afterwards reaching a hand towards her and drawing her down onto the clean sheets, amidst the scent of new love and hope.

With anticipation already quickening both their breathing, Talen ceded, "You know...I'm still not as restored as I could be."

"I know Talen. I don't care. Tomorrow is too uncertain."

Andromeda wrapped her arms around Talen, feeling her too lean frame, breathing in the cedar-like smell of the soap she'd used. She was only just beginning to learn the language of Talen's body, and she would not, could not, envision a future in which Talen was gone, ended in a ruin of charred bone and ashen flesh. "I'm not going to let you die," she whispered. "I've already saved you once, and I'll do it again, as many times as I have to."

"I don't doubt it," Talen whispered back with a smile. "But I promise you, Andromeda, the Dragon will not defeat me a second time. I'll end the curse that binds me."

Talen's hands were warm as she touched Andromeda, stirring Andromeda's blood so she could barely think of anything else. Here, there was no watchful mountain, no glass underfoot, just the softness of the welcoming mattress and Talen's eyes, looking down into hers.

This was the end of two and a half years of loneliness, of too many empty nights spent wanting. "I'll hold you to that promise, Talen," Andromeda warned, as she felt the pressure of Talen's body between her legs, as she saw the flush rising on her skin.

"That's fine," Talen said, fervent and breathless. "I think you know I don't make promises lightly."

Yes, Andromeda did know that. She had crossed the boundaries of many worlds, rewriting her life as she went for this very reason. To gain the promise Talen had given her that evening at the Manor House, which she could not have had any other way.

Talen began to kiss Andromeda, slow but with an undercurrent of rising heat that both teased and promised of gratification to come. Andromeda tangled her fingers into Talen's short, fine hair and met that heat with her own, letting go of everything except the feel of Talen's body against hers and the sound of their hearts beating madly in tandem.

❧

THE COALS HADN'T BEEN ENOUGH to last the night, not that it much mattered. Andromeda could not ever remember feeling as warm as she did as when she woke the next morning, sharing naked body heat with Talen beneath the blankets of their bed.

Only with much reluctance did she disentangle herself from Talen's arms and rise from the snug cocoon, throwing on her clothes as quickly as she could to ward off the morning's chill.

Her movements were enough to disturb Talen, who groaned and shifted to look up at Andromeda groggily with hair falling into her eyes.

"What are you doing out of bed so early?"

"I need to tend to Brownie." Andromeda leaned back over the bed and caressed Talen's cheek. "Sorry, I didn't mean to wake you."

Talen took a hold of her arm, trying to tug her back onto the mattress. "Brownie can wait for a little while. It's barely light out."

With an indulgent smile, Andromeda shook her head. "The days are too short, and I don't know when Lezith is taking us to the Blacksmith. Brownie might be waiting until nightfall if I don't take care of her now."

"Mm, I suppose," said Talen, running a hand through her hair and sounding as if she were trying to find a flaw in Andromeda's logic.

"You can join me, if you would like."

Burrowing back under the covers, Talen closed her eyes. "I will. Soon."

Since Andromeda was quite happy for Talen to rest, she didn't try to persuade her further, and had crossed the chamber and was about to open the bedroom door when Talen murmured from somewhere in the midst of her cocoon, "You're not going to kiss me goodbye?"

The throaty request made Andromeda's stomach tighten, and though leaving would have been the sensible option—the option which did not lead her into temptation—she turned around and went back to kiss Talen.

Talen drew her down hungrily, baring the upper half of her body equally to the cold and Andromeda's gaze. "Are you sure you wouldn't rather stay with me?" she whispered, her eyes promising a renewal of those pleasures they'd shared the previous night.

The offer was as appealing as Talen meant it to be. Before she could think about it, Andromeda was placing her hand against the soft swell of Talen's breast and feeling her chest shudder in response. Andromeda had learned a great deal the night before about what Talen liked, and it took all her self-control not to fall right back into Talen's arms and put that new-found knowledge to good use then and there.

Swallowing hard, she said, "Of course I'd rather stay, Talen. But I can't. I have things to do." After forcing herself out of bed for the second time that morning, she looked down to meet Talen's eyes. "Tonight," she promised. "I'll touch you then."

Talen looked back with a hint of surprise at Andromeda's directness, which was soon eclipsed by discernible approbation of the offer. She didn't voice any of this, however, only gave a weary sigh and bundled herself back up in the cooling covers. "Very well. Let me sleep a bit longer and then I'll come join you like I said. This bed won't be nearly as appealing once you're gone."

Andromeda laughed and gave Talen a final caress, before getting safely out of the room and making her way through the still cottage. She shivered as she stepped out into the cold morning, and hissed at the frigid temperature of the water she drew from the well to clean her face and hands. It was difficult to imagine how Blackheath's inhabitants had lived with this for ten years.

Brownie was delighted to see her, whickering a greeting with ears pricked forward when Andromeda went into the stable. After opening her stall, Andromeda scratched her forelock and then enticed her out into the morning with the apple she'd saved from her dessert the night before.

The mare followed her willingly enough, but had a rather distasteful expression when she saw the chill grey sky and felt the prickle of cold through her coat.

Patting her neck sympathetically, Andromeda said, I'm afraid this is just how things are here."

Brownie expelled air forcefully through flared nostrils; a clear indication she was not impressed.

"Look on the bright side, at least it's not snowing."

Andromeda began to groom Brownie, and as she worked, her mind wandered back to the night before. In her previous life as a Princess, touching another or allowing anyone to touch her had been something she simply could not do. Until a Prince claimed her in marriage, she was to save herself; not for her own sake, but for his.

She'd run away the eve before her wedding as she stared into that endless black tunnel of looming possession, her mother's many lectures about what would be expected of her on the wedding night echoing through her head. Submission. Duty. Silence. Gratitude. *Gratitude.* That had rankled nearly worse than all the rest, that she was expected to thank the person taking away her freedom.

For months as the wedding drew closer, Andromeda's thoughts had become ever more unwieldy as she tried to reconcile herself to her future. She spent days on end arguing with herself, trying to justify why she had to go through with the marriage. Why it wouldn't be as bad as she feared. And still she continued to wake up most mornings drenched in a cold sweat of dread, her own instincts telling her how much of a liar she was.

Sometimes—Rarely—She used to have other dreams as well. Dreams that left her veins on fire, of Talen's hands, her lips, her breasts, her taut stomach shuddering in release. Dreams of touching Talen and being touched by her, as they spent themselves in each other's arms.

The free giving and receiving of pleasure, with a lover she wanted. That was the desire Andromeda had not been able to suppress in the end, for all her world had tried. It was what had driven her to defy everything she'd been told was possible. To find Talen, and start something with her that Andromeda already knew had provided her with a powerful inoculation against ever again thinking of accepting misery to make other people happy.

Keeping her promise, Talen did show up a little later, after Andromeda had finished mucking out the stable and was watching Brownie graze. She drew her hand down Andromeda's back in greeting, commenting, "Lezith is up and making breakfast. She says we can go see the Blacksmith mid-morning."

"Mid-morning? Ah well, I guess we could have stayed in bed."

Talen exhaled an amused breath. "Would have been pretty rude to do that to Lezith anyway. Though I get the feeling she wouldn't have minded. You should have seen the grin she gave me this morning when she asked how we slept. Anyway—" She shot Andromeda a serious glance. "Are you still all right with this plan to visit the Blacksmith? I know you are not over-keen on the idea of attempting another slaying."

"I'm not keen on it," Andromeda agreed. "But I understand we need to keep our options open. As much as I hope to find something that will help us, I still barely know where to start."

Andromeda also thought, but did not say, that she was worried about what might happen if Talen faced the Dragon again too soon. Talen had told the Empress that she only needed a night or two of rest, and she'd had that now (if last night counted). She was beginning to regain more of that robust look Andromeda remembered, losing the fragility she'd had when she woke in her shimmering skin, but ideally Andromeda would have liked Talen to rest for at least another week or two.

"If the Blacksmith agrees to forge weapons for you, how long do you think it will take?"

"I don't know," said Talen. "With all of the shortages caused by the Winter, it might not be a simple matter. But since the Empress herself ordered this, I imagine she will facilitate any materials required. What I'm really worried about is how I'm going to craft a new bow. Given the state of the land, I doubt there is any growing wood from one end to the other I could use."

Knowing Talen's skill as an archer, Andromeda ventured, "When you faced the Dragon before, did you try to take her down with your bow?"

"Try being the operative word," Talen said dryly. "The Dragon is blind in one eye; an old injury given to it by an earlier Hero. I approached from its blind side, downwind, moving as quietly as I could. The arrow I released struck true, I'm sure of it."

"One arrow to kill a Dragon?" Andromeda noticed that Talen had reverted to calling the Dragon *it* instead of *she*, but didn't correct her.

"I studied many detailed drawings of the Dragon at the Imperial Palace. All agree there is a patterned area on the Dragon's forehead positioned between its two normal eyes called the Third Eye. It's not used for sight; it's meant to be for some kind of spiritual seeing. None of the diagrams explained exactly what it was for, but all agreed that the skin of the Third Eye is soft and unprotected, not like the rest of its surrounding scales strong enough to break swords and spears.

"I saw the patterned area on the Dragon's forehead, just as the diagrams described, but when I released an arrow, it simply bounced right off the Eye, as if it were covered with scales as hard as the rest of it. And of course, once the Dragon knew I was there..."

"She burned you, badly, but not enough to kill you outright. Have any further memories returned about that?"

"No," said Talen, shaking her head in frustration. "I was wearing Dragon-scale armour. Not from this land, I'd had it for a while before I came here. But the Dragons of that other world clearly did not have the same degree of fiery fierceness as the Dragon of Blackheath. The armour burned up in the Dragon's fire, though it protected me enough that I survived. I have no idea why the Dragon didn't kill me afterwards." With a worried look, she added, "Conventional armour doesn't work against Dragons. I'm not sure what I will do next time. Wool perhaps, if there is anything like that here?"

Wool against Dragon flame. At most, it might prolong Talen's death to an agonising degree as she boiled inside her slowly burning clothing.

"I will make you something better than that," Andromeda promised tightly. "If it comes to the point where you must ascend the mountain again."

Realising where Andromeda's thoughts had gone, Talen caressed her in apology. "Right. Sorry, this is a miserable conversation to have first thing in the morning. Shall we go inside and let Lezith give us knowing smiles for a while?"

Andromeda gave Talen a smile of her own, glad to get away from the subject of Dragons for now. "Yes, let's get out of this cold, and see if Lezith will tell us anything more of Ferris."

They said goodbye to Brownie, and returned to the cottage. Lezith did give them knowing smiles but would not be drawn on Ferris, saying they would have to make their own judgements when they met her.

That time came soon enough.

⛭

FERRIS PROVED herself to be a tall, powerful looking woman with muscular arms that spoke of her employment. Her skin was considerably darker than Lezith's; in fact she would not have looked out of place in Andromeda's kingdom.

She was at work in the forge that had been closed the day of their arrival, and though Andromeda knew she was expecting their party's arrival, she did not look happy to see them. She ceased her work and stood with her arms crossed, looking them up and down with an unimpressed demeanour as Lezith began the introductions.

Holding up a hand before Lezith could finish, Ferris said, "I've done as much as you asked, Lezith. I've seen them. Now take them away again. I won't be drawn into this business."

Andromeda felt Talen bristle beside her. But when she spoke, she had the sense to keep her annoyance in check. "I can understand it must be an inconvenience to be ordered about by the Empress—I myself feel the same, in some of her treatments towards me. Still, I've heard you're the best Blacksmith there is. If I'm to have any chance of surviving my re-match with the Dragon, I will need the help of a skilled Weaponsmith."

Ferris, who had already turned away and picked up her hammer, seemed to hesitate upon hearing Talen's words. She half-turned back, still with the hammer in hand, and gave Talen a longer look. "You're the Hero who survived," she said, half-statement, half-question.

"Yes," said Talen simply.

Ferris looked at Andromeda next, saying more quietly, "And you're the one who ascended the mountain to save her from the Dragon's jaws."

It was a rather fanciful way of putting things, but Andromeda nodded since it was more or less accurate.

"Ferris does not watch whenever a Hero passes through the town," Lezith put in with seeming casualness. "She says it's a morbid business; like watching a live sacrifice."

Ferris gave Lezith an annoyed look and sighed. "Why did you get yourself mixed up with these two? That damn curiosity of yours..."

"The stars advised me it would be wise," Lezith replied in a pious voice Andromeda hadn't heard her use before.

"The stars?" Ferris snorted. "That's just an excuse you use for things you were going to do anyway."

"Well then, perhaps I have a soft spot for lovers."

For some reason, that answer made Ferris even more annoyed, though there was something else below that. Empathy and a flash of pain.

Grudgingly, she said to Talen, "You don't have the physique of a swordfighter. What weapons do you use?"

"Bows and knives. Realistically, against the Dragon, the need for a bow is probably greater."

"A bow?" Ferris's eyebrows shot up, and she gave Lezith a look of veiled hostility this time. "You know I am no bowmaker. Why did you bring them here?"

"I think you know why I brought them, Ferris," Lezith said. "But perhaps we should go inside to continue this?"

Ferris looked as if she wanted to refuse, but Andromeda could tell she wasn't going to. In spite of herself, she'd been drawn in. She felt some sympathetic connection to Talen and Andromeda's situation, the origin of which was still unclear, and it made her unable to turn them away as she wished.

"Fine," said Ferris, giving in with bad grace. She threw her hammer down with a clang and jerked her head towards her cottage. "We can go inside."

The cottage was neat to the point of being bare. The place seemed little lived-in, and Andromeda wondered where Ferris spent most of her time. Where had she been when Lezith had gone to talk to her yesterday?

Leading the way to a long, wooden table, Ferris sat and indicated the others should too. She didn't offer them any refreshments. Taking a breath, she fixed Lezith with a hard stare, her eyes still angry. "I suppose, Lezith, that what you meant outside is you want me to tell them. About the bow."

"I was hoping you would do more than tell them, Ferris," said Lezith calmly, ignoring Ferris's combative tone. "You heard what Talen said. She is in need of a bow."

"That bow is broken. It is of no use to anyone."

"Andromeda is a Sorceress. It may be she can mend the bow."

With a snort, Ferris said, "I have searched this land from one end to the other looking for what is needed to repair the bow. The enchantments simply do not exist anymore. Why do you think Andromeda, an outsider, would fare any better?"

"Her magic cured the marks of Dragon's fire on Talen's skin. She brought her back from the brink of death. I myself witnessed some of the healing. No one in our land has been able to accomplish as much."

Ferris shifted her gaze to Andromeda. The assessing look in her dark eyes was sceptical at first, but as Andromeda continued to look steadily back, something in Ferris's manner changed. "You came after Talen, you saved her, because she is your lover?"

Andromeda nodded. "Yes."

She saw the pain and regret that came into Ferris's eyes then, and a newfound sense of respect she didn't understand until Ferris said, "In that case, you were more successful than I."

"Your lover was one of the Heroes who fought the Dragon?" Andromeda asked, exchanging a swift look of surprise with Talen.

"The first," said Ferris, the words seeming to be dragged out of her reluctantly. "Many years ago, when we were young and stupid. I moved to this town afterwards to be close to the Mountain where she died."

"The first Hero was much favoured by the Empress," Lezith recalled. "She had a special bow made for her. An enchanted bow, which all thought would ensure the Hero's victory. The loss of the Empress's favoured Hero and the bow were heavy blows to the kingdom."

"The loss of the bow?" queried Talen. "But...I thought you said Ferris still has it."

"The Dragon returned it to me," Ferris said. "After Stasia fell."

"You mean, the Dragon killed Stasia, your lover, then came and returned the bow to you?" Talen's brow was furrowed in confusion.

Ferris nodded. "As outlandish as it sounds, yes, that is what happened. I was on my way to Drakk at the time, fully expecting to see Stasia alive and well when I arrived, victorious against the Dragon. Instead, the great beast descended out of the sky and landed on the road in front of me. It dropped the bow from one of its claws and then it...gave me a vision in my mind." A spectre of never-quite-forgotten horror moved over Ferris's features as she told of what the Dragon had shown her. "I saw Stasia, dying, asking the Dragon to take the bow to me so I'd have something to remember her by."

Her expression hardening, she continued in a low, savage voice, "I wanted to kill it. But I knew if I moved it would kill me first. I could see it in the beast's eye. There was nothing I could do besides let it drop the bow and fly away, back to its mountain." She gave Talen and Andromeda a dark, humourless smile. "And that is the tale of my encounter with the Dragon."

"You never told the Empress you had the bow?" asked Talen.

"No. It's useless anyway. Snapped in two." That may have been true, but Andromeda could tell from the way Ferris spoke that a large part of why she hadn't told the Empress was because she hated her and blamed her for Stasia's death.

"And you never became one of the Heroes yourself?"

Ferris's eyes flashed. "Oh believe me, I wanted to. But Stasia had made me promise I wouldn't if she didn't survive. I can only assume... she had doubts she never shared with me. As it was, I made the promise unthinkingly, never imagining it would become relevant." The edge of pain in Ferris's voice spoke of how much she regretted that decision.

"Why would the Dragon return the bow to you?" said Andromeda. "It must have known what it was. A weapon meant to destroy it." Though she believed her Book's assertion that the Dragon was female, she didn't refer to it that way in front of Ferris. Despite her initial reluctance, Ferris was proving to be a valuable source of information, and there was no need to alienate her with Andromeda's own private speculations. Lezith, meanwhile, was being unusually quiet and not drawing attention to herself. Andromeda rather got the feeling she'd hoped things would unfold like this, and didn't want to disrupt the flow of conversation.

Ferris shrugged and answered in a melancholic tone, "I've spent many years contemplating why the Dragon flew all the way down the mountain to return the bow and give me awful images I've never been able to get out of my head. The answer still eludes me."

There was a short, weighty silence before Talen changed the subject, asking, "What was the bow supposed to do?"

Shaking herself, Ferris said, "It was supposed to destroy the Dragon's Third Eye. As one who has faced the beast, I'm sure you know what I'm talking about. Stasia believed the best way to do that was to take the Dragon's normal sight first. I know she got as far as taking one of its eyes, for the Dragon had lost an eye when it delivered the bow to me. But she got no further than that."

"Why did she think she had to blind the Dragon first? I thought the Third Eye was supposed to be unprotected? The one vulnerable spot on its body?"

"It is. But Stasia believed the Third Eye could only be fully destroyed by taking the Dragon's seeing eyes first. I don't know why, but she was convinced of it."

"Do you think she got that knowledge from the Empress?"

"I don't know where she got it."

"The Empress did not say anything like that to me. Also, the Third Eye isn't vulnerable. I shot my arrow straight into it and it bounced right off. Maybe I should have taken out its remaining seeing eye first."

This news was evidently disturbing to Ferris. "No, if you struck the Third Eye, at the very least that should have wounded the Dragon. I wonder if this has been the case all along. If the Eye isn't vulnerable, none of the Heroes who went up against the Dragon would have stood a chance."

"And I'm the first one to make it back with the news," Talen commented darkly.

"Why did the Empress think the bow could kill the Dragon?" Andromeda put in. "What was it supposed to do?"

"The bow was fashioned by the oldest of the Empress's Sages, who has since passed away. It was made from the rarest wood in Blackheath, taken from the Flame Tree. These trees were near immortal, living for thousands of years, never shedding their bright red blossoms, thriving even in the deepest snows. Legend says the Dragon itself gifted Flame Trees to Blackheath, scattering the seeds from its claws as it flew over the sky at the birth of the world. But over time, the few trees that were known to exist began to die, and they left behind no seeds.

"In time, the only known tree that survived was a sapling cared for by the Imperial Family. The Empress destroyed that sapling and used its wood to create the bow. The wood of the Flame Trees was well known for its magical properties, and the Empress must have known something that made her sure a bow fashioned from the tree would kill the Dragon. I do not think she would have destroyed the sapling otherwise."

Nodding towards Lezith with a rueful glance, Ferris said, "All this I told to Lezith one night when I, like a fool, allowed my tongue to be loosened by too much drink. Ever since, she has sent me on missions up and down the land chasing legends of Flame Trees, but none of them turned out to be real. Lezith is convinced that the bow can be mended if only we can find even the smallest amount of wood from a living Flame Tree."

Andromeda frowned. "But why bother, when the bow didn't work?"

"We don't know that it didn't work," said Lezith, finally breaking her silence. "Only that Stasia did not complete what she started. She only got as far as taking one eye."

"So you think if the bow can be repaired, it might still work, if the wielder first takes the remaining eye of the Dragon before piercing the Third Eye?"

Lezith inclined her head towards Andromeda, before addressing Talen. "If we can find a way to repair the bow, is it a strategy you would be willing to try, Talen?"

"It sounds better than anything else I've yet heard,' Talen said. She looked towards Andromeda. "Andromeda, you are the only one with magic here. Will you examine the bow?"

There was a certain tension beneath Talen's request that caught Andromeda off guard. She didn't understand it at first, until she gave Talen an inquiring look and saw several things in her expression she didn't expect. Worry. Guilt. Fear of what the consequences might be.

After a moment, Andromeda worked it out. Talen was thinking of what Andromeda had said to the Empress; that her continued access to the Book's magic was contingent upon her behaving with honour. Of course Talen wouldn't want Andromeda to become embroiled in something that could damage her powers. They'd both already acknowledged they weren't sure if killing the Dragon was the most ethical route to take.

But what Andromeda hadn't had the chance to tell Talen was that she was fairly sure it was another sort of honour the Book was referring to. She'd only said that to the Empress to put her off.

Andromeda grasped Talen's hand beneath the table, in thanks and acknowledgement of her concerns. She tried to tell her with a look that it was all right, before turning to Ferris.

"Ferris, if you are willing to let me see the bow, I'm willing to examine it."

It was some time before Ferris answered, emotions working through her eyes that Andromeda could only guess at. "All right," she allowed after a long pause. "I'll let you see the bow."

Chapter 12

Ferris laid the bow before them on the table, wrapped and tied in soft leather. She handled the object gently, the relic of a vanished world that had died when the Dragon took Stasia's life. Old sorrow and regret mingled with the scent of the leather as Ferris unwrapped the bow, her face pinched with painful emotion.

Andromeda felt too much as if she were looking at what her own future had nearly been, and might be still if things went ill between Talen and the Dragon.

With the bow unwrapped, Andromeda could see that it no longer had its string, and had been snapped cleanly in two at the mid-point of its riser. It was as bad as Ferris had said. Andromeda had gained enough knowledge from Talen to know that even tiny horizontal cracks in the wood could make a bow unstable and too dangerous to use, and this was much worse.

Talen picked up the broken top half of the bow, running her hands over the dusky red wood gently. "This was once a truly beautiful bow," she said in a low, sorrowful voice.

"Beautiful like its wielder," said Ferris. She picked up the bow's other half, caressing the wood with careful fingers. "We all of us took victory too much for granted, and for that reason Stasia's bones now lie somewhere on the peak of the Dragon's Mountain, never to be recovered." There was a lingering darkness in Ferris's eyes as she handed her half of the bow to Andromeda, the legacy of all that which she could not forget; the life she never got to live with Stasia. "Do not let Talen share the same fate."

Andromeda nodded to her solemnly. "I don't intend to," she promised.

Aware of Ferris's gaze on her, Andromeda ran her hands over the broken bow, nervously hoping the faith which Lezith seemed to have in her would not prove misplaced. She still did not know the limits of her powers, nor entirely understand how they worked.

At first, the bow felt no different to handling any other wooden object. Only when Andromeda closed her eyes and kept her fingers still, near the point of the break, did she begin to get a curious sensation she could not at first decipher. She sunk her consciousness further, exploring the fibres of the wood with her mind, and suddenly understood what it was she was sensing.

The fractured bow felt not unlike Talen's skin when she'd been burned; painful and damaged and longing for healing that could not be completed without assistance. In some way, the wood of this bow was still alive.

Without opening her eyes, Andromeda held out her free hand. "Talen, give me the other half of the bow."

She felt Talen place the other half of the bow in her hand. By feel, she fitted the two halves together, sensing the yearning within the wooden fibres to be whole again. There just might be something she could try to fix this. She wasn't sure if it would work, but it was at least an idea.

Andromeda was taken aback to see Talen, Lezith and Ferris all looking at her intently once she came out of the partial-trance, waiting for her to speak. This was a far cry from her days as a Princess, when her father more often than not silenced her when she said anything at all.

Unconsciously straightening her spine, she turned to Talen. "Talen, do you remember that time you were making a bow and it developed a tiny horizontal hairline fracture the first time you tested it? You said if the fracture was any worse the bow would have to be discarded, but because the crack was so minor and you'd noticed it right away, you decided to repair the bow by adhering rawhide over the fracture to strengthen it."

"I remember. But adhesive and rawhide won't fix this bow. It's well beyond that."

"I know. I was thinking of the Moondust."

Talen's eyebrows rose. "The Moondust? Would that work? I thought that stuff was for healing people."

"Well, the legends of the land where I found it say it can be used to heal any living thing. The wood of this bow feels alive, like a living tree. I'm not sure if it will work, but if we could hold the two pieces of the bow together and apply the Moondust over the break..."

"You want to use rawhide to secure the bow together while it heals. If it can heal."

Andromeda nodded.

"What exactly is Moondust?" asked Ferris.

"A rare and powerful healing substance," said Andromeda. "It's what I used to save Talen when she was close to death. It has magical properties that mean it can cure any illness or injury no matter how severe, as long as the subject is still alive. And this bow...The way the wood feels reminds me of Talen's skin when she was burned. Her body was desperately trying to heal itself and couldn't because of how bad the injuries were. This bow feels the same."

Placing the broken bow back on the table, Andromeda looked at Ferris and waited.

Ferris passed her hand over the two halves of the bow in a long, lingering caress before looking up to meet Andromeda's gaze, her eyes sure and determined. "Very well. If you can find a way to mend the bow, you may take it to use against the Dragon. This might be the last hope Blackheath has. Talen—" She switched her attention to Talen. "I can make you arrowheads. I used to do so for Stasia all the time. But

I'm afraid I have nothing from which to fashion shafts or fletching. You will have to look for those materials elsewhere."

"I still have a few shafts left," said Talen. "They were made before I came to Blackheath. With the amount I travel, I prefer to always have at least some of the materials I need for more arrows. I often find myself in lands where not everything I need is available. Lezith, I've seen geese wandering around Drakk. If I could harvest some feathers, they would work well for fletching."

"That is easily arranged," Lezith replied.

"Very well," said Ferris. "That just leaves the question of daggers. You said you had one already, Talen. May I see it?"

"You don't have to make me daggers as well," Talen protested, though she took her dagger out of its sheath and handed it over.

Ferris gave her a critical look. "If you intend to face the Dragon again, you will need all the weaponry you can muster." She began to examine the dagger, nodding once or twice in approval. "It's nicely made. Is this the balance point you prefer?"

They launched into a discussion of dagger particulars, some of which Andromeda understood, most of which she didn't. The upshot was that Ferris insisted on crafting a pair of daggers for Talen, and Andromeda would get her dagger back from Talen once the new weapons were ready.

With those details settled, there was nothing further to discuss, and Ferris got up to show them to the door. Once they reached it, she and Talen clasped arms in a gesture of farewell. "Good fortune to you, Hero," Ferris said in a sober voice. "You're going to need it."

Talen gave a half-smile, looking towards Andromeda with pride lighting up her eyes. "I have something better than luck on my side. I have a Witch."

Letting go of Talen, Ferris clasped Andromeda's arm in turn. "In that case...make sure you protect her, Andromeda."

"I went beyond the ends of the earth to find Talen. You can be sure I will protect her."

Lastly, Ferris shook her head at Lezith, saying with a small, grim smile, "And you, old woman, you bring me nothing but trouble. But just occasionally, you also make me feel like there is still some use to my existence in this world. For that, I thank you."

Lezith smiled back at her, a kinder, friendlier smile. "It is well, Ferris. Let us hope that soon, the shadow which consumes us all will finally be laid to rest."

With that, Ferris opened the door and the party left, going out into a day that had turned to rain. They hadn't gone far before they heard the ring of Ferris's hammer once more, sharp and clear, not missing a beat.

Back at Lezith's cottage, Talen used some rawhide from her own belongings and a glue made from cheese to bind the two halves of the bow together.

Andromeda made up a salve from most of the remaining Moondust near the kitchen hearth, while Lezith took up her weaving nearby. Lezith watched Andromeda intermittently, though she hurriedly pretended to concentrate on her weaving when Andromeda looked at her and said, "The pouch containing the Moondust powder is nearly empty, Lezith, but I would like you to have what's left. As thanks for all you have done."

Caught off-guard, Lezith forgot to pretend she was weaving, and surprise widened her eyes. "That is worth a kingdom, Andromeda. You cannot give me something so precious. I would not accept it. What little I have done does not warrant so great a gift."

"You have shown Talen and I nothing but kindness, though we are strangers to you. You...accepted us. I know feelings like that which

Talen and I have for each other do not bear the same stigma here, but still...I am thankful. This kind of understanding is not something I have encountered before. It means a great deal to me. Besides, I can always return to the world where I found the Moondust to get more. And there is so little left now that there isn't enough to cure any grievous wounds."

"Like those that might be inflicted by a Dragon," Talen suggested from her place at the kitchen table.

Andromeda frowned at Talen's bluntness, but yes, that had been what she was getting at. "I do still hope to find other spells to help you, Talen. But you are correct. Without the Moondust, I might not be able to save you a second time." She got up and went to sit beside Talen at the table, placing the pot of salve between them.

With an entreaty in her voice, she said, "Don't let the Dragon hurt you when next you meet."

"I'll do my best." Talen grasped Andromeda's hand for a moment, an apology in her eyes as she realised she'd upset Andromeda with her glib statement. She turned to Lezith. "Andromeda is right, Lezith. You should take what is left of the Moondust. I...will admit I did not trust you at first, but you have done much to help us, and asked for nothing in return. I think I was wrong in my initial assessment."

After appearing to think it over, Lezith nodded. "Very well. I will look after the Moondust for now. But I will return it, should it be needed. How do things proceed with the bow?"

Examining the bow critically Talen said, "The pieces are bonded together. I think it is ready for its first application of salve."

Lezith remained by the fire, choosing not to observe the proceedings any more closely as Andromeda dipped her fingers into the newly made mixture of Moondust and prepared to rub it over the bow.

"Andromeda—Wait. You should let me do the rest."

Talen spoke with an odd catch in her voice, and a quick examination of her features confirmed to Andromeda what her concern was. This was about the question of honour again.

"Talen, I didn't get the chance to tell you this before, but what my Book says about honour—the sort of honour it's referring to—it's not exactly as I led the Empress to believe. At least, I don't think it is."

"All right," said Talen, looking a little confused. "Then what kind of honour is it talking about?"

"I'll explain it later," said Andromeda, feeling heat in her cheeks that she knew both Talen and Lezith noticed. "For now…" She offered the pot of salve to Talen. "Will you help me?"

Talen nodded and dipped her own fingers into the Moondust, though there were many curious questions in her eyes.

"We'll need to do this every day for the next seven days," Andromeda said as she began to apply the salve. "The same as when I was healing you," she added with a glance towards Talen. "At the end of that time, the bow should be mended. It will be a weapon fit to take the Dragon's life."

There was a gravity in Talen's eyes as she whispered her reply. "And I will make sure its purpose is fulfilled."

Lezith continued to sit by her loom beside the fire, tactfully silent, a thoughtful expression on her face as her needle wove between the warp of her threads.

⊰§⊱

Not until after they went to bed did Andromeda and Talen return to the subject of honour. Talen brought it up as they lay tangled together in the quiet, sated aftermath of the union they'd enjoyed, saying, "So what do you think the Book of Magic means, when it says you have to live honourably?"

"Well—" Andromeda paused. "The Book came from a Library that was built to protect those who follow the Broken Road. Others like us. I think if I were to do something like go back to my kingdom and marry a Prince, then the Book would desert me. Because by doing so, I'd be dishonouring myself. I wouldn't be worthy to have the Book then. It would belong in the hands of another. Someone braver. Someone who could be true to her own feelings."

Talen shifted to look at her. "Are you sure that is what it means?"

"The Book doesn't explain, but that's the feeling I have."

"You're risking a lot on a feeling, Andromeda."

With a smile, Andromeda stroked Talen's face and kissed her. "I think figuring it out is part of the test. If I don't have the wisdom to understand the Book, then I don't deserve the knowledge it bestows."

"I wish we had more information about the Dragon," Talen said. "All those things Ferris told us didn't make any kind of sense. There's a library at the Imperial Palace, but even that didn't contain much of use."

"We still have seven days before the bow is ready." Andromeda traced the delicate shell of Talen's ear. "If you're right, and the Empress is planning something, it may be that she will make her next move soon. What she does might at least tell us where we should be looking."

Talen nodded. "That's true." She drew her fingers lightly down Andromeda's spine in a languorous caress that made Andromeda shiver. "And in that case, all we can do is wait until the Empress does something. Wait and find something to do to pass the time."

"I can think of something," Andromeda whispered breathlessly, and leaned in to kiss Talen once more.

It was raining again several days hence when the Empress played her next card, sending Valouria to Lezith's cottage wearing a grim expression that did not bode well. Talen was the first to notice her approach, and initially insisted she would go out to meet her alone, until Andromeda told her there was no way that was happening.

After a brief argument, they agreed they would both go out, and instructed Lezith to stay in the safety of the cottage. Lezith snorted and looked rather amused, but didn't gainsay their wishes.

Five guards accompanied Valouria, and given the exchange they'd had at the Manor, Andromeda wondered how she had chosen them. It must have been a weighty selection, for Valouria knew she was potentially leading all of them to their deaths if Talen and Andromeda chose not to cooperate.

Bringing the party to a halt at Lezith's door, Valouria dismounted, deliberately giving up the strategic advantage of height, though the rest of the guards remained mounted behind her.

She bowed to Talen and Andromeda, her lips pursed as if she didn't like what she was about to have to say. "Her Imperial Majesty sends greetings and good wishes to the Hero of Blackheath and the Lady Andromeda, wielder of sorcery. Shortly after your audience with her Illustriousness, the Empress left the Manor to return to the Imperial Palace, but bid me come to you on this appointed day to carry out her will."

With another bow, she handed a scroll to Andromeda, which Andromeda unrolled and read.

"What does it say?" asked Talen, not taking her eyes off Valouria.

"That I am to accompany Valouria to the Imperial Palace to be the Empress's honoured guest."

Though the language was very polite, it was clear the Empress was not making a suggestion.

Valouria's hand hovered over her sword as she watched Talen warily in turn. Andromeda was curious about her willingness to carry out the Empress's orders. Valouria wasn't stupid; nor was she lacking a moral compass or empathy for others. Her behaviour the last time she had been in Drakk was proof of that. She must believe the Empress was acting in the best interests of the kingdom, for Andromeda didn't think Valouria would keep serving an Empress whom she suspected of being corrupt.

Talen was tense. She did not yet have her new daggers from Ferris, but she still had the dagger Andromeda had previously returned to her. Her stance said she was perfectly willing to use it, if Andromeda expressed herself reluctant to leave.

And what would happen then? If Talen attacked Valouria, the rest of the guards would retaliate. They'd have to fight all of them. Andromeda could use her magic to protect herself and Talen; she could already feel the power humming beneath her skin in response to the rising tension. She and Talen had a good chance of surviving the encounter; much better than the guards. But what would be the point of all that death? At the end of it, Talen would still bear the Empress's mark, and Andromeda would be no closer to freeing her.

"Talen," she said softly. "I'll go with them."

"You're sure?" said Talen, not doubting her decision but seeking confirmation of her will.

"I am." Andromeda switched her gaze to Valouria. "On one condition. That you wait two days before taking me."

"Why two days?" asked Valouria.

"I am completing a spell that will help Talen when next she faces the Dragon. It will be ready in two days. I will have no objections to accompanying you once it is ready."

"If I agree to wait, I have your word you will come with me at the end of two days?"

"Yes. You have my word."

Relaxing slightly, Valouria began to edge her hand away from her sword, though she kept her eyes on Talen.

Talen noticed, and said in a soft, lethal voice, "I could have already killed you, Valouria. Andromeda doesn't want that. She doesn't want it for any of us. It's half the reason why she has agreed to go with you. And I'll bet the Empress was counting on that, willing to gamble your life and those of your guards on the chance of Andromeda's mercy."

"It's a good thing the Empress was right then, isn't it?" Valouria answered. Her tone betrayed neither anger nor pride, but she held herself in a wide stance and met Talen's gaze without fear. There was a gravitas to her as she stood there unflinching, the cloak about her shoulders heavy with rain while the semi-circle of mounted guards waited behind her, never doubting where she led.

It was in this moment Lezith chose to appear, disregarding the instruction to stay indoors. "If you have all finished out here," she said in a grumbling voice, "I've just made fresh tea. Come inside and get warm, the lot of you. It's bad luck to argue at the door, not to mention undignified."

Andromeda could only assume this was a usual invitation, since Valouria accepted it without surprise, and seemingly without any fear of retaliatory attack. She ordered her troops to dismount and sent two of them to get the horses settled, evidently familiar with the setup of Lezith's cottage. She led the remaining three guards inside, past Talen and Andromeda, leaving their backs trustingly exposed. Andromeda and Talen followed them in.

The remaining two guards joined them a short time later, accompanied by Ferris of all people, who appeared to know Valouria well. Andromeda was initially surprised by that, until she remembered Ferris used to live in the Imperial City.

Ferris had stopped by Lezith's cottage only once since she gave them the bow. She had called in two days ago to ask how the repairs were progressing, looking with an inscrutable expression at the two halves of the bow held together with rawhide and covered in the shimmering coating of Moondust.

Other than that, she had stayed in her forge working every day, her services obviously much in demand around the township.

Andromeda noticed that Lezith had arranged the seating at the table so that Talen and Valouria were neither sitting too near each other, nor directly in each other's line of sight. It was a clever and non-obvious way of discouraging further hostility, though Andromeda knew it probably wasn't necessary. If anything, they were probably relieved not to have to fight today.

Valouria spent most of the very odd tea party speaking to Lezith and Ferris, politely leaving Andromeda and Talen to their own devices. At one point, she even tried to persuade Ferris to return to her former life, saying, "I know I'm most likely wasting my time by now, but you're welcome to return to the Imperial City any time you choose, Ferris. You were the best Bladesmith we had, and we are still sorry to have lost you, all these years later."

"Adair is highly skilled," answered Ferris, not meeting Valouria's eyes and seeming rather bored. "I'm sure he fulfils all your needs."

Frustration creeping into her voice, Valouria insisted, "Adair is highly skilled, but you were better. You're wasting your talents here, Ferris. Is this really all you want to do for the rest of your life? Playing at being a village Blacksmith hammering horseshoes and fixing pots and pans?"

Ferris looked up from examining the dregs in her teacup, giving Valouria a hard stare. "I won't work for the Empress again. You know that. I have no interest in returning to my old life. What I have made here suits me, and I do not care whether others think it appropriate for me or not."

"Ferris, Stasia's fate—"

"Was not all the fault of the Empress," Ferris finished. "I am well aware. The first Hero to face the Dragon, endowed with a magical weapon from the Empress which none of us thought would fail. It was our own arrogance that led to Stasia's downfall." She glanced towards Talen. "That damn Dragon has blighted so many lives. You

151

will be freeing us all of a crushing burden if you can kill the beast. I pray the stars will grant you great fortune in the battle to come."

"I gave the Empress my word I would rid this land of the Dragon," said Talen. "I do not mean to fail."

Underneath the table, she clasped Andromeda's hand; a silent recognition that she hadn't forgotten Andromeda's doubts, or her own, about the righteousness of slaying the Dragon.

Several of Valouria's guards gave Talen a muted salute. Ferris looked as if she couldn't decide whether to be hopeful or guilt-ridden for potentially helping to send another Hero to her death. Lezith wondered when the rain was going to stop.

"Better rain than snow," said Valouria darkly. She looked at Andromeda. "I'll return in two days. You declare yourself willing to go with me then?"

"Yes, I will go with you," Andromeda promised.

Valouria nodded. She didn't speak to Talen when she gathered up her guards and left.

Chapter 13

In two more days, the bow was ready. Andromeda and Talen had decided the night before they would test it together, and they rode out on their final morning when only the faintest light of dawn stained the sky, heading into the wilderness of the deserted lands beyond Drakk where there was no one to see.

Andromeda watched Talen as she pulled the bow taut and chose a tree trunk to target, as she released the arrow and let it fly. In quick succession, she did it again, and again, testing the resilience of the bow, her arrows arching with deadly beauty through the frosty air.

This was the first time since the palace Andromeda had seen Talen practice her archery, and it put her in mind of those days; how impressed she had been when she first saw Talen wield a bow, how she had asked her eagerly what else she knew. It was sometime after that when Talen had begun to teach Andromeda rudimentary survival skills in the tame palace woodlands, without the knowledge of the King and Queen.

"I can't feel any weaknesses in the bow at all," said Talen, looking towards Andromeda with delight and admiration in her eyes. She lowered the bow and came closer, placing her free hand around Andromeda's waist and pulling her into a kiss. "You truly are an unmatched Sorceress."

Andromeda smiled at her. "I never would have gotten the chance if you hadn't taught me how to survive by myself. I've never told you how grateful I was for that. When I started to think about escaping,

I realised I could actually do it, and survive on my own, thanks to everything I learned from you."

Shaking her head, Talen replied, "I could have taught you everything I know and it wouldn't have meant anything if you were too afraid to step away from your old life. You found the courage to do that on your own."

"I'm glad I did. It was...difficult at first. So different from what I'd known before. But now that I am to return to a palace once more, I find myself disliking the idea."

"Yes," said Talen, her gaze growing troubled. "Are you still willing to go?"

"I am. I gave Valouria my word. But aside from that, this may be our best chance to discover something about the Dragon. We said we would wait for the Empress to make her move, and this is what she chose. She thinks it will be of benefit to her if I am at the Imperial Palace, and I do not believe it is simply so you will be more eager to slay the Dragon. I sense there is some other purpose to it."

"I agree, that seems likely," said Talen. "Remember the library I spoke of? There was one book I found that had a slip of parchment inside. It referred to something called The Wildcard of Fate. There was no explanation of what it was, or how to invoke it, but...someone had written it was the Dragon's spell. A spell that must never be spoken of. If you are determined to go with Valouria, that could be a starting point for your search."

"Thank you." Andromeda leaned into Talen. "This past week, I've felt as if my powers are growing stronger. If there's anything to be uncovered at the Imperial Palace, I promise you I'll find it."

Talen nodded, but said, "I feel well enough to climb the mountain and face the Dragon today, Andromeda. I know how to defeat it now. You don't have to go."

"I know, Talen. It just...doesn't feel right."

"Andromeda, I've been travelling the worlds since I was a child. Most of the time, a monster is just a monster. A dangerous beast that wants to rend flesh. A predator like a wolf or a bear, but bigger and more dangerous. Whatever else is going on here, the Dragon is killing this land, and everyone in it. I think that ending this now is an option we should at least consider. As long as you're sure the Book won't take that to mean you've dishonoured yourself."

"This isn't about the Book, Talen. I've travelled the worlds too. I've seen monsters and demons. I've fought them. None of them showed mercy. But the Dragon did. At least, it seems that way. And because of that, I was able to save you. There is something else going on here."

Andromeda understood Talen's desire to get this over with. She knew Talen felt responsible for this whole situation and wanted to solve it on her own. She knew Talen was reluctant to involve her for fear of what might happen. But equally, Andromeda feared what would happen to Talen if she climbed the mountain before they understood the reasons for the Dragon's actions.

She caressed Talen's cheek. "I would ask that you wait a month before ascending the mountain. It should take me about two weeks to reach the Imperial Palace, which means I will have the two following weeks to try and uncover something. It is not much time, but perhaps it is best not to let this situation drag on for too long. I worry about how volatile things may become, with the Empress being so desperate."

"I can give you a month," Talen agreed. "If anyone asks, I will say the spells you put on my armour still need time to strengthen. And Ferris only gave me the completed daggers last night. I will need practice before I am confident in them."

"Yes, that should work."

With Ferris's help, Talen had acquired new leather armour a few days ago which Andromeda had spelled heavily with protective enchantments. While it was true the spells needed time to reach their full strength, only a day or two was necessary. In truth, the armour was already prepared, but no one else in the town knew that. And if Talen thought her excuse about the daggers was believable, then Andromeda assumed it was so.

"We will need a way to stay in touch," added Talen.

"There was a full moon last night," said Andromeda, glancing at Talen and seeing in her eyes too the memory of what they'd shared; their bodies silvered in moonlight as they took comfort in what neither would admit might be their last time together. "At the next full moon, I will contact you at midnight via the communication stone that Jerrard keeps. I'm sure Lezith will help you gain access if you need it. If I have learned anything, I will share it with you then, and we can decide what to do. If not, then you can proceed to the mountain and face the Dragon."

"Very well," said Talen. She drew Andromeda into a tight embrace. "Watch yourself when you get to the palace, especially around the Empress."

"I will," Andromeda promised. "And I have one more request." She indicated Brownie, who had faithfully carried them out here. "Look after Brownie for me. I don't want to take her to the palace when I have no idea what I might be walking into."

"Of course, but—"

"I know. I know what you're going to say Talen. That's the other reason why I want to leave her here. Even if both of us...disappear, Lezith will be able to take care of her. I think Brownie would be happy with Lezith."

There was a sober look in Talen's eyes. "I wish we could go find that secluded woodland cottage right about now. In a world many worlds away from here."

"Maybe after the next full moon," said Andromeda, smiling sadly, while the shadow of Ferris and Stasia hung between them.

They both knew they did not have time to linger, but they did, sharing several more kisses tinged with the pain of oncoming loss before finally mounting Brownie and riding back to the township.

When they arrived, Valouria and her guards were already waiting at Lezith's cottage, restive at finding their charge absent. Andromeda bid them wait as she went inside to pack up the last of her belongings, and clung to Talen in their bedroom, unexpectedly overcome with emotion now that the time to separate had come. All she could think of was Talen as she had found her on the mountain, burned and dying, fearing such a scene playing out again when she would not be there to change the outcome.

Talen comforted her, looking into Andromeda's tearful countenance with conviction blazing in her arresting blue eyes. "We'll see each other again, Andromeda. I don't know what is to come, I don't know how all of this will end, but I feel in my heart this is not our final parting. I will look for your message next month, at the coming of the full moon."

Pulling herself together and stifling her tears, Andromeda nodded. She forced herself to let go of Talen and stepped away to pick up her travel pack, setting her expression into sober resolution. "You're right Talen, let's go. You'll see me off, won't you?"

"Of course," Talen replied, the soft tone of her voice conveying more than she said.

Outside, Talen helped Andromeda to load up her horse, while Valouria waited with a carefully neutral expression that hid whatever thoughts she might have on her orders. Andromeda hugged Lezith goodbye and shared one last kiss with Talen before mounting and indicating to Valouria she was ready to go.

Talen followed them to the gate and out into the lane. Valouria picked up the pace once they reached the road, but Andromeda still looked back as often as she could, until Talen, standing with her cloak fluttering in the wind, was lost to sight in the distance.

WITHIN PERHAPS FIVE miles of leaving Drakk, the world through which Andromeda travelled with Valouria and the guards deteriorated into a frozen wasteland. Though Andromeda had entered Blackheath from the West and they were now travelling East, the weather was much like that she had first encountered when she crossed over into this land. The air was bitterly cold, and icy winds frequently swept over the deserted hills and fields. Only dead trees and shattered ruins were left to mark the life which had once thrived here.

A week into their journey, they were hit by a bad snowstorm. It roared in violently with unnerving suddenness as the day was drawing to a close, and at a word from Valouria their small party galloped at speed towards a ruined farmhouse that was luckily close by.

The door to the house had long since rotted away, and inside drifts of snow were already building beneath the gaping holes in the roof. Valouria began to order the tents to be pitched, but with so much snow coming in, they would soon be buried.

"Valouria," said Andromeda, "If you would—wait a moment. I think I can erect a shield that will protect us, at least for the night."

Valouria gave her an assessing look before nodding her head. "Very well, if you think you can help, go ahead. But be quick. We'll freeze if we don't get the shelters up soon."

The spell Andromeda intended to try was a shield that could be used to protect either from attack or hostile elements. It was not unrelated to one of the enchantments she had woven into Talen's armour, and she had been practicing it with Dragon's fire in mind. Despite the Empress's assertions, Andromeda still intended to see if she could discover a way to accompany Talen to the peak of the Dragon's Mountain.

During her first week in Blackheath, Andromeda had survived by making a small personal flame she could carry with her at any time, or use to light a fire out of even frozen solid wood. The spell she was going to cast now was much different; an area spell that would take a great deal more energy.

Andromeda had already cast it successfully a few times, but only over herself, succeeding in small achievements like keeping off the rain. Casting a spell powerful enough to protect an entire building was going to be more of a challenge.

This was a spell woven of the caster's will; it had to be so, for it was meant to be used in dire situations when all else might be gone. It needed no words of power, no herbs or powders or crystals. Its strength would be determined by the courage in Andromeda's heart, and as she stood in the middle of the decaying room with her eyes closed and her arms raised above her head, she focused her will. She imagined a stream of golden energy flowing through the arteries of her heart, into the veins of her arms, and travelling out into her tingling fingertips. She gathered the energy and let it burst forth, shooting high above her head into a bright, golden stream, to cover the ruined farmhouse with a shimmering barrier.

Upon opening her eyes, Andromeda stumbled, feeling suddenly drained. Black spots danced before her eyes and her head was swimming, making her feel faint and sick. But the golden barrier was there, above them, and snow was no longer pouring into their shelter.

Andromeda was dimly aware of the stares of the guards as Valouria placed a steadying hand on her arm. "You all right?" she asked.

"Yes. Just drained," Andromeda managed to reply in a weak voice. The spell hadn't taken near as much out of her when she'd only had to create a personal rain shield.

Valouria nodded and addressed the guards. "All of you know better than to stand there with your mouths hanging open when there is work to be done. Unsaddle the horses. Get a fire going and make something hot. Shovel out this snow. Someone check that antechamber."

She jutted her chin towards the farmhouse's one internal doorway, leading through to what appeared to be another smaller room.

There was a flurry of activity as the guards began to carry out Valouria's instructions. Two went to investigate the antechamber, and soon returned, their faces grim.

"Dead bodies," said one shortly, in response to Valouria's query. "Frozen. They've been there a long time. Probably the family who lived here."

Valouria sighed and bowed her head. "Leave them where they are," she said. "There's nothing we can do for them now."

There was now a fire going in the remains of the room's old central fire-pit, and Valouria insisted Andromeda sit close to it on one of the thick furs the guards had started spreading over the cold dirt floor. Most of the snow had been swept away.

"Feeling any better?" she asked, squatting down next to Andromeda and examining her with a slightly worried look in her eyes.

"Less faint," Andromeda said.

She noticed the guards were giving her a wider birth than they had before, and as they hurried about their tasks one or two shot her awed furtive looks. Well, that probably wasn't a bad thing. The guards had been unfailingly polite to Andromeda on the journey so far, as had Valouria, but if they knew she had the power to leave if she chose, so much the better.

As food was being prepared, Valouria got out a bottle and passed it round, allowing everyone to take a sip of the warming amber alcohol it contained. She personally served Andromeda once the evening victuals were ready, though there was nothing unusual in that. She did it most nights.

Andromeda felt better once she'd eaten, warmed by the fire and surrounded by the combined body heat of humans and horses. She noticed that Valouria was still keeping a close eye on her, and took it as an opportunity to ask her something she had always wondered—

how Blackheath dealt with those who had been forced away from their homes.

"Blackheath must have lost many of its people to the Winter," she said, looking towards the dark doorway and thinking of the bodies lying in the next room. "Not long ago in Drakk, you mentioned something about refugees. I've been wondering, where do they go? Isn't everywhere the same?"

"There are a few places in Blackheath that have not been completely decimated by the cold as yet," answered Valouria. "The Imperial City is one such haven. Drakk is another."

"But there seem to be no refugees in Drakk. Surely that is odd."

"Even the most desperate will usually avoid Drakk. No one wants to live in the shadow of the Dragon's Mountain."

"Yet the people who are already there do not try to leave."

"No, they do not," agreed Valouria. "Most of those who live in Drakk come from families who have been there for generations. It was a very different town in the past; many would journey there to pray and look up at the sacred mountain. Even though things have changed, the people of Drakk do not abandon their custodianship. It would be unthinkable."

"The places that have not succumbed, do you know what sets them apart? In Drakk, the people seem to think it is the proximity to the Dragon that provides residual warmth, but that can't be the same elsewhere."

"The sanctuaries do not seem to have any common features. They are scattered randomly, and while the Dragon may protect Drakk, you are correct in thinking nowhere else has that distinction. There has only ever been one Dragon."

"Hasn't anybody tried to figure the mystery out?"

"Naturally," said Valouria, giving Andromeda a swift look of annoyance. "Don't you think we would have stopped this if we could? Our most learned scholars spent many years researching and testing theories. But the Winter kept spreading. Now, most of Blackheath is nigh uninhabitable and filled with frozen corpses." She paused as she looked into the fire. The guards were busy clearing up the dinner things and getting the horses settled for the night. "As much death as there has been, many more would have died if not for the Empress. She gives her guards authority to help those in need, to distribute food, to make sure as many have shelter as possible."

Checking to see they were relatively alone, Valouria looked back to Andromeda and added, "This has probably crossed your mind already, but...the reason why the Empress sent you and Talen to Drakk by yourselves was because she knew the two of you hadn't seen each other in a long time. She wanted you to have the chance to be together, for a little while at least."

This was a possibility that had, in fact, already crossed Andromeda's mind. But it left her unimpressed. She was still being taken against her will, at a time when she desperately wanted to be able to help Talen in whatever ways she could.

However, Andromeda knew that saying as much to Valouria would only antagonise her, so she merely replied, "I intend to see Talen again. I have the rest of my life to spend with her now. A few weeks apart will be lonely, but bearable."

Light and shadow flickered across Valouria's face as she glanced away from Andromeda's steady gaze to stare into the heart of the fire. Her own eyes uneasy, perhaps even guilty, she murmured, "May the stars shine bright upon your future."

Andromeda tilted her head up to look at the snow falling upon the shimmering barrier above them. The barrier she had created out of her own will, her own magic. "I would not scorn the blessings of the heavens, but nor will I count on them. Who knows how long it will be before the stars re-emerge from the storm-torn sky? I will move forward and do what I must, blessings or no."

Valouria gave Andromeda a startled look for a moment before smiling wryly. "Her Imperial Majesty was right in what she said about you. You would have made a formidable Queen."

"Perhaps," said Andromeda with a shrug. "But what is probably more relevant is that I intend to make a formidable Witch. Because that is the path I have chosen."

It might have been heavy handed, but Andromeda saw no reason not to remind Valouria that she had enough power to not be here if she so chose.

Instead of reacting with anger, Valouria said softly, "Given what you did for all of us before, that gives me some comfort."

One of the guards returned then, asking about shifts for the night, and Valouria took up her command once more, leaving Andromeda with a respectful bow. The rest of the night passed without incident.

୰ઙൟൢ

THE SNOWSTORM HAD BLOWN itself out by the next morning, but the cold was even more biting than before. Deep drifts of snow made the road before them practically impassable, and in the end, it was Andromeda who saved them once more. Using her magic, she began to blast the snow off the road as they went, and she kept it up for the next five days, until the snow began to recede and they reached inhabited lands again.

Tired from the continuous use of her powers, Andromeda paid only partial attention to the fields they passed, patrolled by guards and busy with agricultural workers. For two days they travelled through this area, staying at small inns overnight. On the seventh day, exactly two weeks after they'd left Drakk, Andromeda saw the walls of the Imperial City in the distance, and what she assumed to be the Imperial Palace itself sitting high above at the summit of a steep mountain peak.

When they reached the gates to the City late that afternoon, they were open but guarded. Andromeda noticed the continual stream of people passing through in both directions were required to show some kind of signed paper before being allowed in or out.

Valouria led their party to a lane that was mostly clear of traffic, cordoned off and marked with the Empress's insignia. They passed through the gates quickly, with only a few words exchanged briefly with the border watch. Inside the City, the streets were crowded and chaotic. There was evidence of beautiful architecture and what had once been well-planned vistas and views, but all of it was sadly neglected and marred with hasty, cheap building projects obviously meant to deal with the swelling population. The smell was not pleasant.

Looking up to the Imperial Palace presiding over the unhappy City, Andromeda wondered again why no one in the kingdom seemed to direct their anger towards the Empress. Did no one consider whether she and the rest of the Imperial Family were to blame for the Dragon's actions? Did no one ask why she didn't do more than send Heroes to die on the Dragon's Mountain?

Well, she didn't know everything. Perhaps there had been rebellions. It was unlikely Valouria would tell her even if that were the case.

As the ground began to slope upwards, the streets became less crowded and they passed larger houses still clinging to faded glory. Grim-faced guards were stationed at every gate, but Andromeda noticed they were not dressed in the same uniform as Valouria and the others.

"Private hires," said Valouria, noticing Andromeda's observations. From the way she spoke, Andromeda could tell she didn't much like them. She also guessed private hires was a nice way of saying mercenaries.

At the base of the mountain on which the palace was situated, they encountered another gate; closed this time. But the guards on duty quickly moved to let them in when they saw their approach, and a messenger was dispatched at once to ride ahead and inform the Empress of their imminent arrival.

The mountain was narrow, not much more than a rocky peak rising short and sharp above the City with the Imperial Palace built right into its stone foundations. Skeletal trees lined the winding road they ascended, their branches grasping like hungry fingers towards the sullen sky. It was difficult to see it now, but Andromeda thought the approach had probably once been quite beautiful.

The palace itself was a slim, spiralling building constructed of pale shimmering stone. Two intricate stained-glass windows dominated the heavily ornate facade that rose before them; a circular window with a tree that had many spreading roots and branches, and below that a larger arched window inset with several different patterns. One of them Andromeda recognised. The mark of flame that Talen bore on her shoulder.

They passed through the final gate, a massive portcullis hewn from the stone of the mountain, and reached the outer courtyard. There were few people in evidence besides more guards. A ripple went through those present as Valouria rode in with Andromeda and the rest of her company; Andromeda couldn't be sure, but she got the impression there had been some doubt as to whether her mission would be a success.

Still mounted, Valouria went right up to the studded double doors of the palace, and the guards stationed on either side swung them open without her needing to ask. Valouria called to them in thanks and dismounted in a fluid motion, afterwards offering assistance to Andromeda though she knew Andromeda didn't need it.

Andromeda shook her head and dismounted by herself. Turning, Valouria gave a few brief instructions to the rest of the guards who'd accompanied them, before focusing her attention on Andromeda once more.

"My Lady," she said, "the Empress awaits."

"Yes," said Andromeda wearily. "I know." She shouldered the pack that contained her Book of Magic and most of her supplies, and looked at the dark doorway through which they were about to pass. She sighed. "Well, we've come this far. You might as well finish this mission, Valouria. Take me to the Empress."

Valouria nodded, and led Andromeda into the palace.

Chapter 14

The interior of the palace was a maze of winding hallways and staircases built of shining black stone. Andromeda followed close behind Valouria, doing her best to memorise the twists and turns of their route, while wondering at the palace's seeming emptiness. They passed almost no one, and the only sound to be heard was their own echoing footsteps.

There must have been someone carrying messages, however, as Jasper soon came to meet them. He gave both Valouria and Andromeda a fleeting expression of dismay as he took in their travel-stained appearance, but quickly schooled the reaction away.

Bowing to Andromeda, he said, "It is an honour to see you again, My Lady. Her Imperial Majesty has expressed her desire for an audience at once. She promises to be brief; she is aware you have endured a difficult journey."

"How considerate of her," said Andromeda in a deadpan voice.

Nodding graciously as if Andromeda's tone had been polite and not antagonistic, Jasper added to Valouria, "Her Imperial Majesty expressed her desire that you also attend, Captain."

"Yes, I rather expected she might." Valouria stretched her shoulders wearily and ran a hand over her face, then grimaced at the grime she saw on her fingers afterwards. "Well," she gestured with her dirty hand, which Jasper momentarily fixated upon in horror. "Lead the way, and let's hope the Empress is capable of a more tactful response to our appearance than you are, my old friend."

❧

ANDROMEDA EXPECTED to be taken to some kind of grand stately hall or crowded noble court, but instead, she was led up many more flights of stairs and shown into a round room at the top of the palace's tallest tower.

The walls and floor were built of more polished black stone, and the Empress herself sat straight and regal upon a golden throne beset with sparkling jewels; as still as a portrait, as inexorable as fate.

Woven tapestries hung upon the gleaming walls, each depicting a different scene. The Dragon, Andromeda realised, was in all of them. In the first, the Dragon soared through the sky while the land below flowered in the sunshine of Spring. In the next, the Dragon visited a cluster of richly dressed people who held aloft gifts of fruits and grains and meats. In the third, the Dragon was standing in a garden, head lowered while a young girl placed her hand upon the Dragon's forehead, in the exact area where the Third Eye was supposed to be.

But the fourth tapestry stood out from the others. It hung upon the Western wall of the throne room, opposite the Empress's throne, and it depicted the Dragon descending from the sky breathing fire, while the people in the tapestry writhed and burned. This was the scene the Empress looked upon, day after day. The living nightmare that had taken everyone she loved.

"Andromeda, the Sorceress from beyond the frozen sea," Jasper announced, bowing deeply to the Empress and indicating Andromeda with a flourish. "Here at Her Majesty's most gracious invitation, to be Her Majesty's most welcome guest."

The Empress inclined her head towards Andromeda. If anything, the pain etched upon her face was deeper than when Andromeda had last seen her less than a month ago.

"I thank you for your visit, Andromeda," the Empress responded formally. "I am aware the road to the palace is not easy to traverse in these times. The day already draws to a close, and I do not wish to keep you. I am sure your most pressing concern is to rest after your journey. Thus, I shall not trouble you further tonight. Jasper will take you to your chamber and ensure you have everything you need. We shall speak on the morrow, when the sun of a new day shines upon us."

"Very well, Your Majesty," said Andromeda, keeping her reply frostily polite.

She wondered where the Empress's court was, or if she even had one. Not more than a handful of people would fit into this tower room. Was there a grander throne room elsewhere in the palace better suited to entertaining crowds and impressing visitors?

Turning her attention to Valouria, the Empress said, "And you, my loyal Captain, of course you have my thanks as always for conveying Andromeda to the palace safely."

Valouria bowed. "Of course, my Empress. I do not fail in my duty."

"I know, Valouria. I rely upon you always, to be my strong arm of justice." The Empress's voice was almost gentle, as if she truly did value everything Valouria did for her.

Valouria bowed again, her back to the tapestry with the scene of carnage that she had witnessed as a young recruit ten years ago.

Jasper cleared his throat. "Well then, shall I take our guest..."

"Yes, yes," the Empress said, waving her hand. "You are free to go. Jasper will see to your needs, Andromeda. Do not hesitate to ask him if you should require anything."

Andromeda gave lukewarm thanks, then followed Jasper out of the throne room.

They'd reached the bottom of the tower stairs when Valouria caught up with them; rather surprisingly since Andromeda had assumed she'd be with the Empress for some time.

"I'll make sure my guards send over your personal things," Valouria promised, poised to disappear through a different passageway to that which Andromeda and Jasper were taking.

Since Andromeda already had everything essential with her, she was not particularly worried about the rest of her possessions, but she appreciated the gesture none the less. She got the sense from Valouria's manner that now she'd completed her task, she was not entirely easy about having delivered Andromeda after all. Had the Empress said something to make her doubt what she'd done?

"It is well, Valouria," Andromeda said, responding both to the Captain's words and her unspoken misgivings. "I have seen enough of you to know you would not willingly commit an injustice. Do not concern yourself with my fate; I have already learned I must make my own."

Valouria looked as if she wished she could respond, but she only nodded, and bowed a final time before departing. "My Lady," she murmured before striding purposefully away.

As she retreated, Jasper coughed discreetly. "If My Lady has no objections, I shall convey her to her chambers."

"Yes, go ahead," said Andromeda tiredly.

After another circuitous route, Jasper led her to a sumptuous suite of rooms including a bedchamber, a parlour, a private bath, a library, and a dressing room already stocked with gowns too elaborate for Andromeda to want to wear. The Empress was certainly sparing no effort to make her comfortable.

Once he had finished talking up the amenities, Andromeda looked Jasper in the eye and said, "This is all very impressive, Jasper, as I'm sure the Empress intended it to be. But how much freedom am I to have, as the Empress's guest? Am I to be locked into my chambers at night, for example?"

Jasper's look was scandalised. "I assure you, My Lady, you are Her Majesty's—"

"Most honoured guest," Andromeda repeated shortly. "I am aware. But let us be frank here, Jasper. I did not come to the palace of my own free will. I came because I feared what the Empress might do to Talen if I did not. I think we are all aware of that. So I ask again—how much freedom am I to have?"

There was a cold expression in Jasper's eyes now. He did not at all like the bluntness with which Andromeda spoke. "If concern for your lover's welfare is what binds you to the palace, I imagine that Her Majesty would not hesitate to grant you as much freedom as you wish. Under such conditions, an escape attempt is most unlikely." He bowed stiffly. "I must take my leave now, My Lady. I shall station an attendant outside your door should you require anything."

An attendant or a guard? Did it make much difference? Dropping into a plush, upholstered chair, Andromeda simply nodded. "Very well Jasper. Goodnight."

"Goodnight, My Lady."

With the quiet discretion of one whose life had been spent in service, Jasper departed. Andromeda was left in a twilit room of grey and purple, her eyes turned towards the square of sky she could see outside the window.

Rising from her seat, she went to look at the view. While her chambers did not reach the height of the Empress's tower, she was still high in the upper levels of the palace and far below she could see a large inner courtyard. She recognised it at once from the tapestry in the throne room. The site of the Dragon's attack. With a shiver, Andromeda drew back and pulled the drapes closed.

In the half-dark, she rummaged through her travel pack until she found a tiny glass bottle filled with shimmering dried petals. The remains of the Lovers' Star. Andromeda had collected the crushed petals from amongst the sheets the morning after the night she and Talen had spent together. She hadn't told Talen she'd done it, but she liked to think that she would, one day.

She liked to imagine she would pour the petals onto her palm, just as she was doing now, and let the sweet scent rise into the air. She'd look over to Talen, who would be there of course, and ask her with a smile if she remembered. If she remembered the fire-warmed room in Lezith's cottage in the land that didn't know Spring; if she remembered the night they had spent together.

Carefully funnelling the petals back into their bottle, Andromeda placed the object on the table before her, watching the soft star-like glow with a lonely ache in her heart.

It seemed an ache like that was always there, when she was trapped behind palace walls.

⁓❦⁓

A WEEK PASSED, and Andromeda did not make progress. She was given leave to wander through the palace and its grounds as much as she liked without escort; a seeming generosity that did not make sense until she began to realise many areas of the palace were shrouded in enchantments her magic could not fathom.

She saw little of the Empress, and when their paths did cross, the Empress spoke to her only of trivialities. Neither direct nor indirect questioning drew the Empress on her reasons for summoning Andromeda and keeping her here. She would only express, in the blandest voice, that she wished to extend her hospitality to a fellow ruler.

The vague clue Talen had discovered referring to the mysterious Wildcard of Fate was also proving difficult to probe further. Andromeda spent several days searching the library but even though she found the book Talen told her of, it no longer contained the slip of parchment referring to the spell.

Andromeda's own Book of Magic was still silent on the subject of the Dragon and related matters. She'd hoped being in the Imperial Palace might somehow unlock more information, and wondered if the palace's enchantments were preventing the Book from giving her what she needed to know.

On the eighth day of her confinement, Andromeda found her way to the guard barracks, and asked for Valouria. The decision was spontaneous, driven by boredom and loneliness and the vague hope she might glean some information more useful than the nothing she already had. But she half-wished she hadn't come once she realised the discomfort her presence was causing. As soon as she entered the barracks, she was met with stiff backs, hasty bows and shocked eyes, as well as a chorus of apologies explaining that Valouria was absent. The most senior guard present promised to pass on a message, but was evidently relieved to show Andromeda out a short time later.

In Blackheath, it seemed, the guards and the Empress's guests were not meant to socially mingle. Well, Andromeda could not claim any prizes for egalitarianism there; the rules in her own kingdom had been the same.

She half thought that Valouria would choose not to heed her message, or would arrive wearing a cloak of obedience meant to mark rather than hide her reluctance to comply. It was therefore a pleasant surprise to find Valouria at her door that evening, with no resentment in her eyes and a bottle of wine in hand.

"I heard you were looking for me, My Lady," she said. "Since the hour grows late, I thought perhaps you would like to share a drink?"

"Yes, please, Valouria, come in."

Andromeda stood aside to allow Valouria to enter, continuing, "I'm sorry to inconvenience you like this. I realise it is probably not the done thing to take you away from your duties for my own selfish reasons."

Taking the seat Andromeda offered her, Valouria shook her head. She looked tired. "You are not being selfish, Andromeda. I will be happy to assist you, if I am able."

"In truth, I primarily wanted to have some company for a little while," Andromeda said as Valouria took on the task of pouring out wine for them. "The Empress ignores me and she has no court, no family, no guests for me to speak to, and Jasper checks on me daily but will not discuss anything other than my wardrobe."

Valouria laughed. "That sounds like Jasper."

"He keeps pressing me to wear elaborate dresses."

Noting Andromeda's attire of boots, hose, and tunic, Valouria commented, "Well, if you asked him, I am sure Jasper would be delighted to source you some elaborate coats and breeches instead."

"I don't really want to wear that either."

Sitting back, Valouria gave Andromeda a considered glance. "Talen was the same when she was here. She wore the simplest clothes she could get away with. She said no one would take seriously a warrior who dressed as a noble. A fair point."

"I am not a warrior," said Andromeda. "I am just...uninterested in being impeded by fashion."

Valouria's look said she was fully aware of Andromeda's explorations of the palace, which would not go as smoothly in brocade and velvet, but she didn't bring it up.

Taking up her glass of wine, Andromeda admitted, "There is something I have been wondering about."

She noticed Valouria tense slightly. "Yes?"

"Why does the Empress not keep court? In my experience, palaces are usually full of all manner of people—nobles, officials, artisans, entertainers, heroes, magicians—I could go on but I can tell you know what I'm talking about. Did the Empress send them all away, or do they not wish to come?"

The tension left Valouria's body. Whatever question she'd been worried about, it wasn't this one. "I think you are really asking a different question, Andromeda," she said shrewdly. "One that I saw you silently pondering as we crossed the snowy wastelands to get here. You wonder how secure the Empress's hold on the throne is. Many die every year as the Winter advances. What cities we have left are crowded and scarce on resources. You wonder whether there is unrest, rebellions; if the Empress sequesters herself away so that she need not answer those who would oppose her."

"Yes," Andromeda admitted, giving Valouria a frank look. "Those wider issues are what I have been wondering about. But I understand there are limitations on what you can say, Valouria, as one who serves the Empress. I do not wish you to compromise yourself."

Valouria waved Andromeda's concerns away while she took a sip of wine. "None of the answers to this mystery require me to compromise myself, as you put it. So I have no objections to answering. Following the Dragon's attack, the Empress tried for two years to re-gain the beast's trust."

Noticing Andromeda's start, Valouria laughed faintly. "Indeed. I didn't think you were aware of that. It was two years before the Empress sent the first Hero to face the Dragon. In the beginning, she hoped to be able to resolve the situation herself. She made many journeys to the Dragon's Mountain, trying to bargain with the beast. She even went so far as to offer her own life in exchange for the prosperity of the kingdom. But the Dragon didn't want her, and it sent her away.

"Only after all those failures did the Empress turn to thoughts of killing the Dragon. She had made a magical weapon—a bow—and gifted it to a great Hero whom she believed could slay the Dragon. You have met Ferris, who was once the lover of that Hero. So you already know events did not unfold as hoped, and the first Hero did not prevail. But more Heroes stepped forward to take her place, each certain they would succeed where others had failed. There were many for the first few years. After that..." Valouria shrugged her shoulders, an ironic twist to her lips. "Not so much."

She sighed, and gave Andromeda another glance. "At one point, there was a rebellion. But most likely not the kind you're thinking of. It was a faction of nobles who rebelled against the Empress. They were angered as the Empress had sent out a decree requiring all members of the nobility to give up some of their land. We needed desperately to grow more crops and find space for the displaced who had lost their homes.

"These particular nobles were not happy about it. They attempted a coup to usurp the Empress's power, and they were very nearly successful. They took the Empress prisoner here in her own palace, and told her they were going to strip her of her throne. If she resisted, they threatened to kill her.

"What happened?"

In an awed whisper, her eyes large and intense, Valouria said, "The Empress burned them all alive."

Andromeda drew in a shocked breath. This was not the response she'd expected. "How? Who set the Empress free?"

Valouria rose from her seat and went to the window of Andromeda's chamber, looking down on the courtyard below. "The Empress set herself free, My Lady. The traitors took her to that courtyard down there, in view of the whole palace, and gave her the choice to surrender her throne willingly, or be executed on the spot."

After pouring out more wine, Andromeda moved to stand beside Valouria at the window. "And then?"

"The Empress unleashed the Dragon's fire."

Andromeda nearly choked on her wine. "I'm sorry, what? Dragon's fire? What is that?"

"Curious the Empress has not told you already," Valouria said. "The ruling Emperor or Empress of Blackheath is given great power by the Dragon, including the power to wield fire. Being in possession of the Dragon's gifts signifies the right to rule, and the Empress proved that day that she still had the Dragon's blessing when she unleashed the fire. She destroyed those who sought to harm her and destabilise the kingdom. There have been no further challenges since."

"And the Empress keeps the palace empty to minimise the risks."

Valouria nodded. "The Empress trusts very few these days. She spends much of her time in solitude. Too much, perhaps. I know she often dwells on the events of that day." Andromeda did not have to ask which day Valouria meant. The day of the Dragon's attack. Returning to her seat, Valouria continued, "I can tell you do not like the Empress, Andromeda. And I will be the first to confess—I have not travelled to other worlds as you have, I do not know what lies beyond the border of this land. But for ten years, I have watched my Empress do everything in her power to keep what is left of Blackheath together. She will do what she must to save as many as possible, irrespective of rank or wealth. The people know this. They still believe she will deliver us from all this."

Pacing back and forth, Andromeda responded, "Of course I don't like the Empress, Valouria. She used you to bring me here against my will, and she doesn't tell me why. She put a curse on Talen that nearly killed her."

"The Dragon nearly killed Talen," Valouria countered. "And the Empress did not curse her. Talen chose to take the Empress's mark."

Andromeda made a sceptical noise. "Every time I touch that mark, I can feel the threat of death hovering over Talen, coming closer. It's a curse if ever I felt one."

"The Empress would not have sent Talen to face the Dragon unless she truly believed she could win. She told you the truth at the Manor. I have seen her turn down many would-be Heroes. Talen was the first in a long time to be accepted."

Ceasing her pacing, Andromeda threw herself back into her chair, giving Valouria a half-apologetic look. She knew Valouria believed in the Empress, and if the things she said were true, the Empress sounded like a ruler who deserved to be believed in. But Andromeda knew her own opinions were not going to change.

"If the Empress still has the Dragon's blessing, why does it forsake the kingdom?"

"Well, that is the question, isn't it?" said Valouria, with a humourless smile. "The question none of us can answer. But I will tell you one last thing about the Empress. The significance will probably not make sense to you, but I'll try to explain it. You remember the stained-glass windows you saw as we approached the palace?"

"Of course."

"They were not always as they are now. For many centuries, the windows that decorated the palace depicted the Dragon, celebrating its sacred role as the protector of the kingdom. After the attack, the Empress shattered both of them.

"The new designs symbolise the Empress herself taking over the role which the Dragon previously held. The tree with its spreading roots and branches is a promise the Empress will return Spring to the land. The larger window shows the elements of life—earth, water, wind and fire. Fire is largest of all, to represent both the Empress claiming the power of fire from the Dragon, and bringing warmth to the people of Blackheath."

"That sounds like arrogance to me," Andromeda admitted with a grimace.

"I knew you would say that," said Valouria, sounding amused. "It is actually the opposite. It is a promise so enormous that only the most humble and selfless would dare to make it. The Empress knows she will carry a great burden once the Dragon is gone. The stained-glass windows are her word she will not fail us, that she will give everything so this kingdom might have a future."

By this time, the bottle of wine was empty. Andromeda swirled the dregs in her glass, still not convinced by Valouria's faith. She said quietly, "If you are without doubt, Valouria, why did you have that strange expression when you left the Empress's chamber, the day you brought me here? You were not sure then."

This was the question Valouria hadn't wanted Andromeda to ask; the momentary tension that returned to her shoulders made that clear.

Looking into her wine glass, Valouria said, "I should refuse to answer that. I should tell you that you're wrong." She looked up at

Andromeda, eyes shadowed. "Normally, I am without doubt, and I didn't like feeling otherwise that day. It wasn't anything the Empress said, it was just an expression I thought I saw in her eyes."

"What expression?"

"It seemed as if she looked into the future, and saw no pride in an action she knew she was going to take." Valouria shook herself. "I probably imagined it." She rose and bowed. "I must be getting back. I hope I have been of help, My Lady. Good night."

With a hasty assurance Valouria had indeed given her much to think about, Andromeda saw her out.

♦

LATER, as Andromeda prepared for bed, she wondered whether getting that admission out of Valouria was going to damage what goodwill existed between them. She hoped not. But she couldn't afford to worry about upset feelings; not when Talen's life was at stake.

Andromeda fell asleep missing Talen's touch, her desires sharpened by the heady wine, her mind uneasy at Valouria's foreboding. It was too much like her old life, when all her nights were spent frustrated in a lonely bed with a terrible future hanging over her. This sojourn in the Empress's palace could not end soon enough.

Chapter 15

The days kept up their inexorable march towards Talen's confrontation with the Dragon, and Andromeda continued to fail at her task. Frustration was beginning to give way to fear as day after day, hour after hour, she scoured the Empress's palace searching fruitlessly for some crack, some weakness in the enchantments she could feel.

She would stop and whisper spells of revealment whenever she felt a prickle of magic nearby, reaching out to touch the seemingly solid black stone of whatever wall or hallway she found herself in, feeling lies in the reality before her but never able to tear it down.

Andromeda could not even be certain the enchantments concealed that which she wished to know, but she considered it very likely. She was occasionally aware of the Empress's shadow watching her, and she remembered the hunger in the Empress's eyes as she had asked Andromeda about her magic, about how she had healed Talen of the Dragon's fire.

The Empress probably intended to persuade Andromeda into using her powers against the Dragon, but why was she waiting? What was gained by letting Andromeda wander the palace at will? A test to see what she could uncover on her own?

Andromeda was tired of it. She was not even fully paying attention as she walked through a corridor that had drawn her attention on previous wanderings, doing a last circuit before heading back to her chambers after half a night spent loose in the palace.

This particular corridor was in an old and tumbledown wing of the palace which was seemingly disused. The walls were built of pitted grey stone, revealing, perhaps, the ancient bones that underlaid the polished mirror-like black surfaces elsewhere in the palace.

What Andromeda noticed, from the corner of her eye, whilst not fully paying attention, was a slight shimmer in the wall. She stopped immediately and turned her head to look properly. The shimmering continued.

Later, Andromeda theorised that the many hours she'd spent honing her skills of perception finally paid off in that moment. The ability to see and feel effortlessly that which was hidden to others became part of her, and it was far from being the last time she would use the skill.

Placing her hand against the shimmering wall, Andromeda pushed. The enchantment resisted. She pushed harder, and began to whisper every spell of disillusionment she had learned from the Book of Magic. The Book had explained at length that these spells would not work the same for every Witch. Magic came from within, and its manifestations had as many variations as the individuals who held the power. Andromeda would have to be prepared to find her own methods to infuse the spells, to trust her own instincts on what felt right.

And so that was what Andromeda proceeded to do. Dismantling the protective barrier was gruelling work. The enchantments felt as ancient and immovable as a mountain. But little by little she felt the bindings give, and every time it happened, she pushed harder, pouring her own magic into the cracks and increasing the power of her spells until finally the barrier shattered.

Where the wall had been, there was now a stone archway and a worn set of spiralling stairs leading up into darkness.

Andromeda let her hand drop. She was shaking and dripping with perspiration, dizzy and slightly sick, but none of it compared to the heady euphoria of her achievement. She had broken the spell of concealment.

The feel of magic was thick around her, pouring out of the breach in the wall and growing even stronger as she stepped onto the stair. Despite the dangers that might be before her, Andromeda didn't dare wait too long to recover. For all she knew, the enchantments might soon start to repair themselves. Speaking under her breath, she created a small globe of illuminated energy to hover before her and light her way, and began to ascend the stairs.

It soon became apparent that Andromeda was climbing up the inside of a tower. There were narrow defensive slits in the outward wall of the stone every now and then, but they were too high up for Andromeda to see out of and mark her position. All she knew in a general sense was that she was somewhere in the back part of the palace, the part that didn't look towards the City below. And that evidently, this structure had once been part of a fortress, bare and bleak, without decoration or comfort. It belonged to some older, forgotten time in Blackheath's past.

After an interminable climb, Andromeda emerged onto a small landing. Before her was a studded wooden door, that half swung open with a creak as she raised her hand to knock. She looked cautiously around the door's edge, catching sight of a cluttered room brightened by the open flames of a burning fireplace. Set near the fireplace was a desk at which a young woman sat, writing in a large tome with a feathered quill.

Andromeda drew back hurriedly as the young woman began to look up, and readied an offensive spell in her hand as she heard a chair scrape back and footsteps beginning to approach.

A few moments later the young woman opened the door the rest of the way, and stood looking at Andromeda with a friendly expression. She did not appear surprised. "Welcome, Andromeda," she said in a clear, pleasant voice. "I was told by the Empress you might find me. Please, come in. You have nothing to fear."

Without waiting to see if Andromeda followed, the young woman turned away and walked back to the fireplace, not seeming in the least worried by the offensive spell Andromeda still had primed to hurl.

That meant she either already knew Andromeda wouldn't attack unprovoked, or her own powers were such that she didn't see Andromeda as a threat. Whichever it was, the spell probably wasn't going to help much, so Andromeda let it fizzle out and followed the woman into the room.

Shelves lined a good portion of the room's stone walls, cluttered with scrolls, books, jars, dried plants, and all manner of arcane objects. Andromeda let her eyes wander curiously over the assortment, and when she looked back to the fireplace she blinked in confusion.

The desk which had been beside the fireplace before was over near the far wall now. Its place had been taken by two deep plush chairs and a small round table upon which sat a teapot and two waiting mugs.

"Sit down, Andromeda," the young woman invited her, taking her own ease in one of the comfortable looking chairs.

"Excuse me, but did the furniture just shift around?" Andromeda asked, sitting down gingerly on the edge of the empty chair, half-wondering if it was going to start moving with her in it.

"Did it?" The young woman looked around vaguely. "I suppose it might have. Things in this room have a way of being accommodating."

She began to pour out the tea, and her mannerisms were so familiar that Andromeda suddenly understood who this woman was. Lezith poured out tea in exactly the same way.

"You're Sorrel, aren't you? Lezith's granddaughter?"

Sorrel smiled at her, but there was a troubled edge beneath the friendliness. "Indeed I am. My grandmother mentioned she had met you in a letter she sent."

Sorrel's stature was delicate and slight, her loose, tumbling hair a rich red-brown colour from which she had perhaps gotten her name. With the greater light from the fire, Andromeda could see she had Lezith's eyes too, though where Lezith's were sharp, Sorrel's were shadowed and mysterious.

As Sorrel handed her a mug of tea, Andromeda picked up on the earlier comment she'd made at the door. "You said that the Empress told you I might come here?"

"Yes. More precisely, she said that because of the strength of your magic, you might be able to find this place despite all the spells of concealment. She said I was to neither help you nor hinder you in whatever actions you took, but she gave me leave to invite you in if you made it to my door."

"So it was a test. I've been wondering about that since I've been here."

"The Empress was very interested in seeing whether you would be able to find your way through the enchantments that keep myself and the other Sages hidden."

"There are more of you?"

"In other parts of the palace, yes. You might have found your way to any one of them, but...I had a feeling you would make your way here."

That was a curious statement Andromeda would have liked to unpack further, however, she decided it was more important to keep her focus on the Empress.

"What was the purpose of this test the Empress set?"

Sorrel's gaze was not quite easy. "I think you already know, Andromeda."

"The Empress thinks my powers can be used against the Dragon. Is that true? Breaking an enchantment in the palace means my magic will work against the Dragon?"

"All magic in the palace can be traced back to the Dragon. If you can break an enchantment here, then yes, potentially, your magic can be used against the Dragon as well."

"Why does the Empress not just ask for my help?"

"She claims she did. At the Manor."

Andromeda gave a humourless laugh. "At the Manor, the Empress attempted to manipulate me into taking her mark by using Talen's life as leverage." She paused and examined Sorrel's face, looking for signs she was angered by Andromeda's less than charitable report of her mistress. But Sorrel remained calm, nodding slightly towards Andromeda as if hoping she would continue.

Taking a breath, Andromeda went on. "The Empress's behaviour— her secrecy, her use of threats and curses—does not make me trust her. I wish she would be honest with me. Otherwise, how can I assess whether killing the Dragon is just?"

"There are some who might say killing is never just," said Sorrel. "There are also some who might hide from the fact that killing is, sometimes, unavoidable if certain conflicts are to be resolved."

"Sorrel, if you are asking me which of those categories I fall into...I undertook a journey of six months through many worlds before I reached Blackheath. Not all of them were benign. I have already used my magic to kill when I had to, when I was threatened and there was no other way."

Though Sorrel's reactions were subtle, Andromeda could tell she was surprised. As well she might be; Andromeda hadn't even yet told Talen she'd had to kill to make it this far. It wasn't something she wanted to think about very much. She only told Sorrel now because she got the sense Sorrel was trying to get the measure of her, work out the limits of her powers. That might be at the Empress's behest, or it might be for some reason of her own, but either way, it was best she know Andromeda was not limited to healing and defence.

At the same time, Andromeda didn't want Sorrel questioning her too much, especially if anything she said was going to be reported to the Empress. To distract her, she asked, "Have the Sages always been hidden as you are now? It must be a lonely life." This was something she'd been curious about since coming to the palace. Was the Empress trying to limit the Sages' influence? Stop her people from learning what they foresaw? How strictly were they watched?

Sorrel answered readily enough. "The Sages have always been elusive. Most of us tend towards a reticent nature. You are right, however. In the days before the Dragon's attack, the Sages were part of the court. We didn't live hidden away in enchanted towers. The reasons for the current situation are complicated, but it is partly for our own protection. All the people of Blackheath wish to know the future of our unhappy land, and they look to the Sages for guidance. They do not always react well when we cannot answer."

"And why is it you cannot provide them with the answers they seek?"

"Because we do not know, Andromeda. None of us can read in the stars whether Blackheath will survive."

"Couldn't that mean the future is not yet settled?"

"No," said Sorrel, shaking her head. "Blackheath is a world ruled by fate. We just cannot always see clearly what is to come."

"Then what has the Empress seen of Talen's future? And what about the other Heroes? Did she know all of them would die?"

Sorrel gave Andromeda a look that was part compassion, part pity. "I think there is something I should show you." She rose from her chair. "Will you follow me, Andromeda? You will not like what you see, but I think it important you know."

With a flutter of trepidation in her stomach, Andromeda nodded. She followed Sorrel to a pair of latticework doors that definitely hadn't been there before. Sorrel pushed the doors open and led Andromeda out onto a wide, generous balcony.

The night sky above them was filled with stars, and far below in the faint light Andromeda saw snow-covered plains and the dark smudge of trees on the horizon.

"The frozen lands," said Sorrel, following Andromeda's gaze. "The Imperial City is the Easternmost outpost that is still habitable. Everything between here and the sea beyond that forest has been swallowed by the Winter. But that is not what I brought you out here to see. Look up."

"Yes, I know," said Andromeda. "The stars." Stars unnamed and unknown to her, whirling towards an end she could not see.

"The stars rule our fate in Blackheath." Sorrel sounded almost dreamy as she too tilted her head back to take in the sky. "Everything is written up there, for those with the skill to read it. But few are born with that talent, and even those who have it cannot hope to grasp the full complexity of the stars, nor have full knowledge of our future. All we can see are glimmers in the dark. I have spent a lifetime in study of the stars, and there are still many things which are hidden from me. And sometimes...there are things which do not become clear until it is too late."

Sorrel ended in a darker tone, perhaps alluding to whatever she had brought Andromeda out here to see.

"Do you mean something to do with Talen's future?"

Meeting Andromeda's eyes gravely, Sorrel nodded. "When Talen first came to the Imperial City and declared her desire to take on the mantle of Hero, the Empress asked myself and several others to consult the stars. We have done this for every potential Hero, ever since the first. If the stars show an unfavourable outcome, or even if they are clouded, the Empress will not give the potential Hero her mark.

"But as far as I could see—as far as anyone could see—the stars pointed towards Talen being victorious. I had never seen such a favourable reading for a Hero before. Sages older than I said the fortune of Talen's stars even exceeded those of Stasia."

"Stasia died," Andromeda pointed out acerbically. "Exceeding the fortune of her stars would not be difficult."

"The misfortune in Stasia's fate was not revealed until much later," said Sorrel. "At first, it seemed as if she was not going to lose. So it was with Talen too. Once Talen took the Empress's mark, the stars revealed where her journey would truly end. I myself have consulted the night skies many times over regarding this matter, and I have never been able to find another result. Talen's death is written in the stars. Her fate cannot be changed. She cannot be saved."

Ever since stepping onto the balcony, Andromeda had been half-expecting to hear something like this. She wanted to argue, to tell Sorrel about her own world, the fate she had escaped and left behind. It was possible. It had to be possible.

But this was not Andromeda's world. Fairy Godmothers did not exist in Blackheath, yet they did in Andromeda's kingdom. The rules were clearly not always the same from one world to the next. Besides, the way Sorrel spoke touched a cold finger of fear to Andromeda's spine that made her objections die before she could voice them. There was a terrible pain and hopelessness in Sorrel's voice, as if she had already witnessed Talen's death and was simply recounting it.

"Didn't I already save Talen from the Dragon?" Andromeda finally asked, more out of stubbornness than any other impulse. "Talen was dying and I healed her. If that is what you saw, I have already averted it."

"You have delayed Talen's fate. That is all. The next time she faces the Dragon, it will kill her. And even if you somehow stopped that as well, the cycle would go on. Talen cannot opt out from her pact with the Empress. She will keep climbing the mountain and facing the Dragon. No matter how many times you save her, eventually it won't be enough. Talen's fate will claim her life."

Andromeda tipped her head up again to look at the strange constellations above her. So many stars spilling across the dark, freezing sky. They were beautiful, but she hated them. She hated this world that had trapped Talen in its tortured death throes.

"How do I know you speak the truth Sorrel?"

The finger of fear was now more like an icy fist gripping Andromeda's spine. Andromeda had come so far, and fought so hard to throw off the shackles her own world had cast upon her. So too had Talen when she refused to be her people's sacrifice; when she killed the Witch who would have eaten her. But now here they both were with the chains of another world closing in around them. Andromeda could not face losing Talen. She couldn't. Talen was the one who had formed her reality, who had made everything possible.

Sorrel was in the Empress's service. It was possible the Empress had instructed her to say all this. It was almost what Andromeda hoped, though looking at Sorrel, she couldn't see any sign she was lying.

There was a large crystal ball resting on a stone pedestal in the middle of the balcony, which, until now, Sorrel hadn't commented on. She gestured towards it, and said, "The crystal allows the sharing of visions, so that others might see what the Sages do. So that we cannot deceive those we serve. If you touch it, you will see Talen's death."

Andromeda crossed the balcony until she was beside the pedestal. Sorrel stood on the opposite side with a warning in her eyes. "What you see will be disturbing. Are you sure you wish to proceed?"

"Yes, I'm sure," said Andromeda, and placed her hand upon the crystal.

Chapter 16

Andromeda saw the peak of the Dragon's Mountain, distant at first. Then, it felt as if she was flying towards the mountain at great speed, while overhead the stars wheeled, and the sun rose and fell, until there was a night when the full moon shone in the sky.

She saw Talen waiting for a message that never came. Something was going to happen to stop Andromeda from sending it, though the circumstances surrounding that remained murky. The vision spiralled its way up to the mountain peak the next day, keeping pace with Talen as she climbed. And then came the confrontation with the Dragon. Talen and the Dragon were poised, staring one another down, Talen's bow pointed towards the Dragon's one good eye.

Andromeda knew what was going to happen. Perhaps Talen did too, but she had no choice. She could not turn away from the vow she'd sworn to fulfil. She released her bow, and as her arrow flew towards the Dragon, the Dragon released a plume of flame.

The arrow struck true. And so did the Dragon's fire.

Talen screamed and burned; the armour Andromeda had enchanted barely slowing down the flames. She died an agonising death, alone on the mountain, while blood dripped from the Dragon's newly ruined eye. The Dragon had lost her sight, but not her life. She let out a roar, and the sound was nearly as bad as Talen's dying screams. Full of anguish, it was the cry of a tormented being trapped in unending hopelessness.

Unable to stand it any longer, Andromeda released her hand from the crystal. Tears were streaming down her face, and she saw the pity in Sorrel's expression again. The vision itself had been disturbing enough, but that wasn't the worst part. It was the inevitability that was so terrible. The events Andromeda had witnessed now loomed in her consciousness like an oncoming storm, something she could feel in her very bones. Something that couldn't be outrun any more than the wind or the rain.

"So you don't lie." Andromeda wrapped one arm around herself tightly and used the other hand to wipe away her tears. Her cheeks were burning though the cold night air clawed at her skin. "Does that mean the Empress told you to show me this? Does she think it will make me do what she wants?"

"I was not instructed to show you the future," Sorrel replied, "but it wasn't necessary. The Empress knew I would. Perhaps Her Imperial Majesty knows of some way I do not to avert Talen's fate, and as you say, hopes to leverage that to win your support."

The manipulation left a foul taste in Andromeda's mouth. What else was she to do, though? She could spin that tale again about her honour, but the Empress was smart enough to know Andromeda wouldn't leave Talen to die, even if she thought it would result in the loss of her magic.

"If that's all you have for me, Sorrel," Andromeda said quietly. "I will take my leave. Since I have passed the Empress's test, I think it is time for me to find out what she wants."

Sorrel hesitated, then said in a hushed voice, "Let's go back inside."

Once inside, they resettled by the fire. Sorrel poured Andromeda a drink; not tea but warm, spiced wine. Andromeda drank it quickly. Her mouth still tasted of death and ashes.

Looking into the fire, Sorrel sipped on her own wine. When her gaze met Andromeda's once more, every line of her body was fraught with tension. She drew in a breath as if to speak, but couldn't seem to bring herself to do so.

"My grandmother..." Trailing off, Sorrel bit her lip. Andromeda realised she was only just stopping herself from trembling. Her eyes had turned into dark pools of terror. She stared at Andromeda silently, as if in entreaty, and without knowing why she asked, Andromeda said,

"Tell me what you know of the Wildcard of Fate."

Sorrel drew in a sharp breath, her fingers digging into the arm of her chair. "My grandmother said you would ask me about the Wildcard of Fate. How do you even know of it?"

"Talen found mention of it in a book in the palace library. I looked through the same book, but it didn't contain the spell."

"No book in the library speaks of the Wildcard of Fate."

"Talen said there was a scrap of parchment hidden in the book that told of it. But even though I looked through all the book's pages, the parchment was gone."

There was a short silence as Sorrel considered this. A fleeting expression passed across her face that gave Andromeda the impression she had her suspicions as to how that parchment might have gotten into the book, but she didn't share her thoughts.

She appeared to have some internal debate with herself, then finally gave Andromeda a direct look that reminded her of Lezith. "The Wildcard of Fate is an ancient ritual, almost forgotten. Even most of the Sages don't know of it. The Empress most likely wishes it truly were forgotten. Once the Wildcard of Fate is invoked, all futures are thrown into chaos. Everything and anything is simultaneously potentially possible and potentially impossible.

"My grandmother told me you care nothing for fate. You took your fate and you ground it under your heel. You snatched Talen away from her appointed time of death. No wonder the Empress wants you. No wonder she thinks you can save us. You are probably the only one brave enough—"

"You think the Empress wishes me to invoke the Wildcard of Fate?"

"No," said Sorrel. "I'm sure she doesn't. She would never risk it. But whatever plan she has, it will be because you are different. Because you are not bound to this world."

Andromeda tried to choose her words carefully. She could tell that Sorrel was still half-horrified at herself for even speaking of the Wildcard of Fate, and she didn't want to scare her into silence. "Could the Wildcard of Fate potentially be used to set Talen free from her destiny? Is there a way to control it?"

Sorrel shook her head. "The ritual is meant to throw everything into flux. It cannot be directed or controlled. There is no guarantee of what would happen to any of us, or to Blackheath. But...Talen's future would be open. Her fate would no longer be certain. That doesn't necessarily mean you'd be able to save her, though."

"Where does this ritual come from?"

"Unfortunately, very little is known about the Wildcard of Fate." Sorrel's body began to lose some of its rigidity, though she moved her hands restlessly, and then clenched them tightly in her lap. "The few stories and records we have all connect it in some way to the first Emperor of Blackheath; it is thought he created the ritual as some sort of failsafe. But against what...no one exactly knows. Perhaps it was meant for a situation like this. Perhaps he foresaw that one day the pact between the Dragon and the Imperial Family would break. I learned of the ritual from my grandmother. I do not know how she learned of it; she has never told me."

"If Lezith knows about the ritual, why not invoke it herself?"

"She does not have the necessary magical power. Nor do I. Nor does anyone in the kingdom, except the Empress, and perhaps..."

"Perhaps me," Andromeda finished for her. She looked down at her hands. "I was going to say...if all that was needed was a willingness to defy fate, Talen could have done the spell herself. She is the one who taught me to be brave."

"Andromeda, if you invoke the Wildcard of Fate, you may free Talen to change things for herself. But she cannot invoke it. She is no wielder of magic."

"So that is what you are asking me to do. To invoke the Wildcard of Fate, in the hopes of changing Blackheath's future. With the added motivation that it is the only way Talen's life might be saved."

Sorrel got up and paced restlessly. "I hated this plan when my grandmother first told it to me in her letter. If all fates disappear, I will lose the stars. That thought is terrifying to me. I'd feel like I was struck blind. Nothing would have meaning anymore. I could never knowingly invoke that. Not even to save the world. I doubt anyone in Blackheath could.

"But the more I thought about it, the more I understood my grandmother's urgency. We have struggled with the Dragon for ten years, and have little time left before the Winter swallows us all. Every Sage has studied the stars, the histories, the magics, and found no answer. Every Hero who might step forward has already done so, and died. The Empress will have her plan for you, Andromeda, but if you do not like it, you will not help her. On that point my grandmother was certain."

"If I invoke the Wildcard of Fate, Blackheath could end up in ruins. Have you considered that?"

"Of course I have," said Sorrel, her expression bleak. "But I fear my grandmother is right. We cannot wait any longer for the Empress to save us. We cannot wait for the stars to clear. We must no longer trust in fate, but in something else. A future beyond what fate can deliver. You, Andromeda, who have already fought that battle...perhaps you can fight it again, for all of us."

Sitting down again, Sorrel withdrew a small scrap of fabric from her sleeve. There was an incandescent gleam all around the border, as if something shimmering had been sewn into the fabric. She placed the object on the table between them. "You may recognise this."

After a moment of trying to work out what the scrap was, Andromeda nodded. "That looks like the handkerchief Lezith was making. She entrusted Valouria to give it to you."

"Correct," said Sorrel, an approving flicker in her eye. "The tiny shimmering fragments sewn into the border are Dragon scales. Collected from the Dragon's Mountain many years before the current catastrophe. The Wildcard of Fate requires a physical offering from our guardian."

"Why did Lezith not give this to me in Drakk? Why didn't she tell me about the Wildcard then?"

"She felt that if you were the one meant to invoke the Wildcard of Fate, you would come to learn of it yourself. Besides, though she predicted you would end up here at the palace, she wasn't certain. But she told me if you did come, and if you asked about the Wildcard, she was depending on me to help her. Until I met you, I thought she'd gone mad. However, I think I understand what she meant now, when she wrote you have a light in your eyes that none of us have known for a long time. Not even Talen had it, when she came to this palace. The light of hope."

Folding her hands once more in her lap, Sorrel grew sober. She was very calm now, almost unnaturally so. "You will need one other ingredient as well; not easily obtained. A drop of blood from the Empress. Bring that together with the Dragon scales as you invoke the ritual, and the Wildcard of Fate will be unleashed.

"I can give you no guarantees of what will happen then, Andromeda. You might be able to save Talen. You might be able to save all of Blackheath. But there are many other possibilities too. The loss of Talen's life. The loss of your own life. The destruction of Blackheath. Other consequences neither of us can imagine. Do you understand?"

"I understand," said Andromeda. She reached out her hand and hovered her fingertips over the handkerchief briefly before making her decision and picking it up. Though weightless, she knew it represented an unimaginably heavy burden. The future of an entire world now rested on her shoulders.

She let out a breath and met Sorrel's eyes with a steady gaze. "How do I invoke the Wildcard of Fate?"

Sorrel gave her an approving look. She seemed to appreciate that Andromeda was neither arrogant nor excessively fearful in her manner. Sliding a scrap of parchment across the table, she said, "This is the incantation you must speak, once you bring together the Dragon's scales and the Empress's blood. Commit it to memory now. Dangerous enough that you will have the Dragon scales with you; I cannot allow further risks. This parchment must be burned before you leave."

The incantation wasn't long, and Andromeda did not have difficulty memorising it. She'd grown used to remembering spells from her time spent studying the Book of Magic. Once she was done, she rose from her seat and threw the parchment into the fire.

Turning back to Sorrel, she said, "I would give you my thanks, but I know such words can only be inadequate. Please know, I will do all I can to justify your faith in me. If there is a way through this, I will find it. If defying fate is what it will take, I am not afraid."

"I know," said Sorrel, with a faint smile. She got up, and walked Andromeda over to the tower door.

"I won't tell the Empress about any of this," Andromeda promised, somewhat unnecessarily, as she prepared to leave.

Sorrel responded with a shake of her head, and a resigned expression. "The Empress will find out anyway, sooner or later. When she does, I will most likely be put to death for treason. But that is right, perhaps. I am betraying the Empress's trust by helping you, and for that I deserve punishment. As long as Blackheath is saved, it is a sacrifice I am willing to make."

Andromeda was horrified. "Why did you not mention this before?"

"Because I did not wish that to influence your decision." Placing her hand on Andromeda's shoulder, Sorrel smiled, warmly this time.

"Truly, my grandmother and I know the risks of this plan. We are both in agreement it is our best chance. Go, Andromeda, with my blessings and the very best of luck. I imagine the Empress will be calling for you soon. Once you know what she intends, you can make your choice. Farewell."

All Andromeda could do was nod, and echo Sorrel's valediction. She exited the tower, and the door closed behind her. Then she began to descend the long, winding stair back to the hall below.

❦

As THE SUN rose after that night, Andromeda stood at her chamber window looking down upon the scorched cobblestones of the courtyard. The stones had turned pink in the reflection of the flushed dawn sky, as if stained with the memory of blood. She hoped it did not bode ill for the future.

She'd already bathed, and gotten dressed in the maroon robes she'd worn the first time she met the Empress. Andromeda didn't have many outfits to choose from without resorting to Jasper's wardrobe.

The handkerchief was safely stowed away in a pocket at her hip.

Just three nights hence, the full moon would rise. Andromeda had not much time left, and she was done waiting. She was going to see the Empress.

Her breakfast tray was arriving as she left her chambers, but she waved the servant away distractedly. She was in no mood to eat. The servant asked her where she was going, and warned Andromeda the Empress was not likely to be ready to receive her given the early hour.

This Andromeda dismissed. The Empress would be ready. She'd been waiting ten years for someone who could subdue the Dragon.

And indeed, when Andromeda reached the throne room in the tower, the Empress was already there. She was dressed in black and gold and utterly alone, without even Jasper at her side. She did not seem surprised by Andromeda's visit.

"I will not waste time," Andromeda said, after a brief exchange of greetings and pleasantries. "You know I have seen Sorrel. You know my powers are strong enough for whatever you have in mind. I came here to offer my help, on the condition that you tell me what is really going on. If I am satisfied that what you ask does not go against my honour, I will gladly do what I can to save your kingdom."

There was that pleased, hungry glint in the Empress's eye that Andromeda was becoming wearily familiar with. "Of course, Andromeda."

The Empress rose from her throne, her movements fluid and stately, and descended the dais. She crossed the room to the tapestry showing the Dragon's destruction and pushed it aside. She whispered something under her breath, and Andromeda heard rocks grating.

"You did well to find your way to my Seer, Andromeda. There is not a Sage in Blackheath who could accomplish as much. However, know that the secrets I am about to reveal to you are sacred mysteries known only to those of the Imperial bloodline. They are protected by enchantments that not even you would be able to break on your own. Now come, and I will show you everything you wish to know."

A wave of magic emanated out of the dark doorway the Empress had revealed. She threw Andromeda a look of challenge and then stepped into the void, leaving Andromeda to decide whether she would follow.

Andromeda was aware the Empress's speech had been intended to show she had not lost control of the situation. All she said was most likely true; given that it had taken Andromeda the better part of two weeks to find Sorrel's tower, she doubted she'd have been able to break through magic even stronger.

Well, that was fine. Let the Empress think she held all the cards. She didn't know about the Wildcard of Fate. Andromeda could feel the scrap of fabric in her pocket, pulsing and resonating in response to the magic swirling around the tower. It was her insurance against being forced into a course of action she didn't want. Her last resort of defiance.

After stepping through the door, Andromeda heard the rock grate closed behind her. She was now in complete darkness, standing uncomfortably close to the Empress and unwilling to move in case she lost her footing. She'd gotten a glimpse of a steep staircase going down before the door closed.

The Empress drew in a breath, then spoke a strange word Andromeda didn't recognise. Something crackled through the air, and tiny pinpoints of light began to glow around them. Rather disconcertingly, the lights looked like nothing so much as suspended glowing embers, both menacing and beautiful.

With a quick glance towards Andromeda, the Empress said, "Follow me," and began to walk down the stairs.

They went down for a long, long way. By the time the stairs finally ended, Andromeda thought they'd gone deep enough that they must be underneath the palace itself.

The Empress moved confidently through the rough-hewn passage the stairs opened onto, ignoring numerous branches on either side. Soon, the floor began to slope downwards again, and then came yet another staircase to descend. Old magic lingered here, growing stronger the deeper they went into the earth. Andromeda reached out to touch the nearest wall and felt an odd thrill, like a faint electrical current. There was something else, too, a sense of emotion too faint and fleeting to understand.

At last, she began to see light up ahead, brighter than the floating embers still accompanying them. As they drew closer to the light, Andromeda caught glimpses of what looked like a large cavern, containing an enormous skeleton.

"What is that?" she asked in a hushed voice.

"You'll see," said the Empress, and led the way into the cavern.

Andromeda didn't have words to describe the sight that met her eyes. The cavern was bigger by far than the grandest room in her old palace, and that room could hold over a thousand people. Most of the space was taken up by the great skeleton, and even though Andromeda had never seen one with her own eyes, she knew what the creature had been in life. A Dragon.

The walls and floor of the cavern glittered in the light of the many torches that had already been burning when they entered. Andromeda was eerily reminded of the glimmer of the Dragon's scales on the handkerchief Sorrel had given her, and she soon confirmed she wasn't mistaken. Dragon scales were embedded into the very rocks of the cavern everywhere she looked, though whether the process had happened by natural or artificial means she couldn't be sure. Either way, it made the cavern breathtakingly beautiful.

The Dragon's skeleton rested between two massive dead trees, both of which had branches disappearing up into the dark recesses above them. Andromeda immediately knew what they were as well. Flame Trees. The rare, immortal trees from whose wood the Dragon-killer bow had been made. She knew because she could feel the faintest magic from the trees still lingering in the air, and it was the same as the magic she'd felt when she repaired the bow.

Turning, and standing by the skull of the Dragon, the Empress met Andromeda's eyes. "As you see, Andromeda, the Dragon who now dwells on the mountain is not the only one who has ever lived in this world. Dragon bones lie scattered deep within secret caverns such as this beneath several of Blackheath's cities. Those are the parts of my kingdom which still retain their warmth. As the living Dragon protects Drakk and the Barren Mountains from the Winter, so too do these dead Dragons protect their cities from succumbing to the cold."

"How?" asked Andromeda. There were a million other questions she wanted to ask, but somehow, this was the only word she could formulate.

"These bones share a connection to the living Dragon. Some part of her power flows still through them, and by that means the Winter is kept at bay."

The Empress held up her hand as Andromeda drew in a breath to speak again. "I know you have many more questions, but the fastest way to gain the answers you seek is to place your hand against the skull of the Dragon. Right here."

Momentarily, the Empress placed her own hand against the Dragon's skull, in the middle of its forehead above its two gaping eye sockets. In the place where the Third Eye was supposed to be. The area glowed with a soft light at the Empress's touch.

Despite her desire to at last know the truth, Andromeda hesitated. She still didn't trust the Empress, and had no idea what might happen to her if she touched the Dragon's skull.

Noticing Andromeda's hesitation, the Empress gave a scornful laugh. "You fancy yourself a Witch, do you not, Andromeda? Whether or not you trust *me* is irrelevant. What you should trust is your own judgement. Decide for yourself whether it is safe or not. I will lose nothing if you choose to remain ignorant."

Andromeda took one step forward, then another, and another, until she was standing before the Dragon's skull, which was practically the same as her own height. Oddly, the Empress's taunt had galvanised her confidence. If there was ill intent in the Dragon's bones, she would be able to sense that. She had felt evil before, when she ran from the demon with the face of a man, and on other occasions too during her long journey on the Road.

Her own judgement was worthy of trust, and she could feel no evil in this place. As she had reached for the crystal last night up among the stars, now, deep in the earth, she touched her fingertips to the glowing Third Eye of the Dragon's forehead.

Chapter 17

Immediately, Andromeda was thrust into a confusing whirl of image, memory and emotion. Though this Dragon was dead, it still retained an imprint not only of its own life, but of the life of every Dragon that had ever lived in Blackheath. Including the one Dragon still alive who at this very moment guarded the mountain above Drakk.

Very soon that Dragon was aware of her; Andromeda could feel the Dragon's strange alien mind probing hers. She could feel the Dragon's emotions. Anger. Sadness. Pain. Confusion. The Dragon had been living like this for ten years, a broken and tortured being.

"I want to help you," Andromeda whispered, hoping her intention would come across even if the Dragon could not understand her words. "What happened ten years ago? Why did you destroy the Imperial Family? Why will you not let Spring return?"

In response, there was only another wave of anger, sadness, pain and confusion.

"Why are you the only Dragon left?" Andromeda persisted. "What happened to all the others?"

This time, Andromeda received a series of images. While she didn't fully understand them, she began to gain a sense of how the relationship between Blackheath and the Dragon had come to be. She saw a kingdom dying; not of cold, but of heat. There was a man standing in a sweltering desert with his hand upon the forehead of a Dragon, making a pact that would bind both of them for many generations to come. He dissolved and became one with the Dragon, giving up his physical form to gain the strength of the Dragon, and giving the Dragon the ability to reproduce without another of her own kind. For there would be no other Dragons where she was going.

The Dragon, who now carried the spirit of the man as well as her own, drew a great cloak over the fragment of green land still remaining that had not yet been claimed by the desert. She split that land away, severing it from the desert, and from the other Dragons who thrived in the changing climate with no fears for their survival.

The green land the Dragon split away became Blackheath, and the Dragon became its guardian. But Dragons, though long lived, are not immortal. As the end of her life drew near, that first Dragon laid an egg, and brought forth into the world a new Dragon who would take her place.

At the same time, there was a child born to the Imperial Family who bore the mark of the Dragon—a mark that looked remarkably similar to the curse on Talen's shoulder—and all knew it was the destiny of that child to merge with the new Dragon, in order to create a new guardian of the land.

So the cycle had continued on for many hundreds of years. But in the end, something had gone wrong. What it was, Andromeda could not fully understand. She only knew it had resulted in the current Dragon sending fiery death down upon all members of the Imperial Family except for the Empress. It had resulted in the endless Winter for the last ten years.

The connection between Andromeda and the Dragon began to fade, and soon she was only staring at a skull once more, feeling the smoothness of bone beneath her fingers.

Looking to the Empress, Andromeda said, "I still don't understand. The Dragon showed me another kingdom, a desert, and a man merging with a Dragon long ago. They cut off Blackheath from the desert, and the merging of human and Dragon continued for many centuries. But the Dragon still didn't show me why she killed the rest of the Imperial

Family, why she will not come down from the mountain. All I know is something went wrong."

There was a disquieting expression in the Empress's eyes as she looked back. She still had that terrible haunted loneliness that never seemed to leave her, but it was tempered with something else now. Something even more frightening. A kind of demented hope; the hope of a madwoman who believed the impossible was no longer beyond her reach. And always, always, there was her insatiable hunger as she learned more of what Andromeda could do.

"That other kingdom you saw was once the rest of this world," the Empress said. "It was swallowed up by heat and dust three thousand years ago. A natural, though devastating, progression of change my ancestors could not stop. When there was only a small fragment of the world left that was still green and living, the Emperor who ruled that land made a pact with a Dragon. The Dragon had been unable to find a mate amongst her own kind, and so the Emperor said he would give her the ability to reproduce if she would agree to save what was left of the world. She agreed, and the two of them merged into one being inside the Dragon's body.

"The Dragon closed off Blackheath from the desert, but the link between the two worlds could not be completely severed. That is what the portal is on the Dragon's Mountain. It is the way through to that other world. If the Dragon were to leave the portal open for too long, the desert would return to ruin us. Leave it closed for too long, and we die of cold. Apparently the Dragon has chosen the latter for our end."

"Something happened to sour the pact between the Dragon and the Imperial Family," Andromeda insisted. "That is what caused the Dragon to attack ten years ago. What went wrong?"

The Empress's expression grew bitter. "My selfish older brother would not give up his son. His son was born with the mark of the Dragon. He was destined to merge with the Dragon on the mountain, but my brother wouldn't allow it. He refused, and so the Dragon destroyed them all."

"The Dragon spared you because you were pregnant," Andromeda guessed. "She thought that the destiny would pass to your child, and you would honour the pact. Why didn't you?"

With a pained flash in her eyes, the Empress responded, "My labour was not easy, and at the end of it I had no child to give the Dragon. Nor have I been able to have another since. It is impossible for me to give the Dragon what she wants, but she will not believe me. She seeks to freeze my kingdom until I produce a child for her. She thinks I deceive her, but I do not. I will never bear another child."

Andromeda did not know what to make of the Empress's story. Despite giving her a long, searching look, she could see no indications she was lying. The Empress met her gaze without flinching, without blinking, and the sorrow she carried was certainly real enough. But if the Dragon was connected to the Empress, she must have some reason for thinking the Empress could in some way supply her with a child.

"Why is it that no one else in Blackheath seems to know any of this?" Andromeda decided to ask. She asked that instead of asking why the Empress had told her all this. That look in the Empress's eyes was making her nervous. "No one has spoken of Blackheath as being a land split off from another world. No one has talked about members of the Imperial Family having to merge with new-born Dragons. Your people don't even appear to know there have been multiple Dragons. Surely something of that knowledge should have survived, as myth and legend if not history."

"They don't speak of it because they do not remember," the Empress said. "The survivors of three thousand years ago chose to forget the catastrophe that led to the creation of Blackheath. It was too painful for them to remember the old world and all that was lost. Thus it was written in the annals kept by Blackheath's first Emperor, the son who inherited the kingdom when his father became one with the Dragon. Only the Imperial Family have carried the knowledge of Blackheath's true origin down through the years, and now that I am the last survivor of my line, I alone safeguard the truth. Just as I alone bear the consequences for all those choices made millennia ago."

"What of killing the Dragon? You say that without the Dragon guarding the portal, too much heat will be allowed in, and Blackheath will be taken by the desert that claimed the rest of your former world. So why do you seek to end her life?"

"Ah, yes. That." The Empress spoke in a new tone she had not used until now. "With that question Andromeda, we draw closer to the reason of why you are here. I have discovered a way in which Blackheath can be severed from the remnant of the old world, to become a full-fledged world all its own. But it requires a sacrifice. The blood of the Dragon. However, since you came to my kingdom, I have begun to think there might be another way. You have a powerful aptitude for magic, and you are not bound by the rules of this world. I think you are strong enough to take the Dragon."

"To take the Dragon? What do you mean by that?"

The Empress gave Andromeda a chilling smile. "Let me ask you a question first. Now that you know why the Dragon acted as she did, what do you think will happen to your powers when Talen climbs the mountain for her final battle? Do you think aiding her was the honourable thing?"

If Andromeda invoked the Wildcard of Fate, there would be no need for Talen to face the Dragon. And that was not the sort of honour her Book was concerned with. But Andromeda let the Empress think she'd been rattled; pretended she hadn't recognised what was happening as a tactic meant to distract her while the Empress moved both of them towards some goal Andromeda could not yet see.

"You should have told your people the truth about the Dragon," Andromeda said. "They are fighting blind without knowing all the things you have revealed to me. You should have told Talen as well. I don't know how the promise you bound her to can still hold when you deceived her."

"I told Talen no lies," said the Empress coldly.

"Nor did you tell her the full truth."

"I told her enough. She would not still be bound to her fate if I had deceived her as you claim."

Talen's fate. Bound to a painful death which Andromeda had seen with horrifying clarity. How could the Empress speak so callously when she too knew what waited in Talen's future?

"You know," said the Empress softly, "that Book you cling to is a curse, Andromeda. Why should you depend on it for instruction? For arbitrary parameters and conditions? Sooner or later, it will abandon you. It will leave you powerless."

The Empress walked a few paces back and forth before the great skull and then stopped, turning to Andromeda as if struck by a thought. "Would that not be a great shame? To lose all your powers when you barely have the measure of them. How will you ever know what you might have been able to become? Have you not considered a failsafe, in the event your magic in its current form cannot be sustained?"

"I don't need to," said Andromeda. "I have no intention of dishonouring myself."

"How noble." The Empress's voice was faintly scathing. She focused on Andromeda, her eyes stained with darkness. "You will lose your honour, you know. Sooner or later. We all do, no matter how pure we start out. The Book will leave you."

"No, it won't. I will not lose my honour."

The Empress studied Andromeda, probing her. Andromeda stared back defiantly, only to be disturbed when the Empress smiled.

"I thought so," the Empress murmured. "That tale you spun me was a lie. You're not worried about your actions at all. But there is something. Some catch to the Book's magic."

Dismayed, Andromeda did her best to school her features into a bland mask. She should have guessed the Empress wouldn't be taken in by what she'd said at the Manor.

"Hmm." The Empress continued to study her, then let out a laugh. "It is still about honour, though, isn't it? The best lies are closest to the truth. The sort of honour we don't care about in this kingdom anymore. The sort of honour your parents would have sought to preserve in you."

Andromeda shook her head, unable to stop herself from letting out an exhale of amusement. "If that was what I needed to possess the Book, then it would most definitely be gone."

"Still it is the same concept," the Empress insisted. "Honour of the self. Having the honour not to betray yourself, which I suppose must be quite difficult in the world you come from."

"I'm tired of this conversation. What does any of it have to do with the Dragon?"

Drawing closer to Andromeda, the Empress said, "When Talen took my mark, she doubted you. She cried such bitter tears when she told me how she feared you would never leave your world."

Tiny sparkles, glittering like dewdrops, began to appear in the air around Andromeda. Without knowing what they were, she instinctively tried to throw up a protective barrier, but as soon as they started to fall, she couldn't keep the barrier up. She could feel the pain and despair released from the droplets as they rained down upon her, and knew they had come from Talen. These were the tears Talen had cried when she told the Empress her story, and Andromeda couldn't reject them any more than she could Talen herself.

As the tears continued to fall, Andromeda felt her powers, her connection to the Book of Magic, beginning to slip away. "What are you doing to me?" she whispered to the Empress in horror.

"Talen believed you would never honour your feelings for her when she cried those tears. They are washing away your powers, taking away your connection to the Book of Magic. Soon, you will no longer be a Witch."

"No," said Andromeda, the word slipping out with a choking sound. "Such a small thing cannot be enough to undo everything I have."

If Andromeda was no longer a Witch, she wouldn't be able to invoke the Wildcard of Fate. She wouldn't be able to save Talen from dying. She'd be powerless again; a captive Princess chained to rocks and put under spells. A pawn to be manipulated in other people's games.

The thought revolted her.

Andromeda fought the rain of glittering tears, but they ate through every counter curse she tried to conjure, seeping into her, robbing her of the spells she'd come to know as part of herself. The words of magic would no longer come to her lips. Power no longer flowed from her fingertips. She kept trying long after the tears had stopped falling, and all the while the Empress stood and watched her with a pitying but implacable expression in her eyes.

I think you are strong enough to take the Dragon.

Stiff with anger, despair, and confusion, Andromeda closed her eyes. She had to find out what the Empress wanted from her. How could she take the Dragon if her magic was gone? Drawing in a breath, she forced herself to look at the Empress.

"So," she said, her voice dry and raspy, "you want to give me the Dragon in place of the Book. Is that it? Is that even possible if I don't have magic anymore?"

"Oh yes," said the Empress, drawing closer to Andromeda. "You activated the Dragon's skull. That is what matters. You do not need your own powers if you are going to take those of the Dragon."

"And then what? Talen doesn't die?" Andromeda's throat nearly closed as she said Talen's name.

Gazing at Andromeda with an intensity that wouldn't allow her to look away, the Empress answered, "Exactly right, Andromeda. Talen lives, and you gain the power of the Dragon."

"How? I thought you needed the Dragon as a sacrifice to create Blackheath anew." A strange sense of unreality was beginning to descend upon Andromeda. Was she really standing here, talking to the Empress like this, after what she had done?

"I told you, Andromeda," the Empress's voice was soft, and far too reasonable. "I have found a way to sever Blackheath from the remnant of the old world. That spell can also be used to split the Dragon from herself. You take her heart, and I will take her spirit. The spirit will renew Blackheath, and without it, the heart will be more easily controlled. It will be yours, Andromeda. The Dragon will be yours, and Talen's fate will not come to pass."

"If you can split the Dragon and sacrifice her spirit to the kingdom, why have you not done so already? Why do you need me at all?"

"Because it cannot be done without a vessel for the Dragon's heart. The separation must be complete before I can destroy the Dragon's spirit. But I never expected to find a vessel strong enough. That is why I sent the Heroes."

"A vessel?" Andromeda shook her head hopelessly. "No, I don't want that. I have to think this through. My powers can't be gone." She tried to focus, to search the depths of her heart, looking for that core of strength and warmth she had come to know from carrying the Book with her. But there was nothing, only the cold trails on her soul left behind by Talen's tears.

The Empress's proposal was horrific; Andromeda knew that. It made her skin crawl to think of splitting a being in two, of having half of it forced inside herself. Yet she couldn't stop listening to the poison the Empress kept pouring into her ears. These were the things that happened in the world bound by fate. This could be what Andromeda hadn't been able to escape in the end.

"There is no other choice, Andromeda. The Dragon will not willingly give up her role as Blackheath's guardian, even while she destroys the kingdom instead of protecting it. Forcibly severing this sick, dying bond is the only way."

With startling swiftness, the Empress produced a dagger, and slashed the palm of her own hand with barely an outward sign of pain. As her blood began to flow, she moved her hand to the Third Eye of the Dragon's skull, placing it slightly to one side so she was not covering the whole area.

When the Empress's blood came into contact with the skull, the Dragon scales all around the cavern began to pulse with a soft glow, and Andromeda thought she heard the distant echo of a Dragon's roar.

The Empress held out the dagger to her, hilt first. "Let your blood flow, Andromeda, and place your hand next to mine. I will give you everything." Her voice was low and intense, her eyes glinting in the glow of Dragon scales.

She looked beautiful and terrible, and with the feeling of nightmare growing, Andromeda couldn't stop herself from taking the pro-offered dagger. "Empress, if you give me the Dragon, won't you lose your powers? I could kill you once the transfer is complete. You'd deserve it, for what you've done to me."

Did Andromeda mean that threat? She thought she did, but she wasn't sure. If she didn't want the Dragon, why was she taking it? She must want this, on some level. It must be right.

"If you kill me, so be it," said the Empress, her eyes growing dark. "I want to be free of this burden. I want to die knowing my kingdom will endure for many eons to come. Take the Dragon from me. Please."

Her plea was heartfelt; even desperate. Andromeda could feel the Empress's emotions, her intentions, and she knew they were real. The pulsing cavern and the Dragon's skull were linking her and the Empress together, forging the way for the deeper connection still to come. It was no longer even a question in Andromeda's mind whether she would do it.

Andromeda used the dagger to slash her hand and placed it on the Dragon's skull. Her blood, warm and wet, stained the pale bone and began to drip down onto the floor. She locked her eyes upon the Empress's, and gasped at the enormity of the power that slammed into her like a firestorm.

"Don't take your hand away."

It sounded like the Empress spoke through gritted teeth, as if this was hurting her as much as it was Andromeda. But caught as Andromeda was in the midst of raw, dangerous magic, it was difficult for her to be certain she'd heard anything at all.

She felt as if she was being immolated in flame; strange thoughts, knowledge and spells pouring relentlessly into her brain until she feared her head would split open from the pressure. Parts of her were dissolving, being reshaped, until she barely recognised this being in flux as herself. There were screams coming from somewhere that might have been her own.

And then, she stood at the desolate peak of the Dragon's Mountain, eye to eye with the Dragon herself. She felt the hot steam of the Dragon's breath, smelt the sulphur that came from deep within her belly. Loose shale slipped beneath her feet and went skittering down the slopes, and the Dragon stared at her with seething hatred.

For the Dragon was bound, criss-crossed with a thousand golden chains, and Andromeda herself held the end of the chains like a gaoler.

"Use this."

The Empress was there. Perhaps she had been there all along. She placed a heavy ornate padlock in Andromeda's free hand. There was no key.

"What do you mean?" Andromeda asked her. "Use it where? How?"

"Where do you think?"

Following the Empress's gaze, Andromeda looked down at her own chest. Within the cavity of her ribs, a twisted, melded-together heart was beating. Her heart and the Dragon's. The knowledge came to her without having to be told. The padlock had to be used to lock the two hearts together.

"The Dragon's heart will pour into yours and afterwards, her spirit will be left behind. Once I kill it, Blackheath will be renewed and the Dragon's heart will become yours. Owning her heart, you will own her body as well. You will be feared wherever you go with a Dragon at your command."

With the Dragon's heart beating in her chest, Andromeda could feel the Dragon's emotions as if they were her own. She could feel the Dragon's utter loathing of what was about to happen to her. Andromeda understood it, for she felt the same. The Dragon was about to be torn asunder, and there was no way that could be right.

This ritual was an abomination. A sick and perverted thing that never should have been.

"This is wrong," said Andromeda, speaking more to the Dragon than the Empress. "I can't force any living being into this kind of subjugation. Not when I know how it feels. That would truly be an act without honour."

She crushed the gleaming padlock in her fingers as easily as if it had been made of dust. The Empress let out a cry of anger, while the Dragon struggled free of her chains and went soaring into the sky with a roar.

Chapter 18

With great effort, Andromeda tore her hand away from the Dragon's skull, suddenly finding herself back in the underground cavern. She staggered a few steps and fell onto her back, writhing in pain as fire continued to move through her veins. She could see it burning under her skin, eating into her, and wondered with a stab of terror if she was going to burn right away.

She heard the Empress let off an ugly spout of laughter, and then the Empress was leaning over her, despair transformed into triumph as she said, "You're too late. The spell can't be stopped now. The Dragon will be yours."

"No," said Andromeda, still helpless and twitching on the floor. "I don't want this."

In her mind, she had a vision of chains shooting up into the sky, pulling the Dragon back down to the mountain. Her slashed hand was burning.

"There is no way back from here," the Empress said sharply. "I thought you wanted to save Talen? How else can you accomplish it? And think of what else you could do. With the Dragon, you could take back your kingdom. Reclaim your throne."

"I gave up that life. I chose another path."

There was a disturbingly demented light in the Empress's eyes as she continued to try and persuade Andromeda otherwise. "That was not an action freely made though, was it? You ran because you had no choice. Now, you can become the Queen you were always meant to be. You can rule with Talen at your side, and bring forth a glorious era for your kingdom. Without prejudice. Without injustice. Some might say it is even your duty to do so."

"My duty?" Andromeda let out a short bark of laughter. She could barely see through the pain; she could barely think. But she knew that underneath all the propaganda, what the Empress was saying only amounted to being a sacrifice chained to a rock. Her life for the kingdom. Her own kingdom. The Empress's kingdom. Was she really so worthless?

Her connection to the Book of Magic was already gone, and Andromeda had thought she had nothing else left to lose. But she found she was wrong about that as the Dragon's fire continued to burn inside her.

Andromeda's link to the Road was fading. The Broken Road that had led her to Talen. She hadn't even noticed it was still with her, that she could sense it, that she would have been able to find Talen again, any time she needed to. She didn't realise she still had it until it was gone, and she'd lost the last piece of the life she'd been trying to build.

Overwhelmed by the impending destruction of everything she was, Andromeda did the only thing she could. She closed her eyes and retreated deep into the quiet of her own mind; what little of it was left to her.

The pain faded. The cavern faded. She could no longer hear the Empress's voice.

She opened her eyes and it was blissfully quiet. All around her, something glimmered. Air or water, she couldn't tell. But Andromeda floated in it, or she swam in it, and she realised she was not alone.

Turning, she saw the Fallen Fairy.

"Well, you have gotten yourself into a mess, haven't you?"

Andromeda began to feel more grounded, as if there was now a solid floor beneath her feet. She didn't understand how the Fallen Fairy could be here, but she was too grateful to question her presence.

"Please," Andromeda said. "I need your help. The Empress has taken my powers. Without them, I can't save Talen's life. But I won't do what the Empress says. I won't merge with the Dragon. It will destroy both of us."

The Fallen Fairy's eyes glittered. In her low, smoky voice, she said, "If you don't want this, Andromeda, then stop it. You are far away from me in another world. I cannot help you. My powers end at the borders of your kingdom. Find the strength within yourself."

Andromeda hopelessly shook her head. "It's too late. I have to take the Dragon. The Book has already deserted me. This is the only way left to save Talen's life. I can feel the magic changing me. It's all coming back; the chains, the confinement." Perhaps Andromeda had been deluded all along. Perhaps there never was a way out. Freedom was a vanishing dream, and her old life was reaching out for her like black hands pulling her into the dark.

Stepping closer, the Fallen Fairy insisted, "You are *my* charge, Andromeda. You are not so weak as to give up everything you are without a fight. Invoke the Wildcard of Fate."

"I don't have the power to invoke the Wildcard any longer." Andromeda stared at the Fairy in despair, her hands clasped over her chest, feeling the emptiness inside. The Dragon's fire had burned everything else away.

The Fallen Fairy took Andromeda's hands in her own. Her dark eyes shone fiercely. "You do have the power, Andromeda. I promise you it's there. The Empress has placed a shroud over your heart. It blocks your connection to the Book of Magic, but it has not been severed. Perhaps the Empress's spell would have worked if you had still been a Princess engaged to her Prince when Talen cried those tears, but that was not the case, was it?"

"No. I was following the Broken Road. I was searching for her."

"Exactly. Your heart was full of Talen. That's why the Book was helping you to gather all those healing ingredients. As you guessed, it could sense what was happening on the Road far ahead. Remember the courage and the faith you had then, Andromeda. Find it again within yourself."

"Wait." As the Fallen Fairy began to move back, Andromeda stopped her. "There's something else. In Blackheath, no one is free. All are bound to their fates. That's true, isn't it?"

"You are not of this world, Andromeda. Not yet. You can still stop what the Empress is trying to do."

Andromeda met the Fallen Fairy's eyes. "But what about our world? What drew Talen to me as I slept in my rose-covered bower? Was it fate? You said you put me to sleep so I would understand who had the power to wake me. How was Talen chosen to be the one?"

"What makes you ask this now, Andromeda?"

"Because, Fairy Godmother, you keep telling me to find my power, but if none of the choices I've made have ever been mine, then I never had any power to begin with. The Empress has done nothing but manipulate me since I came to Blackheath, and I cannot...I will not continue to trust you if you have done the same."

The Fallen Fairy smiled. "I did not choose Talen, Andromeda. Nor did destiny. Talen chose herself. I already knew that marrying a Prince would not make you happy, and so I did what I was not permitted to do. I cast a different spell. A spell which was...shall we say, an invitation not intended to attract Princes. Talen happened to be the one who heard the invitation and responded, and you responded back to her. But all that did was show the possibility of what might be. Everything that you and Talen became, you did on your own."

Unexpectedly, the Fallen Fairy embraced her. "I'm proud of you, Andromeda. You've come so far since you left the Endless Forest. Don't waste it now. Trust your heart."

"How?" Andromeda asked as the Fallen Fairy drew back. "What do I do?"

"You must discover that for yourself. I can't help you do it. Now." The Fallen Fairy brushed her hand over Andromeda's cheek. "You must go back. If you wait any longer, it will be too late."

Though she was fearful, though she doubted, Andromeda nodded. She knew the Fallen Fairy was right. Back in the underground cavern, the Dragon's fire was continuing to pour into her body, burning away everything she was.

"I won't let you down," Andromeda promised the Fallen Fairy, and saw her sharp, approving smile just before she started to fade.

Andromeda felt herself being pulled back into her own body, and bracing, she let it happen. She screamed as the pain hit her, worse than before, but she dragged herself from her position on the floor and settled into a tight, crouching ball. Now at least the Empress was out of her sight.

As the Fallen Fairy had bid her, Andromeda tried to look inside herself, to find her strength, but all she could find was the Dragon's fire, reshaping her into something else, something she didn't want to be.

Her fingers scrabbled against the cold rock floor of the cavern, and it was then she felt the first stirrings of something that was not of the Dragon. Andromeda caught a scent, a feeling, that reminded her of Talen; that made her feel as if Talen were near.

She focused on that sensation, clung to it. She let it take shape, holding space in her mind, creating a tiny sanctuary for herself where the Dragon couldn't reach, and then it began to stretch out on the floor in front of her. The shining Broken Road, as clear and beautiful as the first time she had seen it many months ago in the underbrush of the Endless Forest.

Hope sprang into Andromeda's heart. If she had the Road, she could find her way back to Talen. That would prove the bond between them wasn't broken.

"Talen," she whispered, speaking her name as if it were a protective spell. Droplets which might have been sweat or tears fell onto the floor in front of her and were soon seared away by the heat of the fire. "Talen." Andromeda spoke again, stronger this time, and for a moment she saw Talen clearly. Standing somewhere in a frozen field, with snow dusting her shoulders and hair, she was practicing her archery. Andromeda saw her start; saw her pause and look to the East, her brow furrowed and her eyes dark with concern.

"Andromeda," Talen murmured.

That was all Andromeda saw. The connection snapped and the Road disappeared, but what Andromeda received from that brief joining with Talen was enough. The Fallen Fairy was right. She could recover her powers. She'd felt Talen's faith in her, Talen's love for her, and Andromeda let those feelings fill up her heart, lifting the shroud the Empress had thrown over her of Talen's lowest moment.

Recognising that Andromeda was as she had always been; that she had not dishonoured herself, all the spells from the Book of Magic came pouring back into her, restoring her. Andromeda uttered a word that came naturally to her lips; one she had previously read in the Book but never understood. A powerful repel.

The magic that had been consuming her, changing her, was expelled, and began to pour back into the Empress. As it went, Andromeda could feel her own powers growing stronger once more, her mind and her will coming back under her own control.

Andromeda rose to her feet. Her limbs ached but she did not allow herself to falter as she met the Empress's eyes. Bound in flames as the Dragon's magic worked its way back into her body, the Empress gave her a look of hatred and spat, "I tried to give you everything, Andromeda. Why wouldn't you take it?"

"Because," said Andromeda. "I don't need what you would give me. And I would not force another being into that kind of subjugation. Not for all the power in the world."

She walked past the Empress to the Dragon's skull, still dripping with blood. Held immobile by the powers re-infesting her, the Empress could only follow Andromeda's movements with her eyes. Andromeda withdrew the handkerchief from her pocket. The stitched border of Dragon scales shimmered in the light cast by the burning brands, and as Andromeda pressed the handkerchief to the Empress's blood on the skull, the scales glowed red.

It was only as she spoke the first word of the ritual that the Empress understood what she was doing. Her face contorted in fear and horror, and with every ounce of her strength she struggled to break free of the magic binding her. "You bring forth that spell, you will be destroying the very foundations of this kingdom! You cannot do it, not for one woman's life!"

"I will not be a sacrifice again!" Andromeda said, her dark eyes flashing with determination. "Nor will I let the Dragon become one. I want to help Blackheath, I want to help your people, but I cannot pay the price you ask. It is too high. If that makes me selfish, so be it. I will not let Talen die."

Andromeda began the ritual again, ignoring the Empress's screams. It didn't take long, and there was a moment of eerie silence after she finished that made her wonder if she'd forgotten or misspoken something.

But then there was a shift, as if the entire world tilted on its axis. Andromeda felt lighter, freed of some weight she hadn't even known was pressing down on her. The handkerchief evaporated, becoming crimson smoke that spiralled into the air, disappearing into the cavern's roof high above them. Somehow Andromeda knew that the smoke, and the magic it carried, would soon grow and be taken by the wind all throughout the kingdom.

The Empress finally gained control of herself once more; her reintegration complete, and she flew at Andromeda with fire streaming from her fingertips. Andromeda blocked her and threw a spell in return.

They battled until the air was alight with magic, warriors without the need of swords, and though the Empress was strong, though she knew her powers more intimately than Andromeda knew her own, as they fought Andromeda noticed the Empress's magic did not flow easily within her. Perhaps it had done once, before the trust between the Dragon and the Empress was broken, but now there was something stilted in the connection.

As Andromeda fought, as she learned with every spell more of what she could do, as she learned to trust the magic inside of her and to meld all into a seamless stream of power, she gradually beat the Empress down.

She launched spell after spell, smashing through the Empress's defences, until a particularly powerful hex slammed the Empress into the far wall of the cavern and momentarily knocked her out. Not squandering the advantage, Andromeda propelled herself across the floor to the Empress's side, touching her just as she began to open her eyes and whispering a spell that encased her in a cage of crystal.

Panting hard, Andromeda stepped back. Dripping sweat and blood, with singes to her skin, and adrenaline still coursing through her, she half thought about killing the Empress. Looking back at her, completely helpless, the Empress knew she was thinking it. Andromeda saw the flash of fear in her eyes.

Instead, not speaking, Andromeda stayed her hand and turned to leave. Perhaps she would regret leaving the Empress alive, but she couldn't kill her when she was in this state, and she wasn't going to set her free.

She had taken several steps when the Empress spoke behind her. "Talen still bears my mark, Andromeda. That much I can feel. She is going to face the Dragon, and you will have no way onto the mountain to help her. She will die up there, alone. Everything you've done will have been for nothing."

It was a bold speech from a woman who had feared she might die moments before. Pausing, Andromeda half turned back. "The mountain belongs to the Dragon. If I need to reach the peak, I will ask her. I don't need your permission. I never did."

Curses followed her as she walked away, but Andromeda listened not. The Road was before her once more, and after she left the chamber, she moved faster and faster through the maze of passages, until she realised she was flying without wondering how she was doing it.

She reached the Empress's throne room and broke through the nearest window. Crimson smoke curled around her, and she could see the Empress's guards watching her and shouting in confusion far below.

Andromeda ignored them and streaked away from the palace, revelling in the space and freedom after weeks of confinement. The boundless sky embraced her, and the Road was her guide, going West, back to Talen. Back to where Andromeda was meant to be.

Chapter 19

Accompanied by Lezith and Ferris, Talen knocked on the door of Jerrard's cottage in the dark before moonrise.

He came to answer the door tutting in indignation at being disturbed, and upon hearing their request, was reduced to incoherent spluttering. Drawing himself up to his full height, (which had the unfortunate side effect of making his rotund stomach stick out even further) he declared he had no idea what they were talking about.

Short on patience, Talen shoved him aside and entered the cottage without his leave, saying, "I'm in a hurry. Everyone in Drakk knows you have a communication stone to keep the Empress appraised of what goes on here. To be blunt, I'm expecting a call from someone and I don't have time to be polite if you are not going to cooperate."

Ferris followed Talen in with a nonchalant shrug at Jerrard's objections, while Lezith patted his shoulder and said comfortingly, "Why don't you come and share some tea while we wait?"

Jerrard made a series of outraged noises and followed the women helplessly as Talen began to search for the communication stone. He raved all the while about how the Empress would hear of this, how the royal guard would be coming for Talen and her accomplices, how she would soon come to regret her terrible mistake.

Having already found the only locked door in the cottage, Talen raised a withering eyebrow at him and said, "I really don't care what you do. Send word to the Empress. Call all the guards you like. It won't stop me from doing what I came here to do." And with that, she kicked down the door.

The communication stone was mounted on a table in the centre of the room. Talen glanced towards Lezith. "This is what we're looking for right?"

"Indeed," said Lezith. She settled herself on a chair and got out her knitting while Ferris lit the candles on the table so they could better see the stone.

"How does it work?" asked Talen.

"It's probably best we wait for Andromeda to contact us," Ferris said. "The stone will begin to glow when activated."

"What if she doesn't? Can we make contact from this end?"

"We can," said Ferris. "But if Andromeda isn't there, someone else may receive the message. And they'll know we're using the stone."

Talen shrugged impatiently. "I really don't care about that. If Andromeda fails to answer then I will be ascending the mountain tomorrow. There's nothing else the Empress can do to me."

Lezith glanced up from her knitting and spoke to Jerrard, who was lurking in the doorway with a scowl. "Why don't you come in, Jerrard? My offer of tea still stands. Ferris, perhaps you'd be so kind as to get a fire going? I need something to warm me up while we wait."

Ferris nodded. She went to the fireplace while Talen temporarily left her position to go and throw the shutters back, so they would be able to see the moon when it rose.

Jerrard muttered several more threats before sulkily withdrawing, refusing to enter the room. Talen neither knew nor cared where he went.

A short while later, Talen stood staring at the communication stone and distractedly sipping her tea as she waited for moonrise. Lezith had said that in this season, the moon would not appear in the sky until shortly before midnight.

For about the millionth time, Talen wished she'd never gotten tangled up with the Empress. When she did so, she betrayed the teachings she'd grown up with. Deciding to pursue material wealth in the hopes of being good enough for the woman she loved devalued everything she was. If Talen had possessed enough faith, she would have returned and offered Andromeda only herself. There was no need for her to have ever entered into a deal with the Empress.

The irony of falling for a Princess was still something Talen marvelled at occasionally. Of all the unlikely things to happen, that had surely been at the top of her list until she met Andromeda. Talen wasn't the sort to pine silently after someone she couldn't have; she knew better than to throw herself into a hopeless unrequited love that could only hurt her. Yet that was exactly what she'd done after she'd woken Andromeda. No matter how she argued with herself, she couldn't bear the thought of leaving.

No spell could create love; not really. A very complex and difficult spell might be able to create feelings that were a simulacrum, but the effects couldn't last long. Still, Talen had been perturbed enough to consult a Witch she knew; another traveller between worlds.

The Witch had visited Andromeda's kingdom once or twice before; she knew about the Fairy Godmothers and the wishes and all the rest of it. She'd laughed when Talen had asked her why she'd agreed to become Andromeda's bodyguard, why she didn't want to leave.

"You need to ask your own heart, Talen. No enchantment is keeping you here. There is not a trace of magic on you."

Which was the answer Talen had mostly expected.

Even after leaving Andromeda, after travelling for two years, Talen couldn't forget her. And instead of going back to find her, she'd gone to the Empress. And now she was in this mess.

Furthermore, Talen was worried. A few days ago, she'd *felt* Andromeda. She'd heard Andromeda speak her name, and she'd gotten a brief sense of her being afraid and in pain. And then a strange reverberation had gone through the earth beneath Talen's feet, and crimson smoke had blown in on a thin, cold wind.

Talen had asked Lezith later what it meant, but Lezith wouldn't tell her. She knew something about it, though. Her expression had told Talen as much.

If Andromeda didn't answer tonight, Talen feared it would be because of whatever had happened a few days ago. The Empress could have hurt her, or worse. Whatever the case, Talen's options were shrinking. Whether it was right or not, killing the Dragon tomorrow might be the only way left to save both herself and Andromeda from this unhappy world.

The moon rose. Cold silver light streamed into the room, touching the communication stone and making it glimmer. Talen shifted impatiently on her feet as the minutes passed and no contact came from Andromeda.

"That's it. I'm going to use the stone." Without giving Lezith or Ferris a chance to object, Talen placed her hand on the stone. "Andromeda, are you there? It's Talen. Please answer me if you can."

A few moments later, there was a response, but it was not Andromeda who answered. "Andromeda isn't coming, Talen," the Empress said, her voice sounding scratchy and weak.

"Where is she?" Talen demanded.

"Dead."

Talen swallowed her growing fear. Even if she suspected something had happened to Andromeda, she would be foolish to trust the Empress's word. "When did this happen? How?"

"I offered Andromeda a bargain. Had she accepted, you would now be free, Talen, and Blackheath would be saved. In addition, Andromeda herself would have gained great power. But she was too afraid, and the power she refused consumed her because she would not accept it. There is nothing left of her. Talen, if you want to free yourself there is only one way. Face the Dragon. Become my champion, and save Blackheath from its curse."

Without responding, Talen removed her hand from the stone, breaking the communication. She looked up to see Ferris watching her with a worried expression.

"Do you believe what the Empress says?"

"No." Talen knew her denial didn't sound convincing. "But I will tell you this: if Andromeda is dead, and the Empress is responsible, then I will find her and kill her after I've taken the Dragon's life. This I swear."

"Then you will face the Dragon tomorrow?" asked Lezith.

"I will wait the rest of the night," Talen decided. "But if I don't hear from Andromeda by morning, then yes, I will face the Dragon as we agreed. Whether her silence is because she no longer lives or for some other reason, it makes no difference to our plans."

Lezith accepted this without surprise, and without any indication as to her opinion on Talen's proposed course of action.

The night passed away. Jerrard came by to bluster a few more times, until eventually Talen threw one of her daggers in his general direction to get him to be quiet. She had no idea how the people of this town endured such an insufferable self-appointed leader.

Andromeda did not make contact.

Once the sun rose, Talen went out into the frosty morning and looked up at the peak of the Dragon's Mountain. She'd always felt in the pit of her stomach that her fight wasn't over; that she was destined to go back there. This time, she couldn't afford to lose.

She turned to Lezith and Ferris who had followed her out. "Let's go back to Lezith's cottage. I need to prepare."

Jerrard didn't appear again. The incident with the knife seemed to have shaken him.

"So I go," said Talen. She was equipped as best she could be, with her enchanted armour and her newly crafted daggers, standing with Lezith and Ferris at Lezith's front gate. It didn't surprise her it had come to this. Talen had every faith in Andromeda's abilities, but this had never been Andromeda's burden. Lurking in Talen's heart, the knowledge had always been there that it was her responsibility to find a way to fulfil her vow.

Ferris handed Talen the bow, and Talen saw in her eyes that she doubted they would meet again. "I would not try to dissuade you from this, Talen, but I hope you do not act in haste. If you fall, you will leave Andromeda with a painful wound that will never completely heal. I say that from experience, and I would not wish what I have endured on anyone else."

"This is all I can do, Ferris," Talen replied. "I started this of my own free will, and so must it end. I know Andromeda will understand." She handed Ferris an envelope. "If I don't come back, this is for Andromeda. Please make sure she gets it."

"I will," said Ferris gravely. "You have my word."

Talen nodded to her in thanks and glanced at Lezith. She had never trusted her as fully as Andromeda seemingly did. She still didn't. But nor could Talen deny that Lezith had helped them, that she'd been kind to them when she had nothing to gain. With a small bow, she said, "Thank you, Lezith, for your kindness to Andromeda and I. It meant a lot; the time we were able to spend here together. I won't forget it. If I don't return, and if Andromeda does not return, please consider Brownie your own. I know you will care for her."

"You can be sure I'll look after her," Lezith promised.

"Do you want us to walk with you to the base of the mountain?" Ferris asked.

"No," said Talen. "I've said my goodbyes. There's nothing to be gained from drawing it out further. The ending will be the same."

She looked away from Lezith and Ferris, glancing at the road that would take her to the mountain. She looked back at them one last time, smiled, and set out, not looking back again. Soon enough, she was on the slopes of the mountain, her eyes fixed on the peak above her, where the Dragon waited.

THE PEAK of the Dragon's Mountain was a chaos of loose shale and shattered stone. Talen's training as a hunter helped her more here than her warrior's skills. Though she didn't know it, her stealth allowed her to get closer to the unsuspecting Dragon than many a Hero before her, whose bleached bones she passed as she picked her way across the peak.

In the grey twilight, Talen crept silently from rock to rock, until the great green bulk of the Dragon came into view. It was curled up asleep like a cat, its nose resting on its tail, its eyes closed. She could hear the rumble of its great bellows-like lungs. Talen could also see something she hadn't noticed last time; a diffuse golden light that was partially obscured by the Dragon's bulk. The portal, perhaps, through which the lost Spring was supposed to enter.

Talen's only chance was to be silent and quick, and she knew it. To dart out, shoot the one good eye the Dragon still had left, and then try to take out the Third Eye and hope for the best. She edged around until she had as good a view of the Dragon's head as she could get.

This could be her best chance. The wind was blowing towards her, carrying her scent away from the Dragon, and if she could be fast enough, she could take out the Dragon's eye in the dark while it slept. It might not be what other Heroes (now dead) would have done, but Talen had only one thought. Successfully destroy the Dragon, and leave this land and its Empress behind. She didn't much care whether her methods would be approved of or not. Hunters did not operate like Heroes.

Taking a breath, Talen stepped out from behind her cover. She didn't allow herself to be nervous. This was a beast to be hunted like any other, where quick, efficient movements were necessary to take down her prey. She drew back her bowstring and prepared to let her arrow fly.

And then the wind changed.

Talen felt it swing around so it was suddenly behind her, causing her cloak to cling to her body while its edges flew out in front of her.

She swore, but it was too late. Her scent had gone right to the Dragon.

The Dragon's one good eye opened, and there Talen stood, caught with her bow cocked, looking at herself reflected in the deep amber of the Dragon's reptilian eye.

The Dragon recognised her; of that Talen was sure. With a roar, it reared back, raising its head and drawing in an ominous breath.

Talen knew she had seen this before. It had happened just like this the last time. She had a sudden memory of standing in front of the Dragon, exactly as she was now, watching the Dragon raise its head before it sent a torrent of flame roaring towards her.

As soon as she released her arrow, the Dragon would strike.

It was cold on top of the mountain, as it was everywhere in this accursed land, but nevertheless Talen felt nervous sweat beading her scalp and trickling down the back of her neck. Her gaze was still locked with the Dragon's, as if it were one of the big cats from the forest of her childhood that would strike if she dared look away.

Then the Dragon let out a huff, and Talen couldn't say why, but she got the sense it was offering her a temporary respite from death. There was something it wanted her to know before it killed her. It snaked its head down, coming closer to Talen, still keeping its one good eye fixed on her.

Talen had stared down many beasts in her time, and she was not so arrogant as to think that beasts did not feel, or understand, or reason in their own ways. But never had she been able to detect her foe's emotions with as much clarity as she could now, looking into the Dragon's eye. She could tell that the Dragon recognised the bow she was carrying. It remembered Stasia, and it remembered killing her. It did not seem a happy memory for the Dragon.

There was fury and betrayal too in the Dragon's eye, which again made Talen wonder how it was she'd ended up outside that mountain hut after the last confrontation. Standing here, Talen knew she didn't want to release her arrow, and she knew the Dragon didn't want to burn her alive, but neither of those things mattered. They were both locked in this killing game now, and neither could bow out.

In that endless second, as the wind blew and the sweat continued to trickle down Talen's body and she held her bowstring taut, humming with the desire to be released, she began to remember.

She remembered striking the Dragon's Third Eye. Her heart had sunk with dismay as she watched her arrow bounce off the Dragon's forehead, for she knew that had been her only chance of victory. She remembered the terrifying moment when the Dragon's flames had come roaring towards her, engulfing her, tearing through her Dragon-scale armour and burning her flesh.

She remembered being crumpled on the ground in agonising pain as the fire ravaged her, the Dragon stepping closer and rearing up its head again, about to finish her off with another blast of flame.

Then Talen had felt something tugging at her mind; something she couldn't understand. Her senses had been pulled right out of her physical form so that she seemed to be floating high above the mountain, looking down on the Dragon and her own nearly-dead body.

What Talen had felt was Andromeda's presence. Out of her body, she could see her, climbing up the mountain. It was impossible but Talen knew it was real; Andromeda was there and Talen's desire to see her overrode everything else—her pain, her hopelessness at being on the losing end of a brutal battle.

Back in her failing body with the Dragon looming over her, Talen had pleaded, "Please, let me see her. Let me say goodbye."

She didn't doubt that the Dragon would understand. It would know Andromeda was on the mountain. It would be able to feel the connection Andromeda and Talen shared.

In making her request, Talen had no thoughts of survival. She knew she was dying. All she'd wanted was to see Andromeda, touch her one last time before she went.

The Dragon had looked at her, rolling its wild eye, torn in some obscure internal battle of its own. And then it had done the unthinkable. It had picked her up in its claw, being careful not to injure her further, and taken her down the mountain. The only reason Andromeda hadn't seen them was because she'd still been on the other side of the slope.

"You showed me mercy," Talen said through dry lips. "Because of you, I was able to see Andromeda again."

She looked at the Dragon, and the Dragon looked back. Knowing the Dragon had shown her mercy, even after she had come onto this mountain with death in her heart, Talen couldn't bring herself to do this. She owed the Dragon too much. She and Andromeda both.

Whatever the Empress had done to Andromeda, Talen would just have to hope she could get herself out of it. Because Andromeda would never accept it anyway, if the death of the Dragon that had brought them together was what was required to secure Talen's freedom.

"Just promise me one thing, Dragon." Talen was surprised her voice was so steady. "Don't hurt Andromeda if she comes up here looking for me. She doesn't want to kill you. She's been against it all along."

As she finished speaking, Talen began to lower her bow. She knew the Dragon would strike her as soon as she did. It couldn't afford to let her live a second time, especially not when she possessed the only weapon that could kill it.

"Andromeda will understand if you show her. She'll be glad I chose as I did."

Talen placed her weapons down, stepped back, and closed her eyes. It was time for her to accept that which had not been averted, merely delayed. It was time to let death take her.

Chapter 20

Andromeda flew through endless white storms, part of the wild fury of Winter. Always she followed the glimmering Broken Road stretching across the sky, her heart pounding with the urgent need to reach the Dragon's Mountain.

That flight was a thing of instinct, born of desperation, and once it was over, it was to be many years before Andromeda would again learn how to harness the power needed to fly at such speeds.

But even as she crossed Blackheath's skies, no matter how fast Andromeda flew, it wasn't fast enough. She saw the full moon rise on the night she had promised to make contact with Talen, and knew she would not reach the mountain until dusk the following day.

By which time Talen may well have already gone to fight the Dragon.

She tried to send her consciousness out before her, hoping to connect with Talen as she had beneath the Empress's palace, but it didn't work. All Andromeda could do was push herself faster, and hope Talen waited.

As Andromeda reached the mountain in the failing light of the next day, however, she knew Talen had not waited. The Road descended from the sky towards the mountain's peak, and unable to reach it, Andromeda was forced to alight as close as she could.

She pressed her hand to the invisible barrier that prevented her from progressing further up the mountain, and whispered, "Dragon, you know me. I am Andromeda, the Witch. I refused the Empress's bargain because I did not wish to enslave you, or myself. Please...

allow me onto the peak of your mountain. None of this need end in bloodshed."

After a few tense moments, Andromeda felt the barrier drop. She passed through, attempted to regain her flight, failed, and cursing, half-ran up the steep trail towards the peak of the mountain. Not until she reached the top did she see Talen and the Dragon.

In the oncoming evening, the Dragon's massive body was a darker blot against the sky, the shine of her deep green scales barely visible. And there was Talen, standing with her back to Andromeda, facing the Dragon with her hands wide and empty.

Andromeda couldn't see Talen's expression, but she could just make out the Dragon's. Her look was remorseless; that of an executer about to carry out her task.

The Dragon had to know Andromeda was there. She'd let her onto the mountain. But she gave no sign she was aware of Andromeda's presence, and as the tense tableau between Talen and the Dragon continued, Andromeda had a terrible fear the Dragon had allowed her to come only to watch Talen die.

As Andromeda continued to stand, debating whether any movement she made could tip the standoff before her into violence, she noticed some imperceptible shift in Talen's body, some slight change in the timbre of her breathing.

"Andromeda?" Talen spoke quietly, without moving, without turning.

"Yes," Andromeda replied, just as softly. "I'm sorry I couldn't contact you. I'd left the Imperial Palace and was already on my way here. I found a way to reach the peak of the mountain."

"It is well," said Talen, an odd inflection in her voice. "I'm sorry I couldn't wait. I feared...something may have happened to you." After a beat, she continued, "Andromeda, listen. I remember what happened. It was the Dragon who brought me down the mountain. She spared me so I could see you. I don't have time to explain it properly but...I can't kill her. Not even if all Blackheath is destroyed. It would be... wrong. It would be the sort of decision that would poison my soul and never let go."

"I know Talen. I learned some things too at the palace."

Talen sounded as if she was smiling fondly when she replied. "I expected nothing less of you. But Andromeda—" There was a catch in her voice that filled Andromeda with dread. "I've already decided what I'm going to do. I'm not going to fight. And the Dragon can't risk letting me go again. Soon enough..." Talen trailed off, then started again. "Listen, you're further away. You can generate that protective shield. Throw it up, get down the mountain as fast as you can, and don't look back. Do you hear me? *Don't look back.*"

"Talen, there is no way—"

"There is no way your spell is powerful enough to protect both of us," said Talen, which was not at all what Andromeda had intended to say. "I have no doubt it will be one day, but not yet. I've felt this Dragon's fire before. You come closer—you try to protect me—we both die. So go now. And when you hear a rumble like thunder—run."

"Talen—"

"This isn't a discussion." Talen's voice was soft and regretful. "These last few weeks, they've all been on borrowed time. If you hadn't found me back then, I would have already died on this mountain. I think...this is just what is meant to happen. But thank you. Thank you for coming to find me. I love you."

Talen's choice of words chilled Andromeda to her very bones. *What is meant to happen.* Exactly what Sorrel had told her. *Talen's death is written in the stars.* No. Andromeda had not come all this way, crossing worlds and defying fate itself, to lose Talen now. She was not going to run.

"I'm not leaving, Talen."

Andromeda crossed the peak of the mountain, kicking up shale and stumbling over loose rocks. She felt the Dragon's eye on her briefly, felt the Dragon's mind brush against hers. It was an experience far more intense than when Andromeda had touched the skull beneath the Empress's palace.

Trembling, Andromeda reached Talen's side. She took her hand, and Talen glanced at her. Andromeda saw concern spring into her eyes, and remembered she must still be covered in cuts and bruises from her battle with the Empress. Her left hand was bandaged too, from the knife slash on her palm.

Talen moved her thumb over the back of Andromeda's hand, tracing the cloth binding and silently acknowledging her injuries, but she didn't ask what had happened. Despite the Dragon towering over them, she smiled, warmth and gladness in her eyes to be with Andromeda again.

As Talen's gaze returned to the Dragon, however, she whispered an insistent, "You shouldn't have stayed."

"The Dragon can judge us both," Andromeda said. Her grip tightened on Talen's hand.

It might have been her imagination, but Andromeda thought the Dragon hesitated. She shifted her great bulk, and a halo of light emerged from behind her. The portal. The Dragon went into silhouette, and Andromeda could no longer see her expression.

Talen didn't take her gaze from the Dragon, but she began to speak to Andromeda softly. "The Dragon didn't kill me last time because she recognised my pain and loneliness. She recognised how much I wanted to see you, Andromeda. She took me down the mountain and left me outside the hut so you'd find me. She thought I was dying anyway; she didn't know you had the power to heal me.

"I think something similar must have happened with Stasia. I think Stasia must have asked the Dragon to take the bow to Ferris, so Ferris would have something left of her. And the Dragon didn't have the heart to refuse, even though she knew the bow was the only weapon that could ever be a danger to her. Have I got it right, Dragon?"

Throwing her head back, Talen searched for the Dragon's eye. Starlight gleamed in her hair; the same stars thrown into chaos by the Wildcard of Fate.

The Dragon snorted through fire-red nostrils, moving again so the glow of the portal disappeared. Her eye was liquid, brimming with too many emotions to name, and then the tension in her muscles began to melt and she lowered her head.

She snaked her neck forward until both Talen and Andromeda were buffeted by her warm, stinking breath. Then the Dragon made a rumbling noise like a purr and butted her snout against their clasped hands, nudging them apart. She looked at them, waiting expectantly, the area of her Third Eye pulsing faintly.

"The Dragon wants to communicate with us," Andromeda said, daring a swift glance towards Talen. "Place your hand next to mine, like this."

Talen looked as if she was questioning her own sanity, but she did as Andromeda asked, placing her hand next to Andromeda's over the Dragon's Third Eye.

Entering into direct communication with the living Dragon was an experience that could have easily shattered both Talen and Andromeda's minds had the Dragon taken less care. But she was gentle with them; even more gentle than she had been with Andromeda before, allowing them to sense the immensity of her power whilst still shielding them from being harmed.

The first thing the Dragon showed them was that Talen had been right about the confrontation with Stasia. It had been beyond the Dragon's comprehension that the Empress would send a warrior to kill her, and both Talen and Andromeda experienced what the Dragon had felt that day. Her boundless anger at the Empress's betrayal, her agony at losing an eye. Her rage as she burned Stasia in retaliation.

It wasn't long before the Dragon's regret set in. Dragons were empathic beings; capable not only of connecting with others, but in certain circumstances even needing that connection in order to live. Feeling Stasia's dying emotions, her sorrow at leaving Ferris behind, the Dragon hadn't been able to refuse her last wish. She'd taken Ferris the remains of the bow, even knowing it might one day be her downfall.

Next, Andromeda saw again what she had seen beneath the Empress's palace; the origin of the pact between the first Dragon and the Imperial Family. This time, however, the vision was clearer, and Andromeda better understood why it was the Dragon needed to merge.

The bond between the Dragon and the chosen member of the Imperial Family born with the Dragon's mark was a much-altered version of how Dragons chose a mate and bonded with their own kind. That first Dragon had been alone; a state that Dragons could not endure in perpetuity, and merging with the Emperor to save his kingdom had saved her from dying.

When their spirits merged, it created a psychological bond that allowed the Dragon to reproduce, and so the pattern had continued on ever since. The Imperial Family knew that when a child was born with the Dragon's mark, that child was destined to merge with the Dragon. The late Emperor's oldest son had been born with that mark, but he had not allowed his son to merge with the Dragon—this Dragon—when the time came. He had broken the pact.

But unless the Dragon merged with a member of the Imperial Family, she would never be mated. She would remain alone until she died in torment, and the Dragon to succeed her as the next guardian would never be born.

What the Dragon showed next finally explained why she had destroyed the Imperial Family. Amongst their own kind, Dragons killed those with defective genes. Those who harmed other Dragons unprovoked; those who repeatedly endangered the tribe. Because Dragons formed not only close physical bonds, but mental bonds as well, it was simply too risky to allow unstable Dragons to propagate throughout the species.

In destroying the Imperial Family, the Dragon had been responding to the Emperor's betrayal in the only way she knew how. Following her instinct as a Dragon, and wiping out all branches of the defective line. She had hoped that the Empress would be the founder of a new lineage that would renew the bond between them, but the Empress too had failed the Dragon when her daughter was born.

The Empress had implied to Andromeda that her daughter was dead, but as Andromeda had half-expected, that was simply another lie. The Empress's daughter had survived. She'd been born with the Dragon's mark. She'd been born the perfect mate for the Dragon. She had longed for the Dragon as the Dragon had longed for her.

Never had the Empress allowed them to come together. She had kept her daughter secreted away in the palace, and the Dragon was once again at a loss. Yes, she could have killed the Empress, and then perhaps merged with the Empress's daughter, but the Dragon alone was not meant to be Blackheath's guardian. The magic depended upon a partnership. Blackheath's continued prosperity was dependent on both the Dragon and the Empress surviving.

It was at this point the Dragon had decided to refuse to bring new life to the land while her own life was not honoured. The Empress had tried to make all sorts of deals; had even offered herself up to merge with the Dragon. That one small part of the story the Empress had told Andromeda was actually true.

But the Dragon hadn't wanted the Empress. In despair with negotiations failing, she had hardened her Third Eye—an extreme act taken only when a Dragon determined there was no suitable mate to be found. To reverse the process, the Dragon would need one of her own kind, and even then, it might not work. With her Eye hardened, the Dragon would never be able to bond with a human. She'd written her own eventual death sentence, but ironically, it was that which saved her when the Empress began to send the Heroes.

Stasia had been the only one to know enough to try and take the Dragon's sight first, but she hadn't succeeded. None of those who came after her realised they should have finished what she started, and so the Dragon kept her life.

Andromeda learned that the Empress's original plan to use the Dragon's death to forge a new era for Blackheath, while risky, probably would have worked. In her last meeting with the Dragon, the Empress had even gone so far as to tell the Dragon it was her duty to die if she would not let Spring renew the kingdom. It was the only way left to fulfil her fate as Blackheath's guardian.

Part of the Dragon had felt the Empress was right, but for all her unhappiness she couldn't sacrifice herself for a being who had treated her with such faithlessness. The Empress had responded that if the Dragon expected her daughter's life, she should be equally willing to give up her own.

The Dragon had tried to explain it was not the giving up of life, but the continuing of it in another form. But the Empress did not want a daughter whose spirit lived within a Dragon. She wanted her daughter to be flesh and blood. Human.

Unable to break her bond with the Empress, unable to fulfil her vow to safeguard the kingdom, the Dragon had mouldered upon the mountain, killing the Empress's Heroes, despairing of escape. What had been founded on faith and trust and love and mutual responsibility had become a sick, broken and twisted thing, locking both the Dragon and the Empress into misery with the kingdom crumbling between them.

Fatebreaker.

The name slipped into Andromeda's mind, given to her by the Dragon.

By invoking the Wildcard of Fate, Andromeda had thrown into flux the enchantments that bound the Dragon and the Empress together. With the magic that held her weakened, the Dragon had the chance to escape. She wished to go through the portal, to the desert on the other side. There had been few Dragons left alive when Blackheath was formed; one of the reasons why the Dragon's ancestor hadn't been able to find a mate. But what few survivors there were had stayed behind in the desert, and the Dragon wished to see whether any of them still lived.

She wanted to find a mate from among her own kind.

Though warmth from the other land could pass through the portal, nothing from Blackheath's side could return. There was a protective barrier not unlike the spells of concealment that hid parts of the Imperial Palace.

The Dragon did not have the power to break that seal, but Andromeda did. If she was able to open the portal from this side, and then fully close it afterwards, the connection between Blackheath, the Empress and the Dragon would be severed. The Dragon would be free. And with the severing of those bonds, Talen's curse mark would vanish too.

What will become of Blackheath then?

Andromeda asked the question half expecting the Dragon to no longer care, but even for that, she had an answer. Blackheath too would have the possibility of salvation. There was a spell the Dragon could fashion; an idea given to her by the Empress's own attempted renewal. If Andromeda agreed to help, the Dragon would entrust that spell to her.

The connecting link began to fade, and soon Andromeda found herself back on the mountain with Talen.

Regarding Andromeda with her one good eye, the Dragon waited.

Andromeda glanced at Talen briefly. Talen simply nodded; an acknowledgement she too had experienced the communication; that she knew what the Dragon had asked.

"I can't deny her, Talen," Andromeda said. "She has suffered so much, being alone all these years. Being a prisoner on this mountain. I know too well how that feels. Besides, this is probably the only way to take away the curse you bear."

Talen gently stroked Andromeda's cheek. The small gesture of comfort meant a great deal in the bleak surroundings. "You don't have to convince me, Andromeda. It is the Empress who has failed Blackheath, not you. Releasing a being from misery is not an evil action."

Andromeda smiled; glad to have Talen's support. But nevertheless, this decision weighed heavily upon her soul. She was gambling with every life in Blackheath, and she wondered how easily she'd be able to live with herself if there was to be no future once the Dragon was gone.

She looked back to the Dragon. "Show me the portal."

The Dragon exhaled a warm, steamy breath and shifted her bulk so Andromeda could clearly see the portal. The brightness of it was so great both Andromeda and Talen had to shade their eyes. Through the golden shimmer, they could just make out the world on the other side; an endless desert of sand dunes, baking under an enormous sun.

A wave of warmth rushed through the opening, and the Dragon launched herself into the air, dragging the warmth after her and sending a great wind spilling forth from the mountain with an ear-splitting roar. This was her last gift to Blackheath. The long-awaited Spring. But it was to be only a temporary relief. If Blackheath could not become a world unto itself, the Spring would fail and the world would go dark.

The Dragon landed back in front of the portal. With an affectionate snuffle, she rubbed her great head against Talen, then Andromeda, almost knocking them over. When she drew back, there was hope in her eye that had not been there before.

Andromeda approached the portal as she had the protective barrier in the Imperial Palace. The enchantments were not the same, but they'd originated from the same magic. She found the fault lines where the magic was woven together, and began to pour her own spell of undoing into the seams.

The magic holding this barrier intact was far stronger than that of the barrier in the palace. If Andromeda hadn't already successfully dealt with this kind of magic before, she doubted she would have known what to do. She'd thought the barrier at the palace was difficult, but this in comparison was nearly impossible.

She felt like she was trying to crack a rock apart with her fingernails, and every bit of progress she made, she could feel the magic pushing back against her, trying to fuse itself together again. Sweat trickled down Andromeda's brow. Her muscles were straining with the effort of breaking through the portal, even though she wasn't touching it. Her mind felt like it might be crushed if she lost concentration for even a moment.

Gritting her teeth, gasping for breath, she kept funnelling her magic into the portal, and suddenly, she felt it give. A great reverberation went through the mountain, and Andromeda experienced sheer terror as she felt the boundaries between Blackheath and the world on the other side begin to collapse.

Dredging up strength she didn't know she possessed, Andromeda held the portal steady, but she knew it wouldn't last long.

"Go," she said tightly, resting her hand briefly on the Dragon's gnarly snout, inches away from terrifying teeth. "I will close the portal behind you."

The Dragon roared and took flight, soaring through the portal without looking back. Andromeda still caught her emotions, though. Her regret at leaving behind the world she had failed to protect, warring with her surging hope at finally being free.

May you find others of your kind, and an end to your loneliness. I will do what I can to save the rest of this world.

Andromeda wasn't sure the Dragon heard her thoughts, but she hoped she did.

Once the Dragon had gone, Andromeda collapsed the portal in on itself, making sure it crumpled inwards. She instinctively knew that would seal the rift between the two worlds, whereas if it had exploded outwards, both worlds could have been torn apart.

The collapse happened with more speed and violence than Andromeda expected. Before she could give Talen a warning, both of them were blasted off their feet from the blowback and thrown roughly across the face of the mountain.

Andromeda knew the portal was no longer there; she had felt the two worlds sever, but she still levered herself up enough to look, to see the mountain illuminated only by the moon and stars, with no trace of the portal, no trace of the Dragon.

"Andromeda!"

Blearily, Andromeda saw Talen coming towards her. She tried to sit up but didn't manage it until Talen helped her, and she shuddered a little when she felt Talen's touch, because the Dragon had spoken truly. Talen no longer had the curse mark.

This was the first touch they'd shared in Blackheath without Talen's fate belonging to the Empress. Andromeda could feel the difference; she could feel that Talen belonged to herself now. It made the touch more intense, Talen offering everything to Andromeda in a way she hadn't been able to before.

"Can you stand?" Talen asked, examining Andromeda's face with a worried frown.

If Andromeda was to be perfectly honest, she doubted it. She shook her head, and leaned into Talen. "I'm glad you're alive, Talen," she whispered, breathing in her scent, never wanting to let go of her warmth.

"Me too," she heard Talen murmur back. "I really thought we were going to die up here."

"I didn't come all this way to die. I didn't come all this way to lose you." Andromeda drew back to look up at the stars. They were spinning overhead as if she'd drunk too much wine. "Not even if it meant defying the stars themselves. It's up to the Empress now whether Blackheath has a future. She can't blame the Dragon for her failures anymore."

Talen nodded, something grim in her eyes. Like Andromeda, she knew what it was going to cost the Empress if she wanted to save Blackheath. The debt of blood was still to be paid.

Chapter 21

After allowing Andromeda a few more moments of rest, Talen got her onto her feet and insisted they make for the mountain hut where they could take shelter for the night.

Andromeda was so drained she paid little attention to their descent, trusting Talen to lead the way and steady her whenever she stumbled.

She must have passed out for a bit once they reached the hut, because she woke up lying on the narrow bed without remembering how she got there.

Talen was turned away from her, concentrating on feeding lumps of coal to the small flame she'd gotten going in the fireplace. It was still dark outside.

Hearing Andromeda stir, Talen turned towards her, a look of relief on her face. "Andromeda, you're awake!" She took Andromeda's bandaged hand, looking like she was struggling to decide whether or not she should ask about it, and the rest of Andromeda's injuries.

"I had to fight the Empress." Andromeda answered the question for her. "A battle of spells. That's how I got like this. But believe me, the Empress came off worse."

Talen nodded. "I thought it was probably something like that. Here, you should drink."

She handed Andromeda a waterskin, which Andromeda gladly accepted. Her lips were cracked from days of riding the wind, her throat full of dust from the blast. Talen must have filled up the waterskins at the nearby stream, because they'd both been nearly empty on the way down.

"Is there any food?" Andromeda asked hopefully once she'd drunk her fill.

With a regretful shake of her head, Talen replied, "No. I didn't bring much with me; I didn't see the point."

As Andromeda handed the waterskin back, Talen's fingers lingered over hers, perhaps in apology for the bleak honesty of the comment. She'd noticed the way Andromeda's eyes darkened when she said it.

"I'm sorry, Andromeda. Forget that. I just meant—"

"I know what you meant, Talen. Dragon Slayers in this land have a zero percent survival rating."

Talen exhaled a breath through her nose, her lips curving into a half-smile. "Well, maybe not anymore, thanks to you." She reached out to smooth Andromeda's hair back from her forehead, examining her eyes with a hint of worry. "What about your magic? Is it as you thought? When the Book spoke of honour, did it mean—"

Andromeda gave a brief nod, trying not to let Talen see how that question affected her. She didn't have the presence of mind right now to explain how she had nearly lost her powers; how she'd fallen for the Empress's trickery despite Talen's warnings. "I was right about what the Book meant. I'm not going to lose my magic any time soon."

She felt Talen's fingers continuing to drift through her curls. Talen had noticed her manner; she knew Andromeda was holding something back, but she didn't ask what it was. The look in her eyes said it was enough right now just to be able to touch Andromeda again.

Half sitting up, Andromeda tangled her hand into the fabric of Talen's sleeve, pulling her closer. They kissed, Talen letting out a half-sigh, half-moan against Andromeda's lips while Andromeda drew her down onto the bed. Talen hadn't even taken off her armour or her boots yet, but Andromeda didn't care.

Taking comfort in one another's bodies, they lay together on the narrow bed; exhausted, covered in dirt and grime, glad to simply listen to one another's breathing.

Last time Andromeda and Talen had lain in this bed together, the world had been facing an apocalypse of Winter; now, the winds of new life were flowing gently through the Barren Mountains, carrying warmth and hope as they went.

It should have felt like an achievement, but it was difficult for Andromeda to be easy when there was more still to come. How would Lezith feel when she learned what the Wildcard of Fate had wrought? What would the Empress do? Would she fight them, try to kill them? There were no easy predictions anymore.

Yet when Andromeda thought back over her choices, she couldn't bring herself to wish she'd done any different. Because Talen was here, alive in her arms, and this was the one future in which that was possible.

The future in which Blackheath no longer had a destiny.

❦

ANDROMEDA AWOKE the next morning still tired and hungry, and dreading the thought of the long, steep descent ahead of them.

Talen was already up and busy heating water over the fire. She insisted they both clean up before leaving, though she paid more attention to Andromeda than herself. With a careful touch she wiped away the accumulated blood and grit from Andromeda's fight with the Empress, being especially gentle with the cut on Andromeda's hand.

"I still have to tell you everything that happened," Andromeda said, trying not to wince as Talen worked off the old bloody binding. "What the Empress wanted from me. Why I invoked the Wildcard of Fate."

"How you found the Wildcard of Fate," Talen added with a swift, curious look before returning to her task. As she cleaned and rebound the wound, she said, "We're returning to Lezith's cottage, aren't we? She deserves to know what has happened here. Explanations can wait until then. If you tell me now, you'll just have to repeat everything in a few hours."

"You were going to die Talen," Andromeda whispered, tears stinging her eyes as she remembered the vision Sorrel had shared with her. "That's why I had to invoke the Wildcard. It was the only way to avert your destiny."

Her eyes dark, Talen said quietly, "I know, Andromeda. I felt my death coming. I'm sorry. If I hadn't taken the Empress's mark, you never would have had to make that choice."

"Talen, no. The Empress nearly convinced me to do something much worse than what you agreed to. She—"

The clatter of hooves outside the hut interrupted them, along with a familiar trumpeting neigh. Leaving the conversation unfinished, Andromeda and Talen stepped outside to see Brownie waiting for them, pawing the ground impatiently.

"Brownie, I told you to stay with Lezith." Despite the scolding, Talen stroked Brownie's nose in thanks. "But I'm glad you didn't listen. We'll get down the mountain much faster if you can carry Andromeda."

With an arrogant head toss and a scornful expression, Brownie let Talen know that she was quite strong enough to carry both of them. Andromeda was rather reluctant, fearing Brownie might hurt herself, but as Talen pointed out, she could always dismount partway and let Andromeda ride alone if Brownie struggled.

Brownie didn't tire, however, and carried both of them down the mountain as sure footed as a mountain goat.

When Talen and Andromeda reached Drakk, it seemed the whole town was there to meet them. First had come the mysterious crimson smoke, and then yesterday all had felt the reverberations coming from the mountain, followed by the warm Spring winds that hadn't returned for ten years.

The people took it to mean that Talen had been victorious, and eagerly offered her a Hero's welcome; most not even questioning where Andromeda had come from.

Jerrard forced himself to the front of the crowd, babbling out some garbled tale Andromeda couldn't make sense of, in which he seemed to think he had done the Hero some essential service and assumed Talen was now his most particular friend. He magnanimously offered her pride of place at the celebration feast already underway.

Talen steered Brownie around him with barely an acknowledgement, and not until they reached Lezith's gate, where Lezith herself was waiting, did she finally answer the many pleas of those who would know how she had slain the Dragon.

"All that matters is that the Dragon is gone. What happens to your kingdom is up to the Empress now. Look to her for your answers, not I."

Lezith opened the gate for them, and Talen rode through with an appreciative nod. Unlike the rest, Lezith was watchful, and she discreetly bowed her head towards Andromeda as if to say she understood what had occurred.

She closed the gate against the rest of the town, heedless of their objections, and led Andromeda, Talen and Brownie around to the back of the cottage. If the people of Drakk wanted to celebrate, they would have to do it on their own.

❧

WHILE LEZITH TOOK care of Brownie, Andromeda and Talen went into the cottage through the back door.

Upon entering, Andromeda saw Ferris, sitting at the kitchen table with an empty tankard before her. There was tension in every line of her body, and her expression said she'd never expected anything less than terrible news to enter through the door. She certainly hadn't expected to see Talen alive again.

"Ferris," said Talen. She spoke to her with a familiarity that hadn't been there when Andromeda left. "I lost the bow. I'm sorry."

Ferris shrugged, the tension in her muscles dissipating. "Better to lose the bow than your life. I'm glad to see you again." Shifting her gaze to Andromeda she said, "It's good to see you too, Andromeda. The Empress told us you were dead."

"What? Talen, you didn't mention that."

"Didn't get the chance. Ferris, when Lezith comes in, would you tell her I've taken Andromeda to get some rest? I know there's a lot to explain, but—"

"Lezith will understand," Ferris said. "Besides, none of this seems exactly surprising to her."

There couldn't not be a certain amount of pain in Ferris's expression as she looked at Andromeda and Talen, Talen with a supporting arm around Andromeda's waist, Andromeda leaning into her for comfort and support.

But when Ferris smiled at them, her eyes were gentle. "I'm glad things ended like this for the two of you. I'm glad...that no more lives were taken."

Andromeda wished she could think of something to say, but the moment passed, and Ferris rose to refill her tankard from the small keg on one of the shelves, turning away from them with a finality that marked the end of the conversation.

It was with a sense of relief and homecoming that Andromeda stepped over the threshold of her old room with Talen. Of course, this wasn't really their room, it was Sorrel's, and this wasn't their house, this wasn't even their world.

But it was here, in this room, Andromeda had been able to attain that which never would have been possible with Talen in her old kingdom.

Talen helped Andromeda to undress, and lent her fresh clothes, and accepted Andromeda's help in return. It was a ritual domestic and comforting, still novel enough not to be familiar, but imbued with elements both knew would come to be woven into the fabric of the shared life they'd lead.

Lezith arrived a short time later with fresh bread and a pot of stew. She didn't ask any questions, nor seem inclined to stay; however, Andromeda couldn't let her leave without telling her something of what had passed.

"I invoked the Wildcard of Fate, Lezith. All futures in Blackheath are now uncertain, and the Dragon is gone. Talen didn't kill her. I let her leave through the portal on the mountain."

It was difficult to tell whether Lezith was surprised by any of this. Giving Andromeda one of her typically piercing looks, she said, "Do you remember the first time we met, Andromeda? I told you then I thought you would find the Spring that had been hiding from us all these years. And you have. I also told you that if Spring came without the Dragon, it would not be the same as all the other Springs that had come before. But we could not stay as we were. Never mind the shrouded stars; it was obvious we were dying. This may be the best chance we have to make ourselves anew."

"I hope so, Lezith, because—"

Patting Andromeda's hand, Lezith said softly, "I know. But try to remember, Andromeda. The responsibility for this isn't yours alone. Sorrel and I enabled you to do it."

"Sorrel?" asked Talen, her eyebrows quirking up in surprise.

"Yes." Andromeda nodded to her. "I saw Sorrel at the Imperial Palace. She's the one who told me how to invoke the Wildcard of Fate."

"Indeed. Now." Lezith walked over to the door, preparing to leave. "Get some rest, both of you. I'm sure you don't need me to tell you that the Empress will soon be coming. Again."

"We know, Lezith," said Andromeda. "Fear not, we'll be ready." Her tone came out grimmer than she intended. That didn't seem to shock Lezith either. She gave them a nod and left, and Andromeda and Talen gladly got to work on the stew.

※

It was probably the sounds of revelry that woke Andromeda, as the people of Drakk celebrated deep into the night. Unusually, the noise hadn't woken Talen, who was turned towards her, one hand half-curled into a fist, her chest rising and falling with regular, steady breaths.

Being a light sleeper probably went with the territory of being a bodyguard, as Andromeda had come to know during her former association with Talen. Talen used to sleep in Andromeda's chamber back then, not with her of course, but in her own single bed placed against a far wall. The King and Queen had wanted their daughter's life, and her honour, to be guarded at all times.

On several occasions a dream or restless night had been enough to waken Talen and bring her to Andromeda's side, knives bristling, eyes wary as she searched for threats. One time, after a nightmare, Talen had held her for a little while, and Andromeda could still remember her own confusion at what she'd felt having Talen so near.

She'd been torturously aware of Talen's body, of the whisper of Talen's breath against her ear, and had almost blurted out an ill-conceived plea for Talen to stay with her.

But before she could, Talen had drawn back. "Go to sleep, Princess," she'd murmured, despite the unmistakable desire in her eyes, and returned to her own bed, leaving Andromeda longing for something she hadn't known was possible.

Now, in their shared bed in another world far away, Andromeda moved closer to Talen under the covers, reaching out to touch her; feeling the softness of her fine golden hair, the warmth of her cheek.

Talen shifted seamlessly into wakefulness, immediately cognizant of her surroundings, looking into Andromeda's eyes with a question. "Is everything okay?"

Andromeda nodded. "The party outside woke me up. Is it still the same night? How long have we been here?"

"It's still the same night," Talen assured her. "There's nothing to worry about." She took Andromeda's hand, and laced their fingers together. "But you look like you're worried about something. What is it?"

Andromeda rubbed her thumb over the increasingly familiar callouses on Talen's fingers. "It's just—I owe you an apology, Talen."

"What for?" said Talen with a frown.

"The Empress. She had me taken to the palace because she wanted to test my magical powers."

"To what end?"

"She wanted to give me the Dragon. She said it was the only way to save Blackheath. I would have lost my own magic, but what I gained from the Dragon may have been even more powerful."

Talen's fingers tightened in hers. "What happened? You refused her?"

"That's just it, Talen. I didn't at first. She—" Andromeda paused. "Listen, everything I'm about to tell you, it's just between us. I'll tell Lezith the broad strokes of what happened tomorrow, but not this part. It's too personal."

"All right," said Talen. Her look of worry deepened.

"The Empress nearly made me think she'd taken my powers away. She figured out what the Book meant about honour, and she had your tears Talen. She said they were the tears you'd cried when you told her why you wanted to slay the Dragon. Tears from when you thought I'd chosen some Prince over you. The tears blocked my connection to the Book of Magic, because—"

"Because the Book thought it meant you'd dishonoured yourself," Talen finished, her eyes turning the colour of gathering storm clouds. "I knew it. I knew something bad would happen if you went there. The next time I see the Empress, I'm going to—"

"Talen, what the Empress did was wrong, but the real fault is mine for allowing myself to be fooled so easily. I couldn't understand how you fell for the Empress's manipulations; why you took her mark. There's a part of me that's been jealous this whole time. Yet when it came down to it, I nearly made the same mistake. Even after you warned me. I'm sorry. I should have listened to you instead of getting caught up in my own feelings."

Talen sat up and looked down at Andromeda in agitation. "Andromeda, I don't care about that. What I care about is that she hurt you, and it's worse that she used me to do it. I never should have gone to her. I never should have let her see me when I was like that."

Andromeda sat up beside Talen and put an arm around her shoulders. "I'm sorry that you went through that pain because of me. I felt what you were feeling then. You really didn't have any hope left, did you?"

"Not then," Talen admitted. "But after you found me, it was different." She smiled at Andromeda. "I knew if you'd managed to follow me across worlds, you'd chosen what you wanted instead of what your family wanted for you."

Smiling back, Andromeda said, "Yes. I figured it out in the end, even if it took me longer than it should."

"So," said Talen, leaning into Andromeda. "What made you realise you still had your powers? The Empress wanted you to take the Dragon's heart, didn't she? I saw that when you and I were connected to the Dragon on the mountain. I assume that's why the Empress tried to convince you your own powers were gone. So you'd feel like you didn't have a choice."

Andromeda nodded. "The Empress's original plan was to use the Dragon's blood to renew Blackheath, but since none of the Heroes could kill her, she decided to split the Dragon in two, and sacrifice her spirit instead. You saw, didn't you, what caused the schism between the Dragon and the Imperial Family? How the Emperor, and later the Empress, failed to give their children to the Dragon as they were supposed to?"

"I saw," said Talen. Her right hand drifted to her left shoulder, where the curse mark used to be. "The mark I used to bear looked similar to the ones on the children. I suppose the Empress found some way to transfer part of the destiny, to bind others to the Dragon instead of her daughter. Only because none of us were meant to bond with the Dragon, we died if we didn't kill her, and the destiny went back to the Empress's daughter."

"Did it hurt when the Empress gave you the curse mark?"

Talen slanted her eyes away. After a few moments of silence, she said quietly, "Yes, it hurt. It was like having fire inside me. Was that how it felt when the Empress tried to give you the Dragon's power?"

"It was like that, yes." Andromeda answered in a stilted voice. She didn't think she wanted Talen to know how bad it had actually been. After drawing in a breath, she said, "You asked before what made me realise I still had my powers. There were two reasons for it. The first was the Fallen Fairy. I spoke to her in my mind and she helped me to resist what was happening. She told me my power wasn't gone. And then when I confronted the Empress again, I found the Broken Road. I was able to connect with you. Do you remember that? You were standing in a snowy field with your bow."

"I remember," said Talen, glancing at Andromeda with a shimmer of intensity. "You called my name. I could tell you were afraid, in pain. A few days later, when you failed to keep our rendezvous, I used the communication stone myself and it was the Empress who answered. That's when she told me you were dead. She said she'd offered you power, but you'd refused it, and that doing so had killed you. I guess she added lies to truth to make it more convincing. That was why I didn't wait for you. I was worried about what might have happened."

"It's fine, Talen. You did what we agreed. Surrendering to the Dragon is probably what saved you."

"The Dragon was going to kill me until you got there."

"I know. But she'd formed a good opinion of you. You refused to fight her once you knew she'd spared you in your previous confrontation. Your last action was to ask her not to hurt me. If we'd gone up the mountain together, the Dragon wouldn't have been able to see any of that. Once I arrived, I think the thought of having to kill both of us was just too much for her, so she let us both live. She really was...quite gentle."

"I hope she's finally able to find a mate in that other world." Talen shifted out of Andromeda's embrace, lying back down again and burrowing under the covers. Tugging gently on Andromeda's hand, she added, "Join me, Andromeda. I can feel how cold you're getting."

Andromeda gladly slid back down into the warmth of the bed, settling close to Talen. "What I was saying before, about the Road. When you answered me, I knew that meant I had to be able to recover my powers. I made the Book recognise that you believed in me, that you knew I hadn't betrayed you. From there, I was able to reforge the connection and repel the Empress."

She placed her bandaged hand around Talen's waist, caressing. "Thank you for giving me that strength when I needed it. Even though you were far away, I didn't feel like I was alone anymore. It's why I was able to prevail."

Talen gave a sigh and drew nearer, whispering into Andromeda's ear, "You don't need to thank me for that, Andromeda. All I did was say your name. But it is pretty funny. One of the tasks your parents charged me with was protecting your honour when I was your bodyguard. Somehow, I don't think this is what they meant."

Pleasure shot through Andromeda as Talen touched her between her legs, causing her to let out an odd sound that was half-chuckle, half-moan. "You're right. It is pretty funny. Mm—Ah—Wait, Talen, wait. There's something else."

Shifting her hand to Andromeda's thigh, Talen nodded to her. "What is it?"

"When I saw the Fallen Fairy, we talked. I asked her what you wanted to know. How she drew you to the castle where I slept."

Talen gave Andromeda an incredulous look. "In the midst of everything else going on?"

"Yes. Especially then. The Empress was trying to make me sacrifice myself for her kingdom. It was like being made into a Princess again. And I didn't want that, but like you, I wanted to know this journey I've been on isn't all down to choices someone else made for me."

"And?" Talen prompted. The slow stroke of her thumb over Andromeda's thigh felt maddeningly good.

"And." Fearing she'd give into temptation before she was done, Andromeda moved Talen's hand to a safer location outside the covers. She ran her fingers over Talen's palm, glancing up to meet her eyes as she repeated what the Fairy had told her. "The Fairy said there was an invitation woven into the magic of the sleeping spell. An 'invitation not intended to attract Princes', to quote her exact words. You happened to be the one who heard it, and responded. And you were able to wake me because I responded back to you. The Fallen Fairy said that showed the possibility of what might be, but nothing more. Everything we've become, we did on our own. I don't think you'll have a problem with any of that, but...since I know now, I thought I should tell you."

Closing her hand over Andromeda's, Talen said softly, "When you invoked the Wildcard, you broke apart every fate in this world, including mine. We both know I was meant to die on that mountain.

So if destiny was all that was holding us together, that would be gone now. I'm glad you talked to the Fairy, I'm glad you told me what she said. And I'm most definitely glad I happened to be passing when your Fairy Godmother sent out her spell asking for a not-Prince to help a Princess in distress. I wouldn't have liked it if I never got the chance to meet you."

Talen took Andromeda's hand and placed it over her heart. "So, of course I don't have a problem with it. I know this is the bond we share. Stronger than destiny because it was freely chosen. Sounds like the Fallen Fairy understands that too."

Feeling the strong beats of Talen's heart, Andromeda admitted in a tight, frightened voice, "I'm not sure I'll be able to live with myself if this world gets destroyed, Talen. I couldn't let you die, and I couldn't leave the Dragon enslaved, but...all those people out there, they have no idea. You said it yourself. I've broken Blackheath apart."

Wrapping an arm over Andromeda's waist, Talen said, "It is the Empress who bears responsibility for this land, Andromeda. For years she has been trying to foist the burden onto others, killing the Heroes, allowing the land to die. These are not your sins."

"It doesn't make me feel any better."

"I know. At least let me take some of your guilt. You had to do all this to save me."

With a thin smile, Andromeda shook her head. "No, I'm not going to be like the Empress, always trying to minimise what I'm responsible for. There were other options, just none that I could stomach." She sighed. "I wish I hadn't left behind my Book of Magic and all my ingredients. I didn't have time to go back to my room for any of it before I left the palace."

"We can recover the Book and everything else, Andromeda. I'll help you if that is what you want to do."

Andromeda thought of the likely way that would turn out; with too many of Valouria's guards dead. "I'll find another Book," she said, though accepting the loss caused a stab of pain. "I can remember what it has already taught me, and in time, I'll learn other spells. As long as I still have my honour, my magic won't abandon me."

She examined Talen's face in the night-time shadows. "Sorry, all of that took longer than I expected. But I just had to get it all out before tomorrow, when we talk to Lezith. I wanted to make sure you knew everything."

"Don't apologise. I want you to be able to talk to me." Talen settled onto her pillow. "Are you tired?"

"No," whispered Andromeda, sliding her hand under the loose shirt Talen was wearing and stroking the warm, soft skin of her stomach.

Talen's eyes went liquid with desire. "Well then, I have some suggestions..."

Andromeda made Talen gasp and leaned in to kiss her, doing what she could not that night in the palace, when Talen hadn't stayed in her bed. Enjoying an honour unknown and incomprehensible in her former life.

She woke the next morning cradling the Book of Magic in her arms, while Talen slept at her back, embracing her.

Chapter 22

The Book of Magic rested atop the centre of Lezith's kitchen table, while Andromeda, Talen, Lezith and Ferris sat ranged around it, glancing between the Book and each other.

Andromeda had just finished telling the tale of her time in the Imperial Palace, of the Empress's thwarted plan for her, of what the Dragon had shown to her and Talen. How the trust between the Dragon and the Imperial Family had been broken, and why it had brought the kingdom ten years of Winter. How all this time the Empress had been harbouring her daughter, choosing her daughter's life over those of her subjects.

She told them the true nature of Blackheath's origin, and the secret behind the pockets of warmth that lingered in the land.

She told them what it was going to take for Blackheath to be renewed and become a world unto itself.

The only parts Andromeda held back were those she had shared with Talen the night before; the nature of the curse the Empress had tried to cast on her, and how she had defeated it with Talen's help. Those details were too personal to share.

Ferris's look became increasingly perturbed the more Andromeda revealed, but Lezith sipped her tea with only one or two mutterings of surprise. Indeed, she'd shown little shock at anything since Andromeda and Talen had returned, and once Andromeda came to the end of her story, she gave Lezith a direct look, and said,

"Lezith, I must ask—How much did you know of all this? I feel as if I haven't recounted anything of which you were not already aware. But if you did know, why not say anything? And what about the Wildcard of Fate? Sorrel told me you thought I would learn of it myself if I was meant to know. Is that right? Why were you so sure I would find Sorrel and ask her about it?"

"I wasn't sure," Lezith answered. "I have been working near blind on this whole matter from beginning to end. But what I do know is that powerful magic follows currents and desires of its own. In the way that your Book of Magic chose you, in the way it returned to you, I knew knowledge of the Wildcard of Fate would find its way to you if it so desired.

"That was why I sent the handkerchief to Sorrel, rather than giving it to you myself. I thought it most likely if you were going to encounter some whisper of the Wildcard, it would be at the Imperial Palace. Though of course I realise now Talen had already told you of it."

"What if Sorrel is imprisoned or put to death?"

Talen started. "Is that likely?"

"She told me it was a possibility. She said Lezith would know that when she asked for her help."

Lezith's lips tightened, and fear darkened her eyes. "Yes, I knew the cost I might be asking Sorrel to bear. But if it comes to that, I'll surrender myself and be punished alongside her. I wouldn't let her die alone."

"Neither of you will die," said Ferris, speaking for the first time since Andromeda had finished her tale. "I still have contacts at the Imperial Palace. If necessary, I can help you get her out of there. I have somewhere that you and Sorrel would be able to hide. You know where. The Empress wouldn't find you."

Lezith flashed Ferris a grateful smile. "Thank you, Ferris. Truthfully, I don't think matters will become so desperate, but I will trust your offer if the need arises."

"Where do you go to hide from the Empress?" Talen asked Ferris curiously.

Ferris crossed her arms with a stubborn expression and looked away with what might have been a blush on her dusky cheek.

"Let Ferris keep her secrets," Lezith said. "It is of no account to our discussion. Andromeda, you asked me before how much I knew of what you revealed to us. The answer is I knew very little. I told you I had never possessed much talent when it came to reading the stars. And that is true. However, many years ago I was able to notice something that many of the better Seers seemed not to see. I realised there were gaps, areas of darkness within the stars, and it made me wonder if something was being concealed. Based on what I thought I understood of magic at the time, I thought it impossible, but once the Winter came, I began to wonder.

"I read some of the research, the speculations, the treatises that were written about the possible origins of the Dragon's behaviour, and I found all of them lacking. All accepted as incontrovertible that what was occurring must be in accordance with destiny, and because of that, the search for a deeper reason was tepid at best.

"As painful as it was to realise, I knew I could not blindly trust in destiny like my peers. I could not place my faith in the stars alone. That is why I began to seek out and learn the humble instincts, and that is how I learned of the Wildcard of Fate. I got the incantation from the last Seer who still remembered it, shortly before her death. Folk have always been good at not listening to that which they don't want to hear, and that is why knowledge of the Wildcard was nearly lost. The thought of defying fate was so terrifying to most they'd prefer to pretend there was no way to do it.

"Simply having the spell was not enough, however. I did not have the power to invoke it. No one did, besides the Empress, and the Seer assured me the Empress already knew of the spell, and did not wish to use it."

"Of course she didn't," said Ferris darkly. "She wouldn't risk her daughter. She preferred to let the entire kingdom fall."

"Well, be that as it may, the Wildcard of Fate was useless to me. That was why I sent Ferris chasing legends of Flame Trees once I learned of the broken bow she possessed. I thought if we could restore the bow, we could at least give the Heroes a better chance."

"What about the parchment I found that referred to the Wildcard of Fate?" Talen asked. "Who placed it there? What happened to it? Andromeda told me she couldn't find it when she looked."

"My guess is it was the same Seer who hid the parchment inside the book, probably spelled in some way so it wouldn't appear until it was found by someone who had the power to do something with it. It was also she who crafted the bow."

"I didn't have the power to invoke the Wildcard, though," said Talen with a frown.

Lezith smiled. "No, but you knew someone who did. Someone who was making her way to you at the time, even if you were not aware of it."

"That story you told Talen and I about your daughter," said Andromeda. "How she met the Dragon, and the Dragon said she didn't have a friend...that must have been in the time of the Emperor, correct? The Empress's older brother?"

"Yes, that's right. I know where your thoughts tend, Andromeda, and I think you are right. The Emperor's oldest son was born when the Emperor was just shy of sixteen. My daughter was born the same year, when I was twenty-two. She met the Dragon when she was seven or eight; I cannot exactly remember after all these years. But after what you've told me, I have no doubt the 'friend' the Dragon spoke of was the Emperor's son who was meant to bond with her."

"If that Emperor had just honoured the pact with the Dragon, so many lives would have been saved," Ferris said in a bleak voice.

"Indeed," agreed Lezith. "We criticise the Empress, and rightly so, but we should not forget there was another before her who failed and left her to inherit a kingdom already broken."

"True. However, the Empress could have shown strength, Lezith. She did not. She was as weak as her brother before her. I'm not inclined to give her sympathy for that."

"Lezith," said Talen, "what do you think would have happened to Blackheath without the Wildcard of Fate? Even if Blackheath's destiny was unclear, it must have had one, if I've understood the rules of this world correctly. Do you think the kingdom was fated to fall?"

With a frown, Lezith answered, "We cannot ever know whether a Hero would have risen who could have done as the Empress hoped— kill the Dragon and save Blackheath. But we had run out of time to find out. When Andromeda appeared and fixed her gaze on the Dragon's Mountain, I knew I had to act, with or without the stars."

She gave Andromeda a regretful look. "I am sorry I did not tell you then as much as I could. What my hopes were for you. I didn't because I feared doing so might inadvertently close off possibilities. I knew so little I thought it best to give you and Talen the space to make your own decisions. But the friendship I offered was genuine; I hope you can believe that much at least.

"I know invoking the Wildcard of Fate has left you with a burden you did not have before, Andromeda, and I am sorry for that. The decision to fundamentally alter this world will always be with you, as will the consequences, whether they are for good or ill. I wish there had been someone else who could perform the ritual, but the people of this world; perhaps even the Empress herself...I think many of them believe that if defying fate is the only way to gain salvation, then it means we are meant to be damned. And we cannot save ourselves if we do not believe we deserve to be saved. We needed a Sorceress who had the conviction to do what we could not. Even the Dragon needed that to attain her freedom."

Andromeda briefly grasped Lezith's hand. "You don't need to apologise, Lezith; I will always be glad of your friendship. Your reasons for not speaking make sense to me, and as you say, you left me to make my own choices. That is more than the Empress did. And invoking the Wildcard; it wasn't a selfless act on my part. In the future Sorrel showed me, Talen succeeded in taking the Dragon's remaining seeing eye before being killed. That would have meant the next Hero, whoever they were, would have had a real shot at taking the Dragon's life. But losing Talen like that was something I just couldn't bear. And the Dragon asked for my help."

"Even if Talen had sacrificed herself to take the Dragon's one remaining eye, another Hero may not have stepped forward. And even killing a blind Dragon is a task beyond most. Had that future come to pass, Blackheath's deterioration might only have been hastened by the Dragon's condition."

"Speaking for myself," said Ferris, "I am glad all the destinies are gone. If I had the power, and could go back in time, I would do as Andromeda did. I would change fate to save Stasia's life. The Empress had ten years in which to act, and she did nothing. She cannot bemoan the outcome."

"The Dragon murdered the Empress's family," Lezith reminded her. "Including her other three children. It is not difficult to understand why she could not forgive the Dragon; why she would not give her the only child she had left. But the consequences of that were terrible for all of us." She gave a sigh, a sound of endless sadness and regret at the broken history of the last ten years. Then, focusing on Andromeda and Talen once more, she asked, "What are your plans now? Do you intend to go to the Empress? She may not like what you have to tell her."

After glancing at Talen, Andromeda answered. "Talen and I discussed that this morning. We've decided we're going to go West, to the frozen sea. We will wait for the Empress there, on the edge of the world."

Lezith nodded, and said, "Yes, I can see how that would be fitting."

"We intend to leave tomorrow night," Talen added. "Go quietly, without anyone noticing."

"I understand," said Lezith. She exchanged a glance with Ferris. "Ferris and I will help you prepare. If we do not see you again—thank you both, for all you have done."

"Don't thank me yet, Lezith," said Andromeda with a thin smile. "I have not yet done that which will ensure Blackheath's survival. And if the Empress chooses not to cooperate, I may not be able to save Blackheath at all."

"The Empress may prove more amenable than you think," Lezith replied. "From what you have told us, her goal has always been to save her daughter's life, and what you are proposing will accomplish that."

In a dark voice, Andromeda said, "Well, I suppose we will find out soon enough."

⚜

WITHOUT FANFARE, Andromeda and Talen slipped out of Drakk late the next night, with only Ferris and Lezith there to farewell them.

Ferris brought one last parting gift—a beautiful black gelding. "Brownie is a special horse, naturally," Ferris said, as Brownie rolled her eye doubtfully at the newcomer, "but she will not be able to carry both of you all the way to the edge of Blackheath and beyond." She handed the reins to Talen. "I know Andromeda will want to ride Brownie, so I thought he could be a mount for you."

"He's beautiful," said Talen admiringly. "Does he have a name?"

"Midnight Storm," said Ferris. She laughed at Talen's raised eyebrows. "It suits him," she insisted.

"We'll have to give Brownie a better name to match," Talen said, looking towards Andromeda.

"We can talk about it on the journey," Andromeda answered, smiling. She was looking forward to the prospect of travelling with

Talen; just the two of them alone together. "But are you sure you want to give him to us, Ferris? You've done so much for us already, and...we lost the bow. The only connection to Stasia you had left."

Ferris looked towards the shadows of the Barren Mountains looming above the town. "With the Dragon gone, I will finally be able to go up there to recover Stasia's bones. I'll be able to bury her and say a proper goodbye. If I can do that, the bow doesn't matter."

Andromeda nodded, wishing she could say something to ease Ferris's loss, whilst also knowing anything she might say could only ever be inadequate.

Lezith gave them some last minute supplies, treats she'd been saving, and then Andromeda and Talen said their final goodbyes and embraced both Lezith and Ferris in turn. Then they mounted their horses and departed into the night, leaving the sleeping town behind them.

⋆⋅☾⋅⋆

ANDROMEDA AND TALEN rode on the heels of the advancing Spring, going West to the frozen sea.

Once there, they made camp in the remains of a town located high on a cliff overlooking the sea. As the world continued to warm, the noise of creaking and cracking ice became a constant companion. Great icebergs broke away or crashed into the sea, and waves which hadn't moved in a decade began to surge along the shore below.

In due course, the Empress arrived, and a large party travelled with her. Among them were Valouria, Jasper and Sorrel, as well as Lezith and Ferris who Andromeda hadn't expected to see again. She was most taken aback, however, by the youngest member of the party. A girl about ten years old with pale skin and black hair who could only be the Empress's daughter.

The Empress instructed her tent to be pitched, and those who travelled with her began to pitch their own tents too, until the ruined town was transformed into an oddly colourful and festive-seeming settlement.

Once her tent was ready, the Empress dismounted from her horse and approached Andromeda and Talen.

Andromeda and Talen had discussed at length how they thought the Empress would appear, what she might do, what they might have to do to defend themselves against her. They'd both been half-convinced she would come at the head of an army, filled with anger and calling for vengeance.

It was difficult to know what to make of the Empress as she was now, strangely calm, her expression giving nothing away.

"Andromeda, Talen, I would speak to you in my pavilion," the Empress said, and without waiting to see if they followed, she turned sharply and went into her tent.

After exchanging a nervous glance, Andromeda and Talen followed her.

The Empress was alone in her tent. She was sitting upon a sort of miniature throne that had probably been assembled, and without speaking, looked at Andromeda and Talen as they stood before her. There was no hatred in her eyes, but her gaze was cold as the sea sighing beyond the cliffs.

"Well Talen," the Empress began, her voice unusually soft, "you have succeeded in your quest. You have rid Blackheath of the Dragon, though not in the way I would wish. However, I cannot fault you for your methods. I am the one who chose you for this task, and thus any dissatisfaction I have is down to my own selection of Hero."

Talen and Andromeda looked at each other. Andromeda could see Talen was torn between wanting to give her the credit for freeing Blackheath of the Dragon, and not wanting to make her the focus of the Empress's anger.

Noticing Talen's hesitation, the Empress made an impatient gesture before she could speak. "Yes, I am aware it was Andromeda who invoked the Wildcard of Fate; I was there after all. I know it was her magic that sent the Dragon through the portal. But Andromeda never would have come to Blackheath if you hadn't been here, Talen. It was my choice to make you a Hero that set all of this in motion."

"Imperial Majesty," said Andromeda, "I wish you would have told me the full truth at the palace. We may have been able to find another solution. As it is…" She trailed off uncomfortably.

The Empress seemed annoyed at Andromeda's inability to finish her sentence. "For ten years, I have concealed all knowledge of my daughter's existence. Both of you know the reason why. I could not risk you betraying me, Andromeda. Had you known, you would have had a far easier way to save Talen's life. Give my daughter to the Dragon. You wouldn't have even had to force her. Ever since she could form words, my daughter has longed to merge with the Dragon. She was born wanting to fulfil her destiny."

"I would not have done that," Andromeda promised earnestly. "And it wouldn't have worked anyway. The Dragon had hardened her Third Eye. It was no longer possible for her to bond with any human."

The signs were subtle, but Andromeda could tell that surprised the Empress.

With a slight sound of derision, Talen added, "That was why none of the Heroes could kill the Dragon. They didn't know they had to take her remaining seeing eye first. Only Stasia knew to take the seeing eyes of the Dragon before destroying the Third Eye. Why did you never share that information with the Heroes? Did you want them to die?"

"Of course not," the Empress answered coldly. "It never occurred to me the Dragon would do something so foolish. It was a self-imposed death sentence. I never told any of the Heroes because I never thought it would be necessary. I am not even sure how Stasia learned that information. I never told her. However, there is little point in going over what is done. What I would like to know is why the two of you are still here. Talen is free. The Dragon is gone. Both of you could have already left Blackheath and been beyond my reach. Yet you came here and waited for me, knowing there would be no warmth in our meeting. Why?"

"Because the Dragon asked me to," Andromeda answered. "The Spring now unfolding was the Dragon's last gift, but it cannot last unless Blackheath is renewed."

"I know that already, Andromeda. I am not fooled by the Spring. My kingdom is still only a partial world, shut off from that which sustained it. In time it will wither and die like a severed limb. Are you telling me you know of a way to change this?"

"Yes, Imperial Majesty." Andromeda's voice wavered. "There is a way Blackheath can become a world unto itself, exactly as you wished. But instead of the Dragon's life, the life that will have to be sacrificed is yours."

Andromeda felt Talen tense beside her, ready to spring into defence if the Empress did not take this news well. Indeed, Andromeda herself was already preparing spells in her mind, expecting a scene similar to that which had played out in the Dragon's cavern beneath the Imperial Palace.

Instead of attacking, the Empress gave a hollow laugh, a bleak look passing over her face. "That is fitting, I suppose."

"Imperial Majesty?" asked Andromeda, exchanging an uneasy glance with Talen.

It was a moment before the Empress answered. "All I ever wanted to do was save my daughter's life. If this is the only way to achieve that aim, then so be it. It is true I tried to use both of you for my own ends, and I am not so much of a coward I will not face up to that. I have no reason to expect sympathy or understanding, and I do not ask for it.

"In my mind, what I did was justified. When my daughter was born and I saw that mark on her arm, I knew I couldn't give her up; not when the Dragon had already taken my other children. So I sent Stasia to free us from the Dragon's tyranny, but she didn't return. And nor did any of the others. Yet no matter the mounting cost to the kingdom, I loved my daughter too much to lose her. I chose her life over Blackheath, as you chose Talen over your own kingdom, Andromeda. We may not like each other, but we are not so different, you and I."

As Andromeda started to speak, the Empress held up her hand. "Yes, I know you will tell me it was different for you." Her dark eyes bored into Andromeda's face, uncomfortably astute. "You will say you were already going to lose your kingdom; that there was no reason to stay. But you could have fought for it, and you did not. You chose your lover over your kingdom, as I chose my daughter over mine."

Compelled by the Empress's unwavering gaze, Andromeda considered what she had said. After a pause, she answered, "If I'd stayed and fought as I was then, I would have lost. I wasn't strong enough. My kingdom will continue without me, so in that respect, I do not think we are the same. But I did choose Talen over Blackheath. I chose my own freedom over Blackheath. I refused to sacrifice myself so this world could have a future. That was expected too often of me as a Princess, and I am weary of it. I will not live like that any longer."

"You were not a sacrifice, Andromeda," the Empress insisted, though they both knew she was lying. "I would have given you all the Dragon's power. You could have done anything."

"I have my own power, Imperial Majesty. That is enough."

Andromeda and the Empress examined each other, their expressions equally unyielding. It was true they were never going to like each other, but they had a certain amount of reluctant respect for one another, a mutual recognition of the struggles they had both faced as rulers.

The Empress smiled, more sad than bitter this time. "This is a pointless conversation, Andromeda. Neither of us will ever depart from our positions, but let us be gracious enemies, like the Queens we are. It's true I could fight you again; I know you have been expecting it, but that would avail me of nothing. The Wildcard of Fate cannot be undone, and now I must lose my life if my kingdom is to survive." She firmed her jaw without a hint of fear. "I will make the required sacrifice, but I must have your word you are speaking the truth, Andromeda. You must swear that with my sacrifice, Blackheath will become a world unto itself. That no one from the Imperial Family— or anyone in the kingdom for that matter—will ever have to die again for the sun to keep rising and the seasons to keep turning. Deceive me, and my vengeful spirit will return to haunt you into an early grave."

"I swear I am speaking the truth, Imperial Majesty," Andromeda said, as the Empress's dark eyes looked unblinkingly into her own. "May your spirit return to wreak vengeance upon me if I am false."

"Very well." A fleeting mix of emotions moved through the Empress's eyes; regret, pain, sorrow, others gone too quickly for Andromeda to name. "There are matters I must settle before we complete this sacrifice. Go, and I will summon you when I am ready."

She dismissed them with a wave of her hand, and Andromeda and Talen turned and left the tent, letting the flap fall shut behind them. Surrounded as they were by the bustle of the small tent city, they couldn't discuss what had happened, but Talen ran her hand down Andromeda's arm comfortingly. It was only just starting to hit Andromeda that she would soon have to conduct the ceremony that would end in the spilling of the Empress's blood.

They went into their own tent, shutting out curious eyes, and Andromeda sat for a while, grappling with what she was going to have to do. When she'd given the Dragon her promise, she hadn't thought this far ahead. Hadn't considered what it would mean to deliberately involve herself in taking another human life.

This wasn't the same as the self-defence she'd engaged in while on the Road. Her instincts and adrenaline weren't going to be flooding her system, making her forget everything except the need to survive.

Talen was about to speak when a call came from outside the tent—Valouria, asking if she might enter.

Wearily, Andromeda indicated to Talen it was all right.

Valouria came in bearing the pack and saddlebags Andromeda had left behind at the palace. After a cursory greeting, she said to Andromeda, "I thought you might want your things. Shall I put them down somewhere?"

"I'll take them," said Talen, unburdening her and finding an area in the tent for the bags.

Standing awkwardly, Valouria indicated one of the chairs Andromeda and Talen had salvaged from the deserted town. "May I?" she asked.

"Of course," said Andromeda. Still thinking of the ritual to come, she felt oddly disconnected from the present. Talen was unpacking a few things from the bags Valouria had brought, looking over to check with Andromeda that all was as she expected.

Jars, pastes, herbs, magical ingredients. Instruments that had irrevocably changed this land. Elements of life and death.

"I brought everything I could find," said Valouria, perhaps mistaking Andromeda's continuing silence.

"I know, Valouria." Andromeda gave her a weak smile. "This is more than I deserve from you, after what I did. Has the Empress told you?"

There was no bitterness in Valouria's look, but there was a doubt in her eyes that hadn't been there the last time Andromeda had seen her. She no longer trusted the precepts of her world as she once did. "The Empress has told all of those she chose to bring with her. About her daughter and the Dragon, and the Wildcard of Fate." She didn't say more, she was still too loyal for that, but Andromeda could see that her faith and conviction was gone. She remembered Valouria telling her of the stained-glass windows, of how sure she was the Empress would fulfil the promise those windows represented. It pained her to see Valouria like this, and wished she could undo it.

"You weren't wrong, Valouria," Andromeda said softly. "What you told me about the stained-glass windows; the Empress's promise to take the place of the Dragon as the guardian of the land—that is why she has brought all of you here."

A spark of curiosity brightened Valouria's uncharacteristically dull eyes, but before she could ask any questions, a guard called from outside the tent, saying that Valouria had been summoned by the Empress, along with Jasper and the Empress's daughter.

With a murmured apology, Valouria left them.

After she'd departed, Talen took the empty chair and moved it closer to where Andromeda was sitting. "Valouria told me the same story about the stained-glass windows," she commented, reaching out to smooth Andromeda's hands between her own. "I wondered back then why the shape of the flame matched the mark on my shoulder. Of course we know why now."

"Talen." Andromeda caught Talen's gaze, her voice cracking, her breaths coming in uneven gulps. "I am going to kill someone to bring forth a world."

Talen's hands tightened over her own. "I know," she whispered. "Is there anything I can do to make it easier?"

"Tell me I'm doing the right thing."

"You saved my life. You freed an unhappy Dragon. You're giving this world a future when it probably had none before." Talen raised one shoulder in a half-shrug. Her left shoulder, where the mark of her fate used to be. "Beyond that...I can't tell you whether it's right, Andromeda. But I'm glad I'm alive. I'm glad you came to find me in this world."

In spite of her unease at what was to come, Andromeda smiled. "I'm glad of that too, Talen. I'm glad I followed your advice and lost myself in the Endless Forest, all those months ago."

Chapter 23

After the sun went down, Valouria's guards lit several fires and the cooks began preparing an evening meal for all those present. Andromeda and Talen accepted their share, but didn't eat with the rest of the party. They took a couple of burning brands for light and walked along the cliff, away from the camp. Finding a promontory, they ate overlooking the sea; listening to the cracking and grinding of the breaking ice, blasted by the cold briny wind coming off the water.

Ferris was the only one who took the trouble to follow them, coming along sometime after Andromeda and Talen had finished their meal. She produced the two daggers Talen had lost upon the mountain, saying, "I found these, and the bow as well. I'm happy for you to have the daggers, Talen, but I'm going to keep the bow. To remind me of Stasia."

"Of course." Talen took the daggers, admiring the glint of steel in the flames of the nearest brand. "Thank you."

"Were you able to recover Stasia's remains?" Andromeda asked, hoping the question wasn't insensitive.

Ferris smiled, looking the most at peace Andromeda had seen her. "Yes, I brought her down the mountain. They are talking of building a mausoleum in Drakk where the bodies of all the Heroes will be laid to rest, but I wouldn't want that for Stasia. I will find somewhere to bury her that is quiet, and beautiful."

"I think she would like that," said Talen.

"Yes, I think so too," Ferris agreed. She joined them in contemplating the thawing sea, but not for long. Rising, she said, "It's too cold out here for me. I'm heading back to camp. I'll see you both tomorrow."

"We should think about heading back too," Talen said after Ferris left. "It is cold, and we should try to get some sleep."

"I don't know if I'll be able to sleep tonight," said Andromeda, a shiver going down her spine. "I doubt the Empress plans to wait long before performing the ritual. It will probably be done in the next day or two."

She didn't relish the idea of lying in the tent, restless, alone with her thoughts in the dark. At least out here she had the sea and the sky; the stars with their broken destinies still shone brightly in the night.

So they stayed, perhaps another hour or two, until even Andromeda had to admit her discomfort was too great.

When they got back to the camp, the murmurs of those still awake around the fires indicated the Empress had yet to emerge. She remained sequestered in her tent, in conversation with a succession of advisors, while the rest wondered amongst themselves why they were here.

Because they still didn't know they had come to the end of the world to witness their Empress die.

❧

VALOURIA SPOKE to Andromeda a second time during the course of the night. This was after her audience with the Empress; once she knew what was to happen.

"I understand what you meant now," she said to Andromeda, referring back to their earlier conversation. "You are right, I suppose. At least, I feel as if I should think you are right. But then I wonder what comfort this can bring to the dead, who needed action from the

Empress years ago. Many, many children in this kingdom lost their lives so the Empress's daughter might keep hers."

She stared into the fire for a time, then continued, "I understand more of Ferris's bitterness now. She saw what I didn't want to see, and I am not sure whether I am appreciative or not at having my eyes opened. At any rate," she glanced towards Andromeda. "I am glad it will be you, Andromeda. You will give our Empress the respect befitting her when the time comes. You will not make it ugly. I can see this responsibility lies heavily upon you, and it is to the benefit of your character that it is so, but if it means anything...I think you are doing the right thing."

To Talen, Valouria said, "I hope we part as friends, Talen. Especially now, I would regret it if the orders I carried out for the Empress were to come between us."

"Of course we are friends, Valouria," Talen assured her. "I always knew you were doing what you had to do as the Empress's Captain. I never held it against you."

Soon afterwards, Valouria was called back to the Empress's tent once more, and left them with a small bow. Andromeda hoped her disillusionment would soften in time; it was painful to think of someone with Valouria's nobility tainted by the dirtiness of the world.

Sorrel and Lezith also came to see them that night. Sorrel explained that she and Lezith had both been pardoned by the Empress; a decision driven more by the Empress's fear of losing what support she had left than because she forgave them, but at least it ensured their safety.

The Sages were in turmoil without the stars, and Sorrel herself had an air of loss Andromeda had not seen in her before. Lezith, however, insisted there were other ways of seeing; that the Sages would have to simply forge a new relationship with the stars and the rest of the world.

And, finally, as the fires that had burned all night began to die down, Andromeda and Talen were called back to the Empress's tent.

⸙

As BEFORE, the Empress sat upon her portable throne. Slightly in front of her, and to one side, a smaller seat had been placed upon which her daughter sat. To the Empress's right, Jasper stood, his face composed but his eyes full of misery. Valouria stood on the Empress's left, quiet and subdued.

The Empress calmly met Andromeda's eyes once she and Talen took their places before her. "All my final preparations have been made. I am now ready to hear how this spell is to work, Andromeda."

Andromeda cast an uneasy glance towards the Empress's daughter. "Are you sure you wish me to speak of that immediately, Imperial Majesty?"

"Yes," said the Empress. "I will not hide the truth from my daughter. I have already explained to her what is to happen."

The Empress's daughter returned Andromeda's gaze silently and nodded her head as if to say she agreed with her mother's assessment.

Unhappily, Andromeda looked back to the Empress. "In the pre-dawn, just before the sun rises, you must stand upon the edge of the cliff and...take your own life. Your body will plunge into the sea below; the sea which flows to the border of this world. As your blood spreads red through the water, I will speak the spell the Dragon gave me. The spell of worldmaking."

"I take it there is only a certain window of opportunity in which this ritual will be effective."

"Indeed. It must be done before the Spring fails. As long as the warm wind blows, there is still time. So if you wish to wait, Imperial Majesty—"

"I do not wish to wait," said the Empress. Her lips tightened, and she rose to her feet with stately grace. "The dawn approaches. We will complete the ritual now." She swept past Andromeda and Talen, her

282

daughter in tow, and the others followed her out into the thinning darkness.

Valouria instructed her guards to rouse everyone. Once they were all gathered, the Empress ascended an outcropping of rock that gave a natural vantage point from which all could see her. "My friends and faithful subjects," she began, "thank you for undertaking this difficult journey with me to the sea that marks the end of our land. Though the Dragon has been successfully vanquished, I must share with you the terrible news that there is one sacrifice yet to be made before Blackheath can return to the prosperity we all remember. I know the last ten years have been difficult. We have all suffered too many losses. It cannot continue, and that is why I am glad to give up my life so that Blackheath might be renewed."

There was a burst of shocked murmurs and cries from the crowd, but the Empress continued to speak, silencing the outbursts.

"I name Jasper and Valouria as my daughter's guardians, and the joint guardians of Blackheath. It shall be their responsibility to watch over the kingdom until my daughter is of age to rule as the next Empress. I know they both love Blackheath as much as I do, and in my absence, I leave them with my full faith and trust.

"As difficult and painful as it is, this sacrifice I make will usher in a glorious new era for Blackheath, and that is why I would have every one of you here remember me with pride and gladness. Do not weep, for this is not a day of sorrow. It is a day of great joy, and as I am honoured to have served all of you as your Empress, so too I am honoured to give my life for our kingdom. I leave each and every one of you with my love, and my blessings. Farewell."

As the Empress stepped down from the outcropping, Valouria's guards had to hold back the surge of the confused and agitated crowd. The Empress answered what additional questions she could, but soon enough she looked towards the sky and said there was no time left.

Upon her order, Jasper and the guards between them organised all those present into two lines, forming a long avenue with a path between them.

The avenue went right to the edge of the cliff, and this was where Jasper bid Andromeda wait. The Empress walked through the path with her subjects on either side, touching each in turn and sharing a few words, drawing ever closer to Andromeda.

All was tinged with the muted grey hues of the world before sunrise, making the scene take on a strange, dreamlike quality. Andromeda trembled as she waited, sweat gathering under her arms as she watched the Empress's steps, wondering how she had the presence of mind to appear as if she were taking nothing more than a leisurely morning stroll.

Talen was standing to Andromeda's left; opposite her on the right were Valouria, Jasper and the Empress's daughter. Andromeda wasn't sure why Jasper had placed Talen in such a prominent position—she was going to be one of the last the Empress spoke to—but she was glad to have Talen by her.

The brief touch of Talen's hand as the Empress approached was enough to let Andromeda know she was not alone in this; that Talen would be there for her through the ritual and its aftermath.

The Empress stopped before Talen and gave her a lemon-rind smile. "I wonder, Talen, whether things would have been better for me if I had never laid eyes on you. But I cannot deny you have helped give this kingdom its chance for a future. You have proven yourself as Hero, and for that I thank you."

Once the Empress finished speaking, Talen bowed to her, a complex expression in her eyes. "It was my honour, Imperial Majesty."

Andromeda could tell the Empress hadn't expected this from Talen. Talen did not recognise hierarchy; she had never bowed to the Empress before. Her bow meant that whatever her wider opinion of

DAWN K. LAKE

the Empress might be, she recognised the Empress's sacrifice as an act worthy of respect.

In response, the Empress touched Talen's shoulder, as if to thank her. It was like a window into another set of possibilities; some alternative that might have existed where Talen and Andromeda and the Empress had been able to build peace and understanding. Maybe in that world, there was another way to save Blackheath that didn't require a sacrifice.

As the Empress turned away from Talen, that flash of feeling faded, and Andromeda couldn't say for sure whether it was even founded on anything more than her own wistful hopes.

Valouria was next to be farewelled. She too bowed to the Empress, but it was listless, without conviction.

"Valouria," said the Empress softly, encouraging her to straighten. "I've disappointed you. I'm sorry. You deserved a better Empress than I."

Valouria started to speak, as if to contradict the Empress, but then she stopped. The disillusionment in her eyes told the truth of what was in her heart, and it was clear she could not bring herself to lie. "I will serve your daughter and this land faithfully once you are gone." This was said after some consideration. The best promise Valouria could offer.

The Empress smiled. "I know, Valouria. Thank you."

After Valouria came Jasper. Taking his hands, the Empress spoke to him in a low voice that few would have been able to hear. "Jasper, I have not disappointed you, but that is only because you are too kind to me, too loyal, to let yourself think of how I have failed Blackheath these many years."

Jasper shook his head, his voice hoarse and his eyes red. "You have not failed, Imperial Majesty. You are about to create a future for all of us."

"I hope so," the Empress said. Something intimate and wordless passed between them, and then the Empress released Jasper's hands, going last of all to her daughter.

The Empress knelt down, and though the Empress's daughter tried to hold back her tears, she broke down as her mother embraced her. All was silent except for the sighing of the sea, the grinding of the ice, and the sobbing of the Empress's daughter as her mother offered her what comfort she could.

Colour was seeping into the world as the dawn neared. Andromeda could see it, and she knew the Empress could too. She knew it was why the Empress soon disentangled her daughter's arms from her neck, stepping back while Jasper and Valouria moved forward to support her daughter on either side.

Her hand lingering on her daughter's cheek, the Empress said, "Do not look away, daughter. An Empress must always have courage."

Stifling her tears, the Empress's daughter nodded. She kept her eyes on her mother's as the Empress backed towards the cliff edge, only restrained from running after her by Jasper and Valouria.

Once the Empress stood upon the precipice, she looked towards Andromeda. "I believe it is time."

"It is," Andromeda whispered. Her stomach muscles clenched tight and she thought she might be sick. Andromeda knew what it was to be turned into a sacrifice. She had never thought she would find herself doing it to another.

The Empress drew the dagger which Andromeda remembered from the Dragon's cavern beneath the palace. Was that what she was going to use? Couldn't she have found a less brutal way? Poison, perhaps? What was it going to do to the Empress's daughter to see this?

Sucking in a sharp breath, the Empress placed the dagger against her throat, about to draw the blade across. But before she could, a spasm passed across Jasper's face and he stepped forward, placing his hand over hers on the dagger.

"No, Imperial Majesty. That is not fitting."

Looking like a man being tortured, he produced a long, thin knife, pointed like a needle. "Into the jugular," he said gently, his voice as personal as a lover's. "Pierce your neck, and it will be over quickly. A dignified end."

The Empress appeared nonplussed by Jasper's intervention, but she allowed him to take the dagger, and accepted the knife instead.

Jasper stepped back, his breathing elevated, his eyes pained, and as Andromeda saw the first rays of the sun spill over the horizon, the Empress plunged the knife into her neck and tumbled over the cliff into the sea.

The Empress's daughter let out a wail of animal loss, and many others too amongst the crowd gasped or cried at what they saw. But Andromeda noticed that Jasper only gave a strange little nod, as if glad he had done the Empress that final service, while tears ran unchecked down his cheeks.

As the sun rose, as the waves surged at the bottom of the cliff, as the sea turned red with the Empress's blood, Andromeda chanted the spell which the Dragon had given her. Its power was phenomenal. With each syllable, each word she spoke, Andromeda could feel the very fabric of this world shifting and changing around her. In comparison, her own existence was insignificant, and she knew the forces she was channelling could have easily killed her.

But the Dragon understood the fragility of humans. She had made sure the spell would unfold with a gentleness that would not cause harm, either to Andromeda or to any creature in the world. It was entirely unlike Andromeda's last encounter with the Dragon's power, when the Empress had tried to force it into her.

As Andromeda spoke the final word of the spell, she looked out over the sea now glittering in the newly risen sun, and she saw what seemed to be a great eruption of light on the horizon. The light raced towards them, reaching the land and streaming over them with the faint echo of a Dragon's roar.

The spell had taken the gift of the Dragon's Spring and the gift of the Empress's sacrifice and woven them together to bring forth a new world, and every person present felt it when that happened, felt the moment when the sun's rays upon their faces became the first morning of the future the Empress had promised.

Before Andromeda could say anything, Jasper stepped forward. His voice rang out over the assembled subjects, gesturing with a flourish to the Empress's daughter. "The Empress is dead. All hail the new Empress!"

He knelt before the new Empress, and all those present followed his example. Andromeda knelt in deference for the loss she had caused to the Empress's daughter, and with her eyes asked Talen to make an exception to her beliefs and kneel like everyone else just this once. Talen did so, though not without a slight roll of her eyes.

The New Empress bid her people rise, and went to the edge of the cliff to look out over the blood-red sea. Turning back, she proclaimed, "Let my mother's sacrifice never be forgotten." Her gaze shifting to Andromeda she continued, "Thank you, Andromeda. You spoke truly, as my mother told me you would. You have kept your word to us."

To her people, she said, "I go now to rest. In my absence, I leave Jasper and Valouria with my full authority. Follow their judgements as you would my own."

With great dignity and dry eyes, the New Empress walked into her mother's tent, and let the flaps fall closed behind her. The only sign of her pain was the paler hue of her already pale skin.

THE SEA WAS NO LONGER red, which was how Andromeda knew they had crossed the border between worlds and left Blackheath behind.

Her Book of Magic reflected the change as well, its text on Blackheath blurring away until new stories began to appear. Back in Lezith's cottage, Andromeda had checked the Book after she'd enacted the Wildcard of Fate, and then the pages had been in flux, text running like water everywhere, completely unreadable. But that had settled after the ritual was done, and new information began to appear, far more detailed than the cryptic clues that had been there before.

Andromeda assumed that prior to the Wildcard, the enchantments that clouded the stars and hid parts of the palace affected her Book as well.

She and Talen hadn't stayed long after the ritual was done; indeed, Talen had been quite anxious to leave. Relief had flooded her face when Andromeda told her she had the ability to call a Ship that could travel between worlds.

That Ship was how Andromeda had originally come to Blackheath, paying for her passage with some of the magical ingredients she had collected during her travels. The Captain had agreed to sail the Ship as close to Blackheath as she could, but warned the thick sea-ice would prevent them from reaching land. Undeterred, Andromeda had told the Captain she would cross the sea-ice on foot once the Ship could go no further, trusting that the Broken Road would lead her safely ashore.

Andromeda had paid the Ship's Captain enough for a return passage for herself and one other, and had in her possession the means by which she could summon the Ship.

She had called for the Ship on the beach below the cliff, Talen and the horses waiting nearby, and they had all been loaded and away before most of the Empress's party even knew what was happening.

They hadn't seen the Empress's daughter again.

"You do know we're on a pirate ship, don't you?" Talen commented, coming to stand beside Andromeda at the Ship's rail after having excused herself to check on the horses.

Andromeda glanced at the black sails above them, creaking in the wind. "I know. But the Captain isn't going to betray us."

"You're very sure of that."

The Captain wasn't interested enough to betray them, was what Andromeda wanted to say, but didn't. Whilst Andromeda couldn't guess the Captain's story, she had an aura of being preoccupied with troubles of her own, and had a haunted expression that made Andromeda not want to look into her eyes for too long.

But it would not be smart to voice any of those thoughts here, so Andromeda changed the subject. "What do you think of renaming Brownie as Dark Star? Dark Star and Midnight Storm—the names go well together, don't you think?"

Talen smiled, slipping her arm around Andromeda's waist. "I'll approve as long as Brownie does." After a pause, she said in a more serious voice, "I know what happened back there wasn't easy, but try to remember—Blackheath's future was the Empress's responsibility all along. She never had any right to try to force it onto you, or me, or any of the others she placed the burden onto over the years."

"I know, Talen. But that doesn't change how I feel about being instrumental in her death. It's going to take me some time to deal with that."

"I'm sorry you had to be the one to do it, Andromeda. I would have taken that burden from you if I could."

Andromeda leaned into Talen. "You've killed to protect me before. You shouldn't always be the one who has to. Nor would I return to being what I was before I started this journey. I would rather live with the responsibility of what I've done than be incapable of doing anything."

"So...Where are we headed?"

Talen asked the question casually, but Andromeda knew there was a bigger question behind it.

"I haven't changed my mind, Talen. I'm not the Empress, and my priorities are not the same as hers. Perhaps one day I'll have the chance to return to my kingdom; to change that world as you and I changed Blackheath. But right now all I want is to go to the Endless Forest to see the Fallen Fairy, and then find somewhere to settle down with you."

The quiet happiness that lit up Talen's eyes warmed Andromeda's heart. Talen leaned in close and kissed her, and it was worth it, it was worth every painful and difficult moment Andromeda had spent transforming herself on the Broken Road to be able to kiss Talen back. Clipping through the waves, the Ship sped on, towards the kingdom of Princesses and Fairy Godmothers, where, unbeknownst to the one who had started it all, Andromeda's rebellion was already beginning to send ripples through her former world.

About the Author

DAWN K. LAKE is a writer of fantasy and science fiction who lives in Australia. She has a PhD in literature, too many books, and shares her home with a grumpy calico cat. Readers can expect to find women, lesbians, and a good splash of romance in most everything she writes. You could say it's her mission in life to combine her love of fantasy with the kind of lesbian-centric stories she wishes she could have had growing up. *Waking Beauty* is her first published novel.

www.ingramcontent.com/pod-product-compliance
Lightning Source LLC
Chambersburg PA
CBHW050030120726
47903CB00006B/1983